FORETASTE OF GLORY

JESSE STUART

FORETASTE OF GLORY

With an Introduction by

ROBERT J. HIGGS

THE UNIVERSITY PRESS OF KENTUCKY

This edition printed by arrangement
with the Jesse Stuart Foundation

Published in 1986 by The University Press of Kentucky
Scholarly publisher for the Commonwealth, serving Bellarmine
College, Berea College, Centre College of Kentucky, Eastern
Kentucky University, The Filson Club, Georgetown College,
Kentucky Historical Society, Kentucky State University, Morehead
State University, Murray State University, Northern Kentucky
University, Transylvania University, University of Kentucky,
University of Louisville, and Western Kentucky University.

Editorial and Sales Offices: Lexington, Kentucky 40506-0024

Library of Congress Cataloging-in-Publication Data

Stuart, Jesse, 1907—
    Foretaste of glory.

    I. Title.
PS3537.T92516F6 1986   813'.52   86-5456
ISBN 0-8131-1594-9
ISBN 0-8131-0170-0 (pbk.)

For

LAWRENCE EDWARD WATKIN

FOR ENCOURAGEMENT AND FRIENDSHIP

INTRODUCTION

Robert J. Higgs

Foretaste of Glory was first published on March 8, 1946, during a decade of amazing productivity by Jesse Stuart that saw the appearance of seven other books by him. Among these were *Taps for Private Tussie* (1943), which won the Thomas Jefferson Southern Award for the best southern book of the year and *The Thread That Runs So True* (1949), voted the most important book of the year by the National Education Association. Immediately preceding *Foretaste* was Stuart's second major volume of verse, *Album of Destiny* (1944), and following it was *Tales from the Plum Grove Hills* in October, 1946.

A wide range of opinion greeted this versatile display of creativity in poetry, novel, short story, and children's literature. Millions of readers bought and laughed at *Taps for Private Tussie*, but *Album of Destiny* went largely unnoticed and unread, an ironic situation in the view of some academic critics. Isabella D. Harris, for instance, in her Duke University Ph.D. dissertation, "The Literary Tradition of the Southern Mountaineer, 1824-1910" (1948), says that *Taps* belongs to the worst aspects of the tradition of mountain fiction, and Frank H. Leavell in his Vanderbilt University Ph.D. dissertation, "The Literary Career of Jesse Stuart" (1966), says *Album* is Stuart's best work. In 1956 Stuart himself wrote an article for *Prairie Schooner* telling why he thought *Album* was his best.

At the publication of *Foretaste* even Stuart's homefolks had mixed feelings. When he returned home in 1946 after a tour in the Navy and after completion of the manuscript in Washington, D.C., the reaction against him in his hometown over the book, he told Professor Ruel Foster, "was terrible." At one time, says Foster in his book *Jesse Stuart*, Stuart thought he would have to leave Greenup County much as Thomas Wolfe had left Asheville after publication of *Look Homeward, Angel* in 1929. But as with Wolfe, acrimony subsided and Stuart was eventually given due honor in his own country in the form of a statue erected in front of the court house at Greenup in 1955.

Stuart, I believe, was always puzzled and no doubt hurt on occasion by reaction to his works, not knowing what to think of a readership that neglected a book such as *Album* that he had worked on so long but swept up copies of another, *Taps*, that he had, comparatively speaking, dashed off. In any event, with *Foretaste of Glory* he returned to a book like *Taps* that had been a favorite with readers. In many ways he used the same type of plot techniques. In both novels the daily lives of characters are interrupted by a sudden and unexpected event which allows for or calls for a dramatic change in modes of living and thinking. In *Taps* the event is the death in World War II of Private Kim Tussie, whose insurance money allows his family to move out of the one-room school where they've lived and which they've wrecked into the finest house in town which they also wreck. In *Foretaste* the event is the appearance in the sky on the night of September 18, 1941, of the aurora borealis or "northern lights," which most of the inhabitants of the town of Blakesburg take as a sign of the end of the world and the coming of Jesus Christ.

As in *Taps*, the central theme in *Foretaste* is the foolishness of man, and story after story illustrates the inevitable discrepancy between the public appearances of characters and their secret lives revealed by action or confession with the coming of the *"lights."* Stuart obviously would agree with Willie Stark in *All the King's Men* who, when asked by Jack Burden if he thinks there's something on Judge Irwin, replies, "There is always something." In *Foretaste* there is always something that even, or maybe especially, the most exalted citizens have hidden from others. Flannery O'Connor has said that the south is "Christ-haunted," and *Foretaste* would seem to reinforce that view. The characters in the novel believe that Jesus will come again in a cloud of glory and how they react when they think that time has come makes for some mighty entertaining reading.

Randall Stewart once said that Faulkner was not writing about conditions in Mississippi but "the human condition" in Mississippi. This is true to a large extent of Stuart in regard to his home state of Kentucky, a point that reviewers and general readers have not always understood. Flannery O'Connor made essentially the same distinction when, in responding to criticism of the grotesqueness of her characters as supposedly representative Georgians replied that she was not seeking verisimilitude in her stories but meaning. Though he differs markedly from O'Connor in tone, intent, and style, Stuart too is seeking meaning in stories by his abundant use of wildly absurd figures and plots. He is not attempting to give a detailed account of the daily lives of Kentuckians, even on judgment day, but to show by means of the myth of comedy something of the fallen nature of man, trying in other words to help us see ourselves, whoever and wherever we are.

The key word here is "comedy," which W.H. Auden in his introduction to the *Selected Poetry and Prose of Byron* has wisely distinguished from satire.

Satire attempts to show that the behavior of an individual or a group within society violates the laws of ethics or common sense on the assumption that once the majority are aware of the facts, they will become morally indignant and either compel the violators to mend their ways or render them socially and politically impotent. Comedy, on the other hand, is concerned with illusions, and self-deceptions, which all men indulge in, as to what they and the world they live in are really like, and cannot, so long as they remain human, help being. The object of the comic exposure is not a special individual and special social group, but every man or human society as a whole. Satire is angry and optimistic—it believes that the evil it attacks can be abolished; comedy is good-tempered and pessimistic—it believes that however much we may wish we could, we cannot change human nature and must make the best of a bad job.

With this distinction in mind we see that few southern writers ever engage in satire. The southerner, especially the Appalachian writer, believes that man is a fallen being, or at least one who is very flawed, and that all we can do is to take stock of our foolishness as often as we can, laugh at ourselves, even as others see us, and go ahead and do the best we can. This in fact was why Faulkner admired Sut Lovingood so much. Sut, Faulkner said, didn't blame his problems on others, and he did the best he could, recognizing himself all along as "a natural born durned fool."

In his tales and novels Stuart, as Randall Stewart and others have remarked, clearly belongs to the frontier tradition that runs back through Mark Twain to George Washington Harris and other humorists of the Old Southwest. When one of Stuart's characters in *Foretaste* takes a swig of homemade whiskey, jumps up, and kicks his heels together, there is no doubt who his literary ancestors are. Certainly they are not descended from the refined and self-conscious gentlemen of the plantation novel such as *Swallow Barn* but from the wild and boisterous frontier.

Frontier humor itself, though, was part of a much older tradition of humor, and I've been amazed at how perfectly almost *Foretaste* follows the age-old formulas. Humor, says Northrup Frye in *Anatomy of Criticism*, is "intimately connected with the theme of the absurd or irrational law that the action of comedy moves toward breaking." In the myth of comedy characters are dominated by what Pope called "a ruling passion" or Ben Jonson the "humor." Central to comedy is the idea of obsession, and this is certainly true of the gallery of characters in *Foretaste*. They are obsessed with making money (Malinda Sprouse), dancing (Mutt Henderson), drinking (Boss Kenton, Noah Billups, Uncle Jeff Hargis, and many others), fighting (Liam Winston and Temp and Ollie Spradling, with Temp doing most of the fighting) scourging sinners and criminals (Joe Oliver), upholding civic virtue (Judge Ollie Henderson), fornicating (Mary Blanton and her pack of lovers), doing nothing (Blue Blood Willie Deavers), and playing the patriot ("Old Glory" Gardner). In short, they are doing the exact same thing that people do today in Washington, Moscow, and everywhere else.

Let me use "Old Glory" Gardner as an example of obsession and the type of humor it evokes. The superintendent of the Blakesburg city schools, "Old Glory" is also a super patriot as Stuart makes clear:

> And if Esther Stableton couldn't conjugate her Latin verb, Old Glory would give her an A for her recitation if she would stand beside her desk and sing the Star-Spangled Banner. If Mabel Cooley didn't have her assignment in English, something which was not very uncommon, she would rise from her seat, stand at attention while she would give the Pledge to the Flag. Then Old Glory would smile as he recorded an A for her in his grade book. If Fiddis Caudill couldn't prove his proposition in Geometry, all he had to do was recite, "Hats Off, the Flag is Passing By."
>
> If any pupil who didn't know his lesson would rise and sing some patriotic song or recite some patriotic poetry he didn't have to worry about his getting a good grade. A

poem about the flag would always get an A, a poem about the state was good for a B; and a poem about the Republic, such as "Sail on, O Ship of State," would pass for a C.

Unfortunately comic treatment of the public patriot and the public Christian has almost disappeared in contemporary society, but in Stuart's writing we can see how such humor once was done. With the appearance of the lights, Old Glory responds in predictable fashion with words that make the scene unforgettable. I'm tempted to share it now but will restrain myself. Stuart no doubt regarded "Old Glory's" patriotism as the kind that Emerson called "maggot's rot" and Dr. Johnson "the last refuge of the scoundrel," though Old Glory is not a scoundrel. Stuart himself, I believe, saw patriotism much as Joseph Conrad did, the noblest sentiment in the heart of man, a quality though, like other virtues, not to be paraded, at least unduly. I'll always remember the New York editor who took a championing interest in *Voices from the Hills* (an anthology of Appalachian writing edited by me and Ambrose Manning) because it contained works of Jesse Stuart whom she, of Italian descent, had always admired because of his "fierce love of his land."

I said earlier that comedy was more concerned with meaning than verisimilitude, but I would like to qualify that briefly. As humorist, Stuart is very much the realist in the same sense that George Washington Harris is a realist in *The Sut Lovingood Yarns* and Mark Twain in "The Notorious Jumping Frog of Calaveras County" and "Journalism in Tennessee." The realism in such tales does not derive from credibility of incident but from the exaggeration itself which highlights recognizable human foibles. It also springs from the graphic use of language which provides the illusion of reality. Note, for example, the following scene in which his sons come to bring Bolivar Tussie home from jail so he can be with their Ma when she goes to glory: "He

[Bolivar] heard the rattle of a jolt wagon and the click of mules' steel shoes against the concrete and he turned to see a scared mule team with their mouths wide open and foam-spittle dropping in big flecks from the corners of the bits as the tall driver leaned back against the leather checklines. . . ." There is something forever appealing about such descriptions for anyone over fifty and from the rural south. Another generation will not even know what a "jolt wagon" is. Even Harold Wentworth, author of *American Dialect Dictionary*, was not sure in 1944 what the term meant though he recorded several uses of it. He guessed that it was a "springless wagon," which it is, but that does not describe it fully. Stuart's works, even his weakest, will remain a rich reservoir of lexical items, many of which are already passing out of use. The same can be said for his use of dialect. Note just one line uttered by one of Bolivar's sons as they try to pull their father away from a barbed wire fence that he has latched onto with mouth and both hands to keep from going back home on judgment day: " 'Be keerful, snail,' Erf warned, 'Ye mought hurt Pap's mouth. Ye might jerk his teeth out.' " Stuart knew that his characters didn't say "mought" all the time—just some of the time. Other times they said "might."

I first read *Foretaste of Glory* in 1950 when I was a freshman at Vanderbilt University. Another freshman recommended it to me—even freshmen in those days recommended books—and I still remember how much I enjoyed it. Reading it again, I found myself laughing at the same stories, relishing the outlandish incidents and appreciating more than before the folklore and dialect. A book of laughter is a joy forever.

FOREWORD

BLAKESBURG IS A TOWN *beneath the Southern sun, fenced in by two rivers, a mountain, and the wind. There Little River, flowing from the south, runs into Big River, headed westward, making a V the shape of wild geese flying. Blakesburg sits on this V like a hen with wings spread out to cover her eggs. Behind Blakesburg is the neighborly mountain that stands eternally from river to river and cuts away the wind from the south, but never the morning sun. For the morning sun glints on Big River, giving the early-rising people of Blakesburg just cause to squint their eyes.*

The two rivers and the mountain form enough of a barrier around Blakesburg to hold cattle not too roguish. But the people of Blakesburg do not need to be fenced in. They are content to stay in a town that is as peaceful as the sighs of the easy wind among the sulphur-stemmed ragweed, or the soft murmur of the lazy rivers.

September 18, 1941, was no different from any other autumn day that came and went at Blakesburg. The sun rose that morning, making of Big River a silver ribbon of light. And on this autumn day the canopy of sky above the sleepy city was as clean as furze fresh from the milkweed pod blown hither and thither by the wind. The morning was beautiful, but it came slowly, like everything else to Blakesburg. Even the city-wise birds did no more flying than was necessary to get their breakfasts.

As the sun, big and round as a jolt-wagon wheel, climbed the sky, the inhabitants of the town bent to their tasks; but when the noon whistle, courtesy of the fire department, sounded its shrill warning, they were more than ready to pause in the midday heat.

Those who could stayed indoors through the afternoon and didn't stir while the splintering rays of the white-hot agate sun beamed down upon their city. Small boys with fishing poles sat with their feet in the water under the sycamores and fished in Little River, and older lads took half-hearted shots with their .22 rifles at turtles and water moccasins sunning themselves on rocks and logs along the riverbank. But among the older folks only a handful of women could be seen. Lacking water in their homes or a well in their yards, they must of necessity wash their clothes on the rocks. All human life that ventured forth in the blaze of afternoon confined itself to the river, where the drowsy water riffled slowly over the rocks, singing a song without words, and the long arms of the willows reached down and combed smooth water.

When at last the sun had journeyed beyond the backbone of the mountain, cool shadows spread across the town. Flowers reopened their blossoms; wilted clusters hanging from the trees became leaves again; the corn in the fields and the sunflowers and the shoemake berries and the ox-eyed daisies stood up. Cows, knee-deep in cool springs under the sweetgum shade, emerged to pick grass hurriedly before the farmer boys came after them. Birds flew slowly through the shadowy walls of evening air, chirruping to each other and singing a few love songs. The people came out too, remarking that today had been a scorcher.

As they began to stir again through their quiet streets, they savored the cool air from the mountain.

It would be a fine night for sleep.

. . . Until in the distant north an arc of icicle-colored light first appeared on a low horizon. In a few minutes long tentacles of white-gold stabbed southward, slitting the velvety darkness with lightning speed. If the dusk had been a solid substance, it would have been slashed as hailstones riddle young burley tobacco leaves.

At first it appeared to be an electrical storm. But in this section of America, south of the Mason-Dixon border, September was late for an electrical storm. And the weather was touched with the chill of autumn. Through the illimitable distance on a sky that looked blue and cold were thousands upon thousands of bright stars anchored in space!

As the arc of light spread southward it became more brilliant than the light of a thousand moons. This world of scary light came down from the north with immeasurable swiftness, and was soon over Big River engulfing Blakesburg with fluxion of multi-colored light. Never had fireworks made so brilliant a display. Never had there been such shafts, tentacles, arms, darts, seas, and mountains of light with such blazing speed and celestial intermingling. Great splinters of light darted across the heavens from the east to the west and from the north to the south. They crisscrossed each other on rolling seas of liquid fire, as God had promised for the last day.

The people of Blakesburg gazed upon this awesome beauty of ten thousand rainbows as a heavenly portent. . . .

1

WHEN THE great lights flashed against the Winston Boarding House windows, Liam Winston, Aunt Effie's old
bachelor son, ran out of the kitchen wearing his white apron
daubed with spots of grease and stove black. In his hand he still
carried the spatula he had been using to turn eggs over in the
skillets on the big stove. He had forgotten to lay the spatula
down or take the skillets of eggs from the top of the stove.

"Liam, ye're a-lettin' the eggs burn," Aunt Effie screamed at
him as he ran wildly through the dining room toward the hallway.

"Let 'em burn, Ma," he yelled as he passed Judge Whittlecomb sitting at his card table in the little reception room playing
his favorite game of solitaire.

"What's the matter, Liam?" the Judge asked, jumping up beside his table, peering at Liam with his big blue-walled eyes from
behind celluloid-framed glasses.

"The goddamned world's a-comin' to a end, Judge," he panted,
making for the door that opened onto Main Street.

Judge Whittlecomb followed Liam to the door. But Liam was
down the street running and the Judge could only distinguish him
from the crowd by the apron he wore and the spatula he waved in
his hand as he was swallowed up among the crowd of confused
people.

Liam pushed his way among the running people, stepping over
those that had fallen in the street, dodging and side-stepping those
who were running away . . . away from the end of the world,

13

screaming their sins to the wind! The great lights were flashing
more than ever. Great rays of light flashed brilliantly, lighting up
the streets of the town until one could see a particle of dust on
the street.

"Has anybody seen Brother Booten?" Liam screamed as he
turned the corner of the courthouse square.

No one had seen Booten Winston. No one cared about Booten
Winston now. Everybody was trying to save his own skin in this
mad scramble. If people hadn't been trying to save themselves
someone could have pointed Booten out to Liam. He was just on
the other side of Main Street, walking up and down the street
screaming, "Has anybody seen Brother Liam?"

Booten and Liam weren't on speaking terms. They hadn't
spoken to each other for three years. Judge Whittlecomb was
boarding at the Winston Boarding House the night Liam and
Booten fought. Everybody had eaten and had gone to their
rooms or out in the street and left Aunt Effie, Booten, Liam
and the Judge in the dining room. The Judge was sitting at the
radio listening to "The Grand Ole Opry" program when he
heard the fight start in the kitchen. There was a wild scuffle of
feet and Booten came from the kitchen door first with Liam behind him carrying a big poker drawn over his shoulder ready
to strike. Aunt Effie came running behind Liam, her gray hair
loose and flying, her arms outstretched reaching for the poker
drawn over Liam's shoulder.

"Liam, Liam," she screamed, "don't hit Booten!"

"I'll kill 'im, I'll kill 'im," Liam screamed. "I'll kill the goddamn son . . ."

Aunt Effie seemed to leap through the air and grab the poker
with her skinny hand and pull it down over Liam's shoulder.
Just then Booten had reached the door and it was shut. His
speed was so great he hit the closed door hard enough to cave it
in. But it didn't go in and he wheeled around to see where Liam
was with the poker. When he saw his mother had hold of it

wrestling with Liam, he turned toward Liam. But while Liam wrestled with his mother, he had his eye on Booten. Liam wasn't taking any chances since he had fought Booten many times before and Booten had won with his fists. He'd beaten Liam's face into a pulp more times than one while the Blakesburg people had gathered to watch their native sons fight each other. It was a sport of the townspeople.

When Liam saw Booten turn on him now that he didn't have full use of his poker and couldn't get it free from his mother who held it with her skinny hands and arms for dear life, he let his hold on the poker go free, ran around behind his mother as Booten made a wild charge. Liam kept going around his mother as Booten followed. He managed to keep his mother between him and his brother until he got his pocket knife out and got it opened.

"Goddamn ye, Booten, I've allus intented to kill ye and now's the time," he screamed, stabbing over his mother's shoulder with the long-bladed knife at Booten's face.

"Don't, Liam, please, Liam," Aunt Effie screamed. "Help! Help! Help!"

Judge Whittlecomb jumped up from the radio but he was afraid of the knife. It was a family fight and he didn't want anything to do with it. But the Judge was drawn into the fight and had to act quickly to help Aunt Effie to keep her sons from hurting one another, or from hurting her. By the time the Judge had jumped from his chair there was a long red mark, curved like a quarter-moon from the corner of Booten's right eye, down across his bulldog face to the cleft in his chin and the blood was oozing down along from the mark and spreading like a line of fire taking off among dry leaves.

"Help me, Judge Whittlecomb!" Aunt Effie screamed when she saw the blood.

Liam could hardly reach Booten's face since Aunt Effie stood between them trying to keep them pushed apart but he was taking one slash after another at his brother's face, slashing it too but the knife blade wasn't going in too deeply.

"I aint afraid of yer goddamned knife," Booten swore. "Ma, get outten my way so I can git to 'im! I'll make 'im eat his goddamn knife!"

In seconds the Judge figured a way so he wouldn't get slashed with the knife. He first thought of using the poker on both and knocking them out but he was afraid he couldn't judge his licks with the heavy iron poker and that he might knock them out for longer than he intended. And he knew if he knocked them out, when they came to their senses they would start the fight all over again. If he hit one a little harder and he was out longer when the other came to he would beat the tar out of his senseless brother. But quickly the Judge ran behind Liam . . . he had to do something . . . he put his hands on Liam's shoulders, then he extended his foot past Aunt Effie and put it against Booten's stomach. He pushed them far enough apart so that Liam's bloody knife blade lacked a couple of inches of reaching Booten's bloody face. Aunt Effie stepped from between them. She grabbed a platter from the table and came over Liam's head breaking the platter into little pieces no larger than cracked corn. But the platter didn't make Liam bat his eyes. He was harder to hold than ever. It just made him madder. Booten tried to wiggle the Judge's foot from against his stomach so he could get to his brother and Aunt Effie ran around to his back and held him by the galluses with one hand while she pounded him on the back with her other. At the same time she screamed for more help. Jimmie Welch, one of her star boarders, heard her cries in his room upstairs and came running to the scene. Jimmie called the town Marshal, Edd Crutch, one-armed, who had just floated into the town and got the job since not many of the natives wanted it. And he had to shoot with one hand and had once shot at a mad dog and sprinkled Nellie Blake and Mrs.

Marvin Clayton, a couple of the town's leading women, with buckshot.

But when he came Liam and Booten both gave up for they were afraid of him. He handled his pistol nervously with one hand while standing at a safe distance. He took them down to jail and locked them in separate cells. Peace reigned at the boarding house. Aunt Effie, exhausted, went to bed. Next day she paid Liam's fine and let Booten pay his own. Aunt Effie always paid Liam's fines for she said she couldn't do without him in the kitchen though he had run off all the cooks but one, with the poker he was trying to use on his brother Booten. The one cook he didn't run off was a big colored woman who brought her poker from home and kept it lying by her side. She warned Liam that if he ever got tough with her she would brain him and she was of the disposition to back up any threats she made.

But Liam Winston had more than his brother Booten or the colored cook to fear now. He trotted around the courthouse and back up the street past the place where he always stopped to get his beer. But Liam didn't stop. He trotted on past his favorite spot. If he had stopped, he couldn't have gotten in for the place was closed and the door was padlocked. This wasn't a night to buy beer in Blakesburg. Even beer couldn't have settled the nerves of the inhabitants of the town as the end of time approached.

After Liam circled the courthouse square many times looking among the bewildered and wild faces for his brother, he cut across the street toward the Drug Store where he ran into Booten.

"Booten, I've been a-lookin' fer ye everyplace," he said excitedly.

"And I've been a-lookin' fer ye too," Booten growled.

"I want to make everything right with ye, Booten," Liam repented. "I've had a lot o' enemies and fights with 'em in my life but ye've been the worst enemy I ever had!"

"I still am," Booten roared. "I've been a-huntin' fer ye just to tell ye!"

While they stood facing each other, the great lights and signs in the sky seemed to come closer and get brighter. Liam would look up at them and then he would look at his brother. The scars his knife had left gleamed white on his brother's flushed red face.

"Won't ye let me make things right with ye tonight?" Liam asked.

"No, never," Booten roared, spitting as the words flew from his mouth. "Anybody that won't fight any fairer than ye, I never want fer a friend! I'm sorry we nursed the same mother's milk. I know the end of time has come but I don't give a damn. I can go with the rest! Thar'll be a lot a-goin' to hell with me. And the Devil will know I've been a fair fighter! He won't be afraid of old Booten! But by-god he'll be afraid o' you! Ye'll be a-lookin' fer a soft place to stick yer knife in his back. . . . And ye know damned well Jesus Christ won't have ye! And the Devil will be afraid of ye! I don't know what the hell's a-goin' to happen to ye, Liam!"

The spatula shook more in Liam's hand, more than it did when he used it to turn eggs in the skillets. His teeth rattled until he couldn't speak as he stood there watching his brother cross the street to hear "Old Glory" Gardner give his last talk on Blakesburg and the flag.

2

THERE WAS a time when the Greenoughs and the Dinwiddies controlled Blakesburg. But they didn't control it at the same time for they were of different political beliefs. For more than a century and a half these two families had not only controlled Blakesburg which was the county seat of Blake County, but they had controlled the county. People over the county had either joined the Greenoughs or the Dinwiddies. And they had faith almost equal to their religious faith, in their political parties. They looked upon these families as natural-born leaders and they were just that to a certain extent. If practice makes perfect, they were at least good leaders. It was hard for any person to be elected to any of the city or county offices unless he was either a Dinwiddie or a Greenough or unless he was backed by one of them.

Even the women of the two families were envious of each other. If and when a prominent person came to the town, both families fought over who should entertain him. The women vied with each other in dress and for the society column in the paper. It became such a fight that this small city had to have more than one paper. The Society Editor on each paper tried to outwit her rival and give the women of the family for whom she worked more and better publicity. And the editor of each paper expounded his owner's political views. Certainly the Greenoughs and the Dinwiddies who fought each other for social prominence and on political views, could not have the same religious beliefs nor could they be buried in the same plot on Lonesome Hill.

They were two separate families from the beginning of Blakesburg. And each family claimed the honor of having founded the
town, and his newspaper constantly reminded its readers of the
fact.

Not until 1910 had there ever been a case of love between a
Greenough and a Dinwiddie. Pat Greenough, aged seven, and
Aliss Dinwiddie, aged six, looked at each other eagerly across
the schoolroom aisle. Though they were children, this information spread about Blakesburg. It was something unusual. The
teachers talked about it and the pupils went home and told their
parents. This was the beginning of the finish and fall of both
families who had fought each other since the beginning of
Blakesburg. People whose faith, future and fortunes had been
linked with one of these families, began to lose faith when they
saw their dream begin to disintegrate and collapse. They even
wondered if in the future they wouldn't be burying Dinwiddies
and Greenoughs in the same plots on Lonesome Hill. When a
seven-year-old Greenough was sweet on a six-year-old Dinwiddie, that was something. It was shocking news to followers of
both families.

Many people thought this case of puppy love would blow over
and each of the families would regain its prestige and power and
the confidence of its followers. But when Pat Greenough failed
a year in the graded school on purpose so he could enter Blakesburg High School with his Aliss, they thought it was more than
puppy love. Through high school Pat and Aliss loved each
other, further destroying each family's prestige, honor, and
power. And, even before they were graduated from high school,
Pat and Aliss were seen riding up Blakesburg's Main Street in
their swank two-horse surrey behind fringed curtains while the
embarrassed driver fidgeted on his seat nervously twirling his
quirt. People knew now this wasn't a case of puppy love. And
everybody thought the wedding bells would soon be ringing,
joining these families' bitter rivalry in marriage.

In 1922 Pat graduated with highest honors in his class and Aliss graduated with second honors. This too was something to gossip about. The two oldest families were still in there pitching. Pat and his Aliss became the darling couple of Blakesburg among the younger set. They were looked up to and kowtowed to by everybody. Even the enemies of one or the other family started looking upon the situation, despite all the unfriendly gossip, with admiration. Pat and Aliss were in the glorious days of their youth, in the tumbling twenties. Pat decided to make it more glorious and his father, Didway Greenough, after consulting Eddie Birchfield, bought him, for a graduation present, the biggest automobile ever brought to Blakesburg. Then his father sold the two horses and the rubber-tired silken-fringed surrey.

But the automobile was faster than the surrey. Pat found this out when he tried to make a short turn on one of the city streets, when he was showing his Aliss how fast the "newfangled thing" would go. They went over the bank toward the slough and would have dropped to the bottom if a grove of wild plum trees hadn't caught them. Aliss and Pat were badly bruised and scratched and Eddie said the car was wrecked beyond repair. Thus ended their days with such newfangled modernity as automobiles! They went back to the two-horse surrey.

Pat and Aliss continued to be Blakesburg's darling couple until 1929. Then came the depression, the year Charlie Allbright had prophesied the world would come to an end. This year did end the world of the Dinwiddies and the Greenoughs. Each family lost its small fortune. And strange as it may seem, the older Dinwiddies and the Greenoughs died off one by one, a few taking their own lives, leaving only Pat Greenough, the last of his line, and the Dinwiddies didn't have a male heir to carry on their name. Only Aliss was left of her family. Now people knew they should marry and they wondered why they waited. They had "sparked" all through the teens, the twenties and they were going into their thirties.

Aliss lived alone in her big house, and Pat sold his homeplace
for what it would bring and lived on the money. He didn't
work; he just walked about the town. He dressed in fine clothes
and lived at the Winston Boarding House. He had a room there
and a few family belongings that he didn't sell at auction. Two
nights each week he went to see his Aliss and they were always
together on Sunday afternoon after each had gone to his separate church. Then the talk of the town started. They wondered
why they didn't marry in the thirties. They were not spring
chickens any longer. It was time for them to marry. The youth
of their generation had married and they had families and another generation had come along and married. And now there
was another crop of young lovers. Pat and Aliss were no longer
looked upon as the darling couple but they were eyed with sus-
picion in Blakesburg where a woman unmarried at twenty-two
was considered an old maid and a man twenty-five was really an
old bachelor. Everybody started referring to them as Mister
Pat and Miss Aliss, which was a kind reference to old age.

Blakesburg gossip had many reasons why they hadn't married. Many said it was because of the depression. Others said the
ghosts of their ancestors came back from Lonesome Hill to
haunt them. While others thought the political faith of their
fathers was still so strong within them, that the word marriage
could not be mentioned without fuss. A few had the audacity to
intimate Miss Aliss was afraid Mister Pat couldn't make her a
living since he had lost the influence of his people. They didn't
marry through the thirties. They were just growing old together, one living in a boarding house in one end of town, and
the other in her ancestral home in the other end of town. They
were living this way, still dating two nights a week and on Sunday afternoon until September 18, 1941.

Long before Liam Winston had left his mother's boarding
house, Pat had seen the great lights from his room window
which was on the north side. As soon as he saw these lights,

something seized him like a great sweep of wind big enough to root up a century-old oak. His first thought was, naturally, his Aliss. He left the Winston Boarding House in a hurry without anybody's seeing him leave.

But when people in Blakesburg saw Mister Pat running down the street from the wrath that was coming, they knew the very foundation of their city was shaken. And they became more excited. If Mister Pat was a-running from the things to come, then they should be running. But Mister Pat didn't pay any mind to anybody. He was heading for the Dinwiddies' ancestral home. Strange that a Greenough could be running there in time of the world's ending, many of the older people in Blakesburg reasoned. But this was a case of love and maybe he wanted to be there and depart from the world into Judgment with Miss Aliss, a Greenough.

Again people saw Miss Aliss and Mister Pat running hand in hand. They were heading toward the west end of town and the riverbank. They watched them, still hand in hand, go over the bank where the thin-leafed branches of the willows swayed gently in the bright evening light. These willows whose leaves were upturned by the wind showing their little bellies of silver made a good place for their last retreat. Lester Langley, whose family had been associated with the Greenoughs since Blakesburg had been a town, thought Mister Pat and Miss Aliss might have gone to jump in the river. He put aside his worries of the Judgment and took off toward the willows.

When Lester approached the willow grove, he didn't hear a sound except the swish of the willows in the wind and the murmur of the quiet river reflecting a sea of light. He listened for the sound of a human voice but didn't hear one. So he parted the willow branches and walked into the grove where the bright light penetrated between the limbs and the leaves into pockets and pencil streams of light. He could see among the willows all right and he had hopes that he would find Mister Pat and less hopes that he would find Miss Aliss, whose family his people had hated for more than a century.

When Lester peeped over a barrier of willow branches, he saw Miss Aliss and Mister Pat safely hidden from the excited eyes of people running over the wrinkled skin of a collapsing world. Behind these unsure willow walls of velvety green, they were lying upon a carpet of lush grass near the murmur of the water, under the whisper of the wind.

I never thought a Greenough could get so intimate with a Dinwiddie, Lester Langley thought. I didn't think I'd ever live to see this even on Resurrection Day.

Lester wasn't sure that he was awake. He thought he might be dreaming and that when he awoke he would laugh about his dream of love as beautiful as mountains of light reflecting in the river.

3

AT ANY TIME between six and seven in the evening it wasn't an uncommon sight to see Judge Allie Anderson walking down the back street to his hogpen with a big bucket in each hand. He wore a black broad-rimmed hat that shaded his red face like an umbrella and to make him feel more optimistic about his pants, he wore a big broad belt and a heavy pair of faded galluses because his hips were small and his stomach pouched over like a bulging cliff. He would swagger slowly down the walk, stop at a little stable in the far corner of his lot, mix middlings into his buckets of table scraps and slop. Then he would pour it into a chute from the outside of the pen and it would run down into the hog trough. His two big red hogs would stick their noses under the chute as soon as the mixture started pouring through it into their trough. And as soon as the Judge was through pouring he would stick his toes into the crack between the first and second rails, spread his arms along the top rail, bend over and watch his hogs eat. And while he watched his hogs eat, men of his Greenough party from both the town and county, would drop by and talk to him.

This hogpen was the rendezvous for more county transactions than his office in the courthouse. Men would come and ask him about putting a drain pipe under one of the county dirt roads, about running the grader over a road, digging a ditch or building a bridge. And many would come to seek help from the county. All would come wanting something. But they would brag on the Judge's hogs first telling him he was the greatest hog raiser in the county. But before they left they would be sure to state their business. And they hadn't come just to brag on the Judge's hogs either. They had come to get something, and these who were wise enough to come to the pigpen usually got it. For during the Judge's hours at his office, people who came to see the Judge usually found his office full. And in a well-decorated office, they didn't feel at home to state their business where there was a crowd of people always around listening.

The Judge's opponents in the Dinwiddie Party said this pigpen had brought him more votes than anything else he could have done. They even accused him of being a politician. They went so far as to kick on his having a hogpen with fertilizer around it, only one street from Main Street. They said it smelled in summer until one had to hold his breath when he passed.

They said if he wanted to be a farmer he should get out of the office and get him a farm. But the Judge came back and said such was propaganda his political enemies had started on him. He made good use of everything said about him, by giving it to Charlie Allbright to "put on the air lines" on the courthouse square. And the news went over the county, up each little hollow and to the tops of the ridges. It made him votes among his political opponents. This made Judge Allie "jist a common man" to Blake County voters.

The people from the hills elected Judge Allie. He knew that. And they knew the hogpen wasn't the only place they could go to see him. They knew it was better than his crowded office in the courthouse where he had a big shiny table and plush-bottom chairs for his visitors. He had a big plush-bottom swivel chair for himself so he could spin comfortably around to face another of his supporters quickly after he'd just finished with one. They didn't like the noise of a telephone ringing and the clicking of a typewriter.

At the Judge's home the farmers' wives who smoked pipes

could go and smoke when they made a trip to Blakesburg which was very seldom. They could sit on his porch facing Main Street and smoke their long-stemmed pipes while they watched the people pass. Men could go there too and talk about farming, for the Judge, they knew, was a farmer at heart or he wouldn't raise a big garden in town, keep a couple of cows and fatten a couple of hogs each year. They felt at home in his house for it wasn't furnished with a lot of good furniture paid for by the taxpayers' money. But it was furnished with simple things just like they had in their own homes. Often when he had his crowd at the hogpen his wife was entertaining a half-dozen farmers' wives on the front porch of their home who sat talking, smoking, watching the people pass. Another thing that made them feel kindly toward the Judge, he had a big family just like so many of them had. He was what they called "a good old-fashioned family man." The Judge had fourteen children. And with a family this large in town they knew it was all right for him to keep his hogs and cows and raise his garden. He just about had to do it, they thought. And one of the best things about the Judge, he belonged to the church of the majority of hill people's faith and he was a religious man, who didn't cuss, smoke or drink.

With all of these things in common with the voters, he ran on the Greenough ticket when it looked like this party was dead. One of the Dinwiddie Party men had said the Greenough Party was a dead duck, roasted and ready to stick a fork in until Judge Allie Anderson ran. And he said hell couldn't beat a man like Judge Allie, that he had not only revived his party but he would be the head of it and would be re-elected until he died if he chose to run. Although he always claimed he didn't choose to run but his followers, so many of them, had come to him persuading him and that he couldn't "let them down."

Though he wasn't wholly disliked by the people in Blakesburg, they thought him a little "too generous with the taxpayers' money" to be a judge. Even the people who belonged to the

Greenough Party in Blakesburg didn't see eye to eye with their Judge and didn't approve the way he kept his hogs in the town and the way he lived; yet they admired him for reviving their Party. They admired him for raising good children as well as good hogs; fourteen of them with good health, good religious and moral training and "not a blemish on one of thar characters." Even the ancient Greenough families admired him, though Judge Allie was a Red Neck, for regaining the power they had lost. They were just a little embarrassed when they passed his place at six or seven in the evening and saw so many people gathered with him looking into his hogpen watching his hogs eat. They thought his business transactions should be done at the courthouse. But they reasoned it was better to do business here and keep the party in power than to let the Greenough Party down.

On the evening of September 18th when Judge Allie went down the back walk with his two big buckets, there was a smile on his face. He went to the little stable as was his usual procedure like he went through his daily routine at his office. Here he mixed his slop and table scraps well with middlings and stirred them into a gruel with a stick he kept at the stable door for this purpose. Then he went to the pen and poured the mixture from his buckets into the chute. After he had done this, he stuck his toes through the first crack and pulled his big body up where he could look over and watch his hogs eat. As soon as a group of men, walking around waiting for the Judge to come, saw his big umbrella hat bob up above the pen, they knew he was there and they made for the pen to brag on his hogs and to get from him a few promises. They knew if they got the promises, he was one judge who would not break them.

No fewer than ten men had gathered at this rendezvous. They had climbed up all around the pen looking down at the hogs, watching them eat. They hadn't got down to business with the Judge yet. They were listening to him tell about the good hogs he had fattened in this pen, one had "weighed eight hundred pounds after it was dressed." And that "hit was some larder." Then he went on to tell one of his greatest enjoyments was watching his hogs eat. The Judge said he liked to watch them eat because they were "sich hearty things." He hadn't got through with his lecture of past experiences and pleasures with hogs until one of his fellow Greenough Party members happened to look up from watching the hogs to pop the Judge a question about "the little favor he'd come to ast" when he noticed something was wrong with the sky. He forgot the favor he was going to ask of Judge Allie. "Look at that sky, won't ye!" he screamed.

"I thought hit wuz awful light fer some reason down in the pen," Judge Allie commented as he beheld the spectacle.

At about this time there were shouts in the Blakesburg streets. People were running like frightened rabbits shot at in a weed field. People were running in different directions screaming as they ran.

"I believe it's the end of time," one of the men shouted as he jumped down from the pen and took off running toward the riverbank with his hat in his hand.

"The end of time comes in the twinkling of an eye," another shouted, leaving the pen. "Not even the angels in heaven will know when it comes!"

Like young birds leaving a nest the other Greenoughs followed leaving the Judge still standing there quivering and flabbergasted with his toes in the cracks and his hands clinging to the top rail. He stood there a minute listening to the wild wails of prayer, shouts and songs going up from the people. Then the Judge got down and stood with the empty buckets in his hand. He knew that he had nothing to fear for he was a "saved man." He hadn't wronged any man. He had been honest and God-fearing. And as he had often thought, he wouldn't mind to face his Savior any time. So he stood with his empty buckets watching the skies while the screams of the unfortunate and the damned rang wildly in his ears.

I will go to help my people, he thought.

He had helped them as their Judge and he would help them now. He was positive the end had come. But something came over him. He didn't think he'd have a fear in him in a time like this. He thought he could face it like a man and help lead his people. But when he tried to move his leg to take a step, he couldn't do it. His legs were frozen beneath him as stiff as January icicles. When he tried to drop his empty feed buckets, his hands wouldn't let go. They were frozen to the bucket bails in a death-grip.

"O Jesus," he wailed with a trembling voice as he lifted his face again toward the skies.

And he stood there with his face uplifted watching approaching doom while tears streamed down his clean-shaven jolly red face. . . .

But, Jesus, I can meet You here at my hogpen, he thought in his minute of meditation, his face growing radiant with joy. I can meet You here, dressed the way I am, same as I can meet You in the finest tabernacle in Blakesburg.

4

R UFUS LITTERAL lived alone in a little shack not far from Main Street where a flourmill had burned, a blacksmith shop had stood and a stavemill had sagged to decay. This part of Blakesburg, which ran from Main Street to the railroad tracks, was used now for stacks of railway crossties and the "jockey ground" where Red Necks came to do their swapping. Animal deposits had fertilized this earth until rank crops of ragweed grew, hiding the trash dumps, rusty cans and culled crosstie stacks. It wasn't an inviting place for a man to live. And any way he looked he could see junk, railroad tracks, tiepiles, ragweeds and animals tethered to posts for trading.

Rufus was born in this shack. His unmarried mother had died at the time of his birth and he was raised by his grandmother, who at the time of his birth was sixty-one. When Rufus was seventeen his grandmother died and he lived on where he had always lived. He cleaned his shack, did his own cooking, washed his own clothes besides the odd jobs he did around the town to earn his living.

The people talked about what a strange young man Rufus was. But they gossiped more about who his father was. Gossip had Bruce Livingstone, Franklin Foster, "Old Glory" Gardner, Boliver Tussie and Charlie Allbright. People would look at Rufus and then at one of these men and start making comparisons. They said Rufus had Charlie Allbright's eyes; some said he had Old Glory Gardner's voice, while others said he walked "ezackly" like Franklin Foster.

"Hit makes no neverminds who my Pappie wuz," Rufus would tell any boy who was nosy enough to inquire.

After Rufus had done a day's work and had finished his chores, he would go down to Bill Simpson's Restaurant to loaf. He would seldom go inside. He would stand outside and watch the people come and go. He would talk to anyone who would talk to him. But few people bothered to talk to Rufus. People in Blakesburg didn't take to him very well. He was a lonely figure, who could be seen standing in front of Bill's Place watching the happy people with eager eyes. He wanted to be friendly with them but they were reluctant to speak to Rufus. What he desired most, since his grandmother had died, was human companionship. He lived in a town where there was plenty of it but none for him.

Maybe it was because the people remembered the stories that were circulated at the time of his birth. Many of the women who heard he was their husband's child, threatened a divorce suit. His birth had caused a bigger stir than the birth of any child in Blakesburg. It had caused more threats of divorce. Franklin Foster's wife left him for two weeks when the gossip spread Rufus belonged to her husband. But he told his wife Marvin Clayton had rumored this thing against him to hurt him in business.

And after his birth, people had never forgotten seeing Rufus when he was a little boy wearing long dirty dresses walking along beside his wrinkled grandmother who was slender as a beanpole and wore her skirts long enough to sweep dust from the streets. Rufus had lived close with her; he never played with other little boys his own age. They fought him, and his grandmother would try to protect him for she knew she was the only one left to fight his battles. Even she didn't know who his father was. Only Rufus's mother knew and her secret had died with her.

When Rufus's grandmother sent him to the Primary Schools,

she would take him in the morning and bring him back in the afternoons, though they lived only a few blocks from the school. But she knew how the boys would fight "her boy" and as soon as he came out of the schoolhouse she would be there, feeble as she was, to bring him home. In the schoolroom his teachers protected him. They didn't exactly take to Rufus but he was one of the best pupils in his class. Once he turned down all eight grades in a spelling match when he was only in the fourth grade. He could work any problem in his arithmetic. And he was good in history.

He finished primary school and had started to high school while Old Glory Gardner, one of the men supposed to be his father, was Superintendent of Blakesburg City Schools. Many of the high school pupils, who had heard their parents talk about this situation, picked out many similarities between their Superintendent and his pupil and they whispered to each other about them while "Old Glory" stood before them giving an oration on the flag or on man's patriotic duty to the city, county, state and Republic. But as soon as Rufus's grandmother died and was buried in Potter's Field at Blake County's expense, Rufus left high school and went back to the shack.

"I can't make my living and go to school," he told Bill Simpson. "I have to spend too much time in my house. And I don't get much for my work."

Rufus made more money in the spring when people plowed their gardens. He was a good gardener, knew how to plant, when to plant and what to plant. His grandmother had taught him how to do these things by the signs in the zodiac. And Rufus had followed them since her death. Rumor had it that he could grow the biggest potatoes in Blakesburg and people sought his help each spring to plant their potatoes as well as tend their gardens. But gardening was only for a short season and when work was over in these gardens, Rufus had to walk the streets to find a little job to do. He often picked up paper from the streets and swept the streets; he wasn't "choosy" when it came to work. He would take any job that was offered him.

When he loafed on the streets there was one thing people would talk to him about. He knew more about baseball than any man in the town. When an argument would start in Red Wampler's Barber Shop about what team won the pennant in 1908, and who pitched for the winning and losing sides, Red would send the shoe-shine boy, Curley Vine, to find Rufus. Rufus would hurry to the shop, proud somebody had sent for him and not only would he tell them who won the pennant in 1908, and the losing teams and the pitchers but he would tell them the story of the entire game. How many pitchers each team used and who got a home run. He could tell them how many were fanned on each side, who made the runs. . . . He would tell them what they wanted to know about baseball. If there was anything he knew as much about as raising potatoes, it was baseball.

After the potato and baseball seasons were over, Rufus had very few people ever to say a kind word to him. In the winter the nights were very long and lonely and he started reading his Bible as he had read baseball news. When he read the Bible he began to have ideas about eternity and the direction he was going. Then he went to every church in the town.

"I found all of them cold as ice," he said. "And they didn't follow the Word. Only one preacher did," Rufus went on to explain to Red Wampler. "But he made one mistake when he preached hell was nineteen miles, straight, straight under the ground!"

But Rufus started going to this church, known as the Church of the Old-Fashioned Faith; he found warmth among the old men who came walking on canes. They were kinder to him than the young people who smiled at the way these people conducted their services without any musical instruments. No organ, guitar, nor tuning fork was allowed. They would read a line from one of the hymns in *The Old Sweet Songster* and then they would sing it. But Rufus was delighted with this church. He got acquainted with these old-fashioned people who said "the old-fashioned religion is good enough fer us."

Rufus never missed a meeting at his Old-Fashioned Church. Instead of keeping up on baseball news, he devoted all his time to the Bible. When the preacher didn't "preach the Word," after his sermon was over Rufus would walk up and show him where he had departed from the Scriptures. Rufus sat silently and concentrated on every word the preacher preached and when he was through with one of his long sermons, he could tell the contents of his entire sermon.

In the evenings Rufus would sit at home with his Bible. He would read several chapters and then he would get the *Old Sweet Songster* and read a line from one of his favorite hymns and then he would sing it. Often there would be a crowd of boys gathered outside his shack, for he would draw his window shades so they couldn't see inside, to listen to him pray, read lines from the songs and sing them.

People thought Rufus had "gone batty on the Bible." One thing that made them think this, his grandmother Fannie Litteral, just a few weeks before she died, had carried a basket of cats all over Blakesburg. And one day people noticed Rufus with a white rooster under his arm. He carried the rooster all over town that day. Next day they saw him carrying the same white rooster around over town. And, on the third day, he had caught the Blue Goose Bus with his white rooster under his arm. They didn't know he had taken the rooster for a chore he had done and when he tried to sell the rooster in Blakesburg he couldn't find a sale. Nor could he sell him to the Produce House. So he had gotten on the bus and had taken him to another town where he had soon disposed of him. But not everyone knew this. And the people said Rufus had "fooled with the Old-Fashioned Church" among the old-fashioned people, wearing old-fashioned clothes like them until he'd gone off in the head.

Rufus had drawn his shades for the evening. He had read a

chapter in the Bible and had sat more than an hour meditating over its meaning. He had prayed a long evening prayer. And then he had finished his evening services by reading lines from his favorite hymns in *The Old Sweet Songster* and singing them to himself. After he was through with the religious service he had conducted by himself and for himself, he took his basket and started to get potatoes from the little smokehouse he had built on the other side of his potato patch. But, when Rufus opened the door, he saw something he had never seen before.

The Heavens are showing the handiwork of the Lord, Rufus thought, his eyes blinking, as he looked toward the fiery skies. This is the end of the world! No need to get potatoes now!

He turned, walked back into his shack and closed the door. Then, he lifted all the shades so the jeering mocking young Blakesburg boys could see him with his Bible in his hand on this last night. But when he lifted his shades, there were none of their faces against the windowpanes.

When the end of time is here, Rufus thought, they have something else to think about.

Rufus was reading his Bible in his last hours on this earth when he heard someone pecking on his windowpane.

"I'm too busy to be bothered now," Rufus said, thinking the boys had returned to look in at him and laugh.

But when the pecking grew louder, Rufus looked toward the window. It was not a boy's face against his windowpane this time! It was the face of Judge Allie Anderson. Rufus got up, laid his opened Bible on the standtable and went to the door.

"I've got to see you, Rufus," Judge Allie said when Rufus opened the door.

"Come in, Judge," Rufus said.

"This is enough to shake a man to his foundations, Rufus," Judge Allie said, shaking his head as he entered the door. "When I first saw the end comin', I jist froze in my tracks. I couldn't move! And then I thought of something that made me move! Somethin' I had to do before I meet my Maker!"

"It's the right time to finish your business here on this earth, Judge," Rufus said, looking at the Judge's beet-red face, "but I wouldn't think you'd have anything betweext you and the Lord, Judge," Rufus continued. "You've been a righteous and upright man!"

"But I've got a confession to make," Judge Allie said, looking down at the floor. "I am yer Pappie, Rufus, I'm the only man in this town who hasn't been accused. And I'm the right man!"

Rufus stood silently looking at the Judge who was now looking down as he shuffled his brogan shoes on the clean bare planks, making a screaking noise.

"I know Frank Foster, Bruce Livingstone, Charlie Allbright, Boliver Tussie, Old Glory Gardner and others 've been accused o' bein' yer Pappie," Judge Allie continued, "but these men 're innocent. I started these things myself to hep me politically. I told the fellars gathered around my hogpen these things. They spread 'em all over the city 'n the county!"

"Confess it to God," Rufus said, breaking his silence. "It don't bother me none!"

"But I thought you ought to know, Rufus," Judge Allie said. "You've got several half brothers and half sisters. You're not alone in the world."

"It's a poor time to tell me now," Rufus snorted. "You've never bothered to help your son! Not even to give him a job, digging ditches along the county highway! Not even o' a-hoein' 'taters in yer garden! And you've caused a heap of misery among the families in this town! You shore have enough betweext you and the Lord! You've sown a seed bed of sin!"

Judge Allie couldn't speak. He couldn't look his son in the face. He stood, looking at his feet.

"I'd never profess to be a Christian, 'Pappie'," Rufus continued. "I'm not proud of you, 'Pappie'! I'm very busy here myself with my own soul . . . and if you don't mind. . . ."

5

EVERYBODY IN Blakesburg knew Attorney Joe Oliver had many enemies and that was why he kept his window shades drawn at night. Joe was afraid one of the men he had sent to the pen back in the Twenties for making moonshine would slip around his house at night and shoot him through one of the windows. He had made a specialty of sending men to the penitentiary. Joe had always been against whiskey, especially moonshine. And it was his greatest delight to fight a chicken thief hard enough in the courts to send him to the pen, even if he had only stolen one chicken.

Other Blakesburg lawyers could send men to the pen and after they had served their sentences they returned without a lot of malice for the lawyers who had sent them. But they all had malice against Joe for the way he had bullied them in court, the names he had called them and got by with. That was why Joe had a premonition of death. He thought one of these petty lawbreakers he had bullied in court and had sent to the pen would return and bump him off.

But the good people in the town thought Joe one of their most prominent citizens. They knew he wouldn't defend a moonshiner or a chicken thief or gambler. They knew he wouldn't take a divorce case unless it was one of immoral charges against the husband or wife. People knew that Joe was a "clean, decent and upright gentleman of great moral integrity." He had taught most of the town's young people in his famous Sunday School Class.

There was only one thing the people held against him. He was a little old-fashioned about his house. He was a leading citizen in a city of two thousand inhabitants and he didn't have modern plumbing. When he was approached on the subject of why he didn't have running water and a bathroom in his house, he quickly informed the meddler his house was beyond the slough and it was very difficult and expensive to get pipes from the city's water works to his house. And he went on to inform him the place belonged to his father before him and his grandfather before his father and they had lived in the house without plumbing and had raised fine and decent families and he and his family weren't any better than his people that had lived here before him. And due to the feeling in this town for the old families, Joe Oliver was let alone.

Even when the WPA was making outdoor privies for the poor and made one in the far corner of Joe Oliver's backyard, there wasn't anything said about it; yet Joe had made all sorts of remarks about the WPA's privy builders. He had criticized such silly adventure into Public Works when the taxpayers' money in the end had to pay for it. Had any other man as well-to-do as Joe Oliver in Blakesburg had the WPA to build him a privy, he would have been jeered at by all the town's people. But because of the "good" Joe Oliver had done in the city by sending petty thieves and moonshiners to the pen, by his refusal to take divorces except on immoral grounds, people didn't criticize Joe. He was one of the most respected men in the town and he probably would have been to this day if it hadn't been for his having the WPA to build him that privy in the far corner of his backyard. If he had had a bathroom in his house, his story would surely have been a different one.

Joe had finished eating his supper behind locked doors and drawn window shades. And then he had sat in his soft rocking chair and had read the *Dartmouth Times*, his favorite out-of-town paper. This was his routine evening after evening. And naturally, before bedtime he made his regular trip to the privy.

On this particular evening Joe went out at the back door and started down the little sidewalk bordered with late-blooming flowers. At first he thought he had drawn his blinds too early and had missed the time of day. He could have reached down on the little sidewalk and picked up a pin, even though his eyes were not as good as they had been—due to ransacking his old-fashioned lawbooks for law to back up his cases. But when Joe Oliver looked up at the sky, he wondered if he were asleep or dreaming . . . or if he had died and had awakened in another world. He had never seen anything like this in his life.

He stood there, yet he had the urge to go on. But he was almost paralyzed with fear. He wasn't dreaming for this was his home and there was the WPA privy with the little ventilation pipe sticking up from its roof. And there was where he had the urge to go but his legs wouldn't take him forward. They were weak and trembling and would hardly bear up his two hundred pounds of weight! This man who didn't have any fear of another lawyer shaking his fist under his nose and who didn't have any fear of shaking his fist under his opponent's nose, a man whom the people of the town believed without fear except of the sneaking petty criminals trying to shoot him through a window, was now about to go into hysterics.

He knew as well as anybody these strange signs in the sky meant the end of time. Never had he seen anything like this. But he had read somewhere in the Bible when he was looking for passages to quote in his trials against the moonshiners and the chicken thieves that there would be strange signs in the skies before the end of time and now they had come. He tried to think of the exact words he had read in his Bible but his mind wasn't the same under these circumstances. His legs weren't the same . . . and he was about to go to pieces. Suddenly he obtained enough control of his body to do a perfect about-face on the little walk; then his two hundred pounds seemed lighter than a bag of duck feathers for he leaped through the air like a night-prowling tomcat. And he was on the back porch. He jerked the door open and ran inside. One more leap and he sprawled across the bed, flat on his stomach with his face against the spread.

"Joe, Joe," his wife, Arabella, said as she jumped from her chair and ran toward him, "what's wrong? Heart attack?"

"Ah, my God no, Arabella," he panted. "It's the end of time!"

"Joe? . . ."

"That's right. Look at the signs in the sky!"

"Oh, Joe," she said, her face pained with fright as she ran toward the window and peeped from behind a blind.

When Arabella got one peep at the sky she screamed and ran back toward the bed where Joe lay sprawled and was muttering words Arabella couldn't understand. They sounded like a prayer . . . but Arabella had heard him pray in public where his words were distinct and the ring of them was as musical as the soft ring of church bells on a Sabbath morning.

"You're right, Joe," Arabella wept. "The time has come! The end of the world is here!"

"Have you got any confessions to make, darling?" Joe asked.

"No, my dear," she said. "I've been on Jesus' side since I've be :n sixteen!"

Then Joe continued his mumbling words she couldn't understand.

"What's wrong, Joe?" she asked, standing with her mouth open.

"Have you allus been true to me, darling?"

"Always, Joe!"

She watched Joe wiggle and writhe on the bed as if he were in torture. And then she remembered how the men moved restlessly and writhed when Joe had questioned them on the witness stand. Joe was now moving in the same manner as she had seen them move, wiggle and writhe while her powerful husband shot the questions to them, tangled them in their evidence and made them liars. He seemed to be in as much agony as she had ever seen anyone her husband had persecuted in the past while spectators packed the courthouse, filling all the seats, standing in the aisles, sitting in the windows and cheering the great lawyer as he cleaned the county and town of its bad men. And she thought that Joe, in this hour of the earth's being swallowed into eternity, was repenting over the things he had said and had done to these men.

"Have you been loyal to me, Joe?" she asked, suddenly, after thinking these other thoughts.

She knew that Joe had been loyal to her but since he had put this question to her now after they had raised a family of seven children and they had married off and left their nest, she thought she might as well be polite and ask him. Now she watched Joe's going through great contortions and drops of sweat big as grains of corn popped out on his neck and the sides of his face. She couldn't see all of his face since it was against the bedspread.

She thought it strange that Joe just muttered more words and didn't answer her question directly.

"Have you been loyal to me, Joe?" she repeated.

More sweat popped out over Joe's face and neck and she watched it run onto the bedspread. He rolled restlessly and moaned and muttered. And Arabella knew now that she had never seen a witness her husband had persecuted take on like her husband . . . even though he had vilified them and made them look small as ants while hundreds cheered. But only she was beside Joe and he was taking on more than any witness she had ever seen at the hundreds of trials where the people of the town went since trials were one of their favorite forms of recreation and her husband had been the people's greatest entertainer.

He had given thousands thrills in the jam-packed courtroom.

" 'Bella," Joe said softly, "I must confess."

"Do you have a confession to make, Joe?" Arabella screamed, surprised that her good husband had one to make.

"Yes, I have, darling!"

"I just hope it's not one thing," Arabella wept. "I don't think I could stand it!"

Joe lay silent now while his hysterics ebbed slowly away. Arabella knew the confession was coming.

It can't be a woman, Arabella thought. Joe is a moral man. Everybody knows that!

"Darling, I hate to tell you," Joe said. "But I must be right. The slate must be clean in Judgment. There's nothing I can hide there! There's not anything I want to hide when I'm judged. It's a woman!"

"A woman!" Arabella screamed. "Who is the strumpet!"

"Don't weep now," Joe whispered. "It's too late to weep!"

"But who is she?"

"Mattie Pratt!"

"Oh! That buxom Red Neck thing!" Arabella screamed. "My housemaid that cleaned my house and cooked for me and my children! Oh, that thing!"

"But, darling. . . ."

"Don't darling me any more," she wept hysterically as Joe started moving restlessly on the bed again. "When did this happen? How long has it happened?"

"For years," Joe confessed softly.

"No wonder you didn't rant and rave like a lot of the other men in this town," she screamed at him. "You! Living with two women . . . your wife and the hired girl! She worked for me fifteen years, Joe! All that time?"

"Yes, 'Bella."

Arabella gave a wild scream as she ran to the press to get

her coat and hat. But Joe didn't notice until he heard the door slam and then he jumped up from the bed and ran to the door. But when he got to the door she was running toward Main Street amid the fluxions of yellow light. He could see her plain as day as she ran into the approaching doom.

6

DeWit Addington's coming was an event in Blakesburg's social life never to be forgotten. Dee, as he was later called by the people, wasn't a native of Blakesburg or of Blake County. If his county had Greenough and Dinwiddie Red Necks and Blue Bloods, no one knew. And the young women didn't bother to find out. He was the most handsome man ever to come to Blakesburg. The girls spoke of him as "bein' better-lookin' than any movie actor." They compared him to Clark Gable and Charles Boyer. The Blakesburg girls no longer held to these celluloid favorites, since they had in their midst a very much alive and handsome dream man.

Dee Addington wasn't a movie actor either. He came to Blakesburg to clerk in a store. Maybe Winn Fields was a better business man than people thought. He had been losing his grocery business, a little each year, until his store had dwindled from one of the well-established places of business to one "about to go under." But after he hired Dee as a clerk, he came back by leaps and bounds until he had not only regained the business he had lost, but he had become the leading merchant of the town. There was so much talk about Dee's looks that when mothers sent their young daughters to buy bread, they would go to Winn Fields' Grocery just to get a look at this handsome man behind the counter. If he waited on them it was a thrill and they went out of the store with "oo's" and "ah's" such as people had never heard before in Blakesburg.

Young men had heard their sweeties talk so much about this

Romeo they visited Fields' Grocery just to get a look at him. When they went to the store, naturally, they bought something. They didn't want anyone to know they were making special trips to see the "handsomest man in town." Many of these men remarked he was a little "sissy" or, "he held his head so high it was dangerous for him to walk in the rain." They found fault with him, and as the women said, it was because all the men were jealous. Even married women spoke about Dee to their husbands. They said he should be in Hollywood in front of a movie camera instead of being in Blakesburg behind a grocery counter.

The boys found out Dee wasn't exactly a "sissy" as they had often said he was. He smoked cigarettes behind the counter, a pipe in the evenings at the Winston Boarding House and on Sundays he'd stroll down the street smoking a big cigar. He would take a drink with the boys. They soon found him to be fond of Tid Fortner's "pure corn." Said he held the horsequart bottleneck a long time in his mouth while his small Adam's apple run up and down his smooth swan-like neck. And when Toad Blevins called him a "sissy" once because he was jealous of him, Dee said, "I'm not a sissy, Toad. I cuss, smoke, drink and I go out with women."

All the mothers in Blakesburg with daughters eligible to be married, dressed them in as fine clothes as they could afford to buy, to attract the big blue eyes of Dee Addington. They knew he was a good catch and each wanted him for her son-in-law. For Dee was six feet tall, fair-complexioned with black curly hair, neat black eyebrows that looked like they had been mascaraed, perfect white teeth, long "musician's hands." But the fathers of these husband-seeking daughters speculated that this new Romeo of Blakesburg had some faults.

At first Dee was rather reluctant about going with any one girl. He was often with many boys and girls at the Drug Store which was a popular place among the sons and daughters of the old families. He was seldom seen at Bill Simpson's Restaurant, although he did go since he couldn't afford to let any place go untouched where there was a possibility of drawing more business to Winn Fields' Grocery. He was working for Winn and his salary had been increased time after time until he was now the best paid grocery clerk in Blakesburg. And maybe that was one reason why Dee didn't choose a girl and go steadily with her. If he had, many of the girls who considered him their dream man, would have gone to one of the other stores.

The time came when Dee found his choice. She wasn't the best-looking girl among the eligible list. Nearly everyone was surprised when Dee started dating Ena Tillman. "W'y, she's not a bit pretty," Roxena Barton said. Every girl didn't come out and say so but she knew in her heart she was better looking than Ena. And she couldn't understand why Dee had chosen her. But his going with Ena didn't exactly hurt Winn Fields' business . . . not then. . . .

Maybe many of the fathers had guessed right. Maybe the other girls were proud they hadn't been Dee's choice. Dee hadn't been going with Ena, a respectable girl from a respectable family, seven months until everyone in the town knew what was going to happen. Ena would come downtown to the store every day with a basket on her arm. She would walk inside and just stand with her empty basket and stare across the counter at her dream man as he sliced beef or weighed sugar. She wouldn't speak to him, but she would stare at him with woebegone blue eyes that made all the women sorry for her.

"I told you so," women whispered to each other behind Ena's back.

Since Ena's dream man wouldn't come from behind the counter to ask her what she wanted, she would stand and look at him until she was tired enough to fall before she walked out of the store with her empty basket on her arm.

Winn Fields talked to Dee about it. Winn knew that Dee

was hurting his business and he told him he should marry Ena. But he wouldn't marry Ena, not "at the point of a gun." And that was that. People thought this would hurt Dee's chances of ever going with another girl. But it didn't. He was going with Sibbie Day when Ena had her baby. People wondered how Sibbie felt when she walked down the street and saw Ena pushing a perambulator. They wondered how Dee felt when Ena pushed it inside the store and looked at him behind the counter. Dee never came from behind the counter to look at his daughter. He didn't look up unless he had to. Ena would stand and stare at him then she would roll her carriage with her sleeping or crying infant outside. On many occasions Ena and Sibbie were in the store at the same time.

When Sibbie became pregnant, another girl from one of the old families, there was plenty of talk. There was the talk of a rope, a horsewhip, feathers and tar. Two girls from the same town were too many, something the people didn't intend to stand. The men talked. They didn't give a damn if Dee did look like Clark Gable and talk like Charles Boyer. They went to Winn Fields and told him to get rid of Dee. After Dee had told the young men of Blakesburg he wasn't a sissy, that he drank, smoked, cussed and went out with women, only now did they understand what he meant.

When Winn told Dee to get out of his store Dee told him he would put up a store of his own in Blakesburg and that he would run him out of business. Then Winn laughed a mean laugh and told Dee he would do well to get away from Blakesburg in one piece. Everybody thought this but Dee. He went down the street and rented himself an empty store building that no one else would rent because an evil eye had once been cast upon this building and no one had ever had any luck with a grocery store in this place. Many had rented it and had to take the Bankrupt Law in the end. When Dee rented this store, everybody thought he was not only immoral but he had lost his mind. Here was a man who had wronged two Blakesburg girls, had married neither, and was now going to compete with Winn Fields, a popular Blakesburg merchant, and run him out of business.

Dee had saved enough money to stock his dilapidated store with a few necessities. As Dee told a few of the county Red Necks, he had "started on a shoestring now" but later he would buy their eggs, butter, beans and chickens and give them a better price than any merchant in Blakesburg. Such talk pleased these farmers. And they returned to trade with Dee.

Another event in Dee's life that surprised Blakesburg was when he found himself a wife. They knew he'd never be able to marry a girl from Blakesburg; they doubted he'd be able to find one in the county. They wanted to see his young bride who was out of the state. She had been sent to Blake County by an agency.

Dee and his beautiful bride, Grace Blenner, went to house-keeping in the back room of their charmed store. He and Grace worked hard together through the late Thirties. And, maybe, what caused Dee to take to drink more than usual was the way his past in Blakesburg came back to him. No doubt he often thought it would have been better if he had left the town when he left Winn Fields' Grocery. For Ena Tillman kept rolling the perambulator into his store where she would stand and look at him first and then at his wife. She would often stay thirty min-utes and stand and look. And then she would roll the perambu-lator out the way she had come without saying a word to Dee or Grace. Sibbie Day walked into his store with the baby in her arms one day.

"Have a look," she asked Dee, pulling the blanket from over the young infant's face.

There was nothing for Dee to do but look.

"One thing, I'm glad he doesn't look like you, Beautiful," she said and walked out.

The people of Blakesburg knew this must be hard on Grace.

"Poor girl, married to that ornery thing," more than one woman said. "She didn't know what she was a-gettin' into. She drove her ducks to a bad market!"

As the spider had spun his web to trap the fly, life had spun a web to trap Dee. Here were Sibbie and Ena and here was his wife Grace pregnant and now he had taken to drink to drown his recurring past. But his beautiful Grace was not only a pretty woman, she was a practical woman. While Dee lay drunk in their one room in the back of the store, Grace went ahead with the business. She was a Northern woman who worked more than she talked. Talk was all right with her except when she had work to do and her husband was too drunk to help then she rolled up her sleeves and went to work no matter if she was pregnant. Blakesburg women had never seen her like, this beautiful woman they felt so sorry for but who didn't feel sorry for herself. Grace was fighting "to make a go of their marriage." She wouldn't let it go on the rocks even when Dee was drinking more as the months passed.

Their first child was born and another was on the way and Dee had become one of the best customers Tid Fortner had. He had to have his pure corn. He had become a "quart-a-day man" and was now classed with Jeff Hargis, Bass Keaton, Bill Simpson, Oll and Temp Spradling, Willie Devers and Boliver Tussie. Everybody said Dee was a goner. But something happened right before their second child was born.

Thursday, September 18th, Dee had lain down on the bed in back of the store. Grace, though heavy with child, had not only waited on their increasing Red Neck trade from the county, but she had made Dee hot toddies all afternoon to sober him. She carried him buttermilk to drink. She also took care of their small son. It was a lot for one woman to do, the people thought, and they wondered how she did it. They respected her more than ever for her fight and her courage. It was more than any one of them could or would do.

At approximately eight o'clock that Thursday evening when the people were getting excited about the lights in the sky, Grace went to the door to see what the commotion was. She saw something which she believed to be the same she had seen many times in her native Wisconsin. The lights didn't bother her. She stood observing the electric flashes in the sky remembering how they had flashed over Wisconsin lighting up the fertile farmland on long dark lonely nights. She, too, was amused the way Blakesburg people were taking on. She had never seen anything like it in her life. As she stood in the open doorway, the noise of the shouting people, their prayers and screams went back into the room where Dee was still lying on the bed.

"What's that, Grace?" Dee asked, getting up and sitting on the side of the bed and rubbing his head.

"Come and see for yourself," she said. "It's something . . . I can't tell you!"

Dee heard the wild screams, shouts, guitars playing, and people singing hymns. The tumult grew louder and Dee hurried to the door. As soon as he had had one look at the sky he screamed, "My God, what is it?"

"What do you think it is?" Grace asked calmly.

"The end of the world," he screamed. "Let's go to the church!"

"I'm all right," Grace said calmly.

"Oh, my God," Dee screamed, leaping wildly into the street. "Save me, O Jesus, until tomorrow!"

Grace watched him run toward the Drug Store on his way to the closest church.

"O Jesus, my God and Saviour, will you be merciful on me a sinner vile and vain," he screamed before he reached the Drug Store.

He was running stiff-legged like a buck rabbit through deep snow, his black curly hair bouncing up and down like potato-filled sacks on a jolting wagon. His hands were above his head.

"O my God, have mercy on me," he screamed as he turned the corner, heading up an alley that was without a street light toward the oldest church in town. But this alley was no longer a well of darkness. It was brighter than any afternoon sunlight could have made it.

When Dee ran up to the church house, he found the doors were locked and that it was a pool of darkness inside. He pounded on the doors with his fists but all he heard was his knocks against the silent doors and the screams, shouts and prayers of people running in every direction over the town.

"O God," Dee pleaded falling to his knees at the church-house door, "if you will only save me until tomorrow, I will come here and publicly confess my sins! I will wipe the slate clean! I will work for you, God! O Jesus," he prayed as he pounded the door, "I'll be a different man! Save me, a sinner, on this night from eternal torment!"

7

" 'Around my neck's a golden chain,
And every link in Jesus' Name," Muff Henderson sang as he danced down the street.

"That ain't so, Muff," Dave Doyster yelled to him. "Ye're still a-doin' that two-step! And this ain't a night for dancin'!"

"A-dancin' right into eternity!" Bertha Skaggs said as she took one look at Muff and hurried on her way.

"Wonder where old Muff thinks he's a-goin'?" Boliver Tussie said then he spat a sluice of ambeer on the street. "Thinks he's a-goin' someplace, don't he?"

"Right into Satan's arms," Arabella Whitaker told Boliver as she hurried by. "That's where he's a-goin'! He'll git enough dancin' thar!"

" 'Around my neck's a golden chain,
And every link in Jesus' Name!' "

"Ye won't be a-wearin' hit much longer, Brother, in a time like this," Booten Winston said as he came up the street from Haddington's Beer Parlor and met Muff. "Ye've been a-dancin' too long!"

"Fer thar won't be no dancin' in Heaven," Addition Bennet said, shaking his head sadly as he took one fleeting glance at Muff then at the sky and hurried on his way.

"He's done that two-step so long he don't know no other way to walk," Windie Griffie said, rubbing his big rough hand over his sandy-colored beard as he watched Muff two-step into the swirling mass of hysterical people. "No matter how much he sings now hit won't do him no good!"

Muff Henderson had come from old Blakesburg stock. His grandparents had been born in Blakesburg, had lived their lives in this city and had died here. His parents had been born in Blakesburg, had lived here all their lives and had never been away from the city a hundred miles. But neither his parents nor his grandparents were known to dance very much. Not one of them could be called a great dancer. And everybody wondered why Muff had taken to dance as other prominent Blakesburg citizens had taken to chawing and smoking the "filthy weed" or drinking honorable herbs. Like Bass Keaton's taking to hoss swapping when there wasn't a horse trader among his people, Muff had taken to dancing when there wasn't a dancer among his people.

When Muff was a little boy he would go to Uncle Sweeter Dabney's house and listen to Uncle Sweeter's magic fiddle. When he played the old dance tunes young Muff would dance all over the yard. Many people said his listening to Uncle Sweeter's fiddle had put the fire in his feet. For when Muff heard the fiddle he always had to dance, even if it were on the street or under a shade tree on the grass. Many people said they had seen Muff out dancing at night on the streets when the wind blew through the leaves on the elm trees.

But there was only one step he could do well. And that was the two-step. When he walked down the street he didn't walk straight like other people. He sorta shuffled along and did the two-step. He had done this step so much in his forty-five years of living that it had become a habit to him. Dancing was as great an enjoyment to Muff as the raw burley tobacco leaf was to Boliver Tussie or a horsequart of pure corn was to Jeff Hargis. Muff didn't drink, "chaw," or smoke . . . but he danced. It was the greatest enjoyment in his life. Yet, his enjoyment had caused him much trouble.

When Muff married Victoria Slackburn, his first wife, he started taking her to dances where they did the two-step. Vick was a tall slender girl with plenty of stamina but she couldn't do the two-step with Muff as fast and as long as he wanted to do it. For Muff set a fast pace—faster than anybody on the dance floor. And he never stopped to rest as long as the music lasted. He would start dancing at dusk and if the music went on all night he would still be going strong at daylight. There wasn't a woman in Blakesburg or in Blake County who could dance with him. The first night Vick and Muff danced together they danced all night. Vick stayed with him this one night but she was in bed for two weeks after the dance.

But Vick wouldn't give up. She went back to the dances with him, since she wanted to make him a good wife. She wanted him to be satisfied. Though she didn't like the two-step she danced it with Muff because she knew it was his favorite step, and that it was habitual with him as much as coffee, tobacco, or whiskey could be with other men and women. She would dance with him as long as she could stand it and then she would have to rest.

At first she hated to see other women dance with him while she rested, but she soon became accustomed to this. For as soon as she started resting, Muff would ask another strong vigorous woman to dance with him. And he could take her over the floor at a tremendous pace . . . always far ahead of the fastest music. It wasn't long until Vick grew friendly toward any woman who would dance with her husband and give her a rest. And by the friendly co-operation of her women friends, she was able to continue dancing with Muff and thereby continue marriage for eight years. But as the years passed, she began to see signs of fatigue and worry, and lines grooved her face. Also, when she walked down the street people noticed she had begun to do sort of a two-step in her walk.

After Vick had stood all she could stand of this sort of life and her physical vigor had begun to wane, she sued Muff for a divorce.

"If I don't git away from a-dancin' that two-step," she told Attorney Joe Oliver, "I'll be a dead woman before I'm thirty! Look at me now! I do the two-step when I walk down the street! I do it in my sleep! And I look old enough to be your mother!"

Joe Oliver took the case and that was as good as a divorce.

Just as soon as the divorce was granted, Muff married Rinda Salyers.

"I've got somebody to dance with me now," he said. "I wasn't fooled this time! I went a-dancin' with 'er the other night and she was a-goin' strong at four in the mornin'!"

But Vick didn't marry another dancer. She married a farmer, much older than herself.

"I'm not a-gettin' fooled again," she said. "I've watched Jim Turner work. He moves at a snail's speed! And that's what I want after all I've been through. I need a long rest! I pity poor Rinda!"

Rinda didn't have as many women friends as Vick. And she only thought she could dance with Muff. Maybe she had partly judged him by his appearance. He was a small man with a sandy-colored mustache, spider legs, winking blue eyes, and long dangling arms. He didn't look like the man of action that he was. But he could outdance any man or woman in Blakesburg or Blake County. He had the stamina and he exerted it in full force in these supreme moments of enjoyment on the dance floor.

It took Rinda exactly four years to find out she couldn't keep up with Muff's pace. She looked at herself in the mirror one day.

"Honest, child," she said, "I didn't know my own self. There were grooves in my skin beneath my eyes as big as quail's tracks in the snow! And right then I went to see Joe Oliver! And Joe

Oliver said to me, 'Rinda, child, you'd better get a divorce as much as I hate to see people divorce. If you don't, you'll be a dead woman before you're thirty years old!' And then I thought about poor Vick!"

Two months after Rinda had divorced Muff, he married Daisy Stableton, a big buxom woman who was the very picture of health. Everybody thought Muff had a woman who could dance with him now. She started off like a whirlwind picking Muff up and swinging him like he was a small boy. But before their first year of marriage was over, everybody learned that dancing would remove surplus flesh. And Daisy Stableton was no longer a big buxom woman with apple-colored cheeks. She was getting as thin as a whippoorwill in the spring. Her cheeks had lost their bloom. In two years Muff had divorced her. He said she hadn't come up to his expectation. He didn't have what he had expected to find in the woman he wanted for his helpmate in life.

After Muff had divorced Daisy, he waited a year before he took unto himself his fourth wife. "I ain't exactly soured on marriage," Muff told Booten Winston, his boyhood friend. "I think I can find love yet, a wife who will go through life with me and dance to the end!"

And Muff married a young Red Neck girl, Doshie Kegley, whom he found plowing a mule in the tobacco patch one day. She had strong muscular legs and strong arms. She had enough wind to run down a pig that had gotten out of the pen. Muff had watched her catch it going uphill. He knew Doshie was built for a dancer.

"She's my wife! I said to myself right there," he told Booten Winston. "I knew I's a-goin' to marry her! And she's stayed with me six years! Doshie's a powerful dancer if I ever danced with one!"

But Doshie was in the bloom of youth. She wasn't half as old as Muff, whom the years had been very slow to change.

His hair was getting gray but he could still do the two-step all night. And his fourth wife, Doshie, young as she was, was beginning to walk like she was doing the two-step. However, no one laughed at her for walking this way as they had laughed at his first wife, Victoria. They had a feeling of pity for Doshie because they knew what a struggle she would have in her future years of marriage with Muff. Until this night when the Creator of the Earth had sent His warning. And now they knew that Muff's dancing days were over.

"'Around my neck's a golden chain,

And every link in Jesus' name,'" Windie Griffie heard faintly above the shouting crowd. Windie stood stroking his long, sandy-colored beard with his big hand, looking in the direction from which the sound came.

8

A T THE age of ninety Uncle Sweeter Dabney was the last leaf clinging to his family tree. His wife, who had borne him eleven children, had been dead for thirty years. Eight of his children had died in infancy. Of the three who had survived infancy, his only daughter died of typhoid before she was seventeen; one of his sons was drowned at the age of thirteen while trying to swim the river and his oldest son was stabbed to death in a fight before he was twenty. Uncle Sweeter may have had some distant relatives somewhere in the world for a few of his people through the latter part of the eighteenth and through all of the nineteenth century had followed the sunset toward the west. But Uncle Sweeter wasn't interested in any of his relatives who had moved away. In the first place, they weren't any good. Such relatives he wouldn't claim nor have any part of. Blakesburg had always been good enough for him, his father, grandfather, and his great-grandfather before him, whose ancestral home with very little improvements except a change of roof every half century, he had inherited; and it was in this house he had brought his wife, his children were born and had died. Upon the hill above Blakesburg they were buried.

Though Uncle Sweeter was a direct descendant of the founding fathers and a Dinwiddie in political and religious faith, he never did any boasting about his family tree. He had just lived in his old home after all his family was gone. Citizens in the town would pass by his house and see him out with a sickle cutting his yardgrass for he wouldn't use a lawnmower. It was a newfangled invention that scared his chickens, his cats and his dog. Sir Robert would run at a lawnmower and bark and try to sink his teeth in it same as he would a passing bicycle, motorcycle or a car. And Sir Robert, like his master who was the oldest citizen in Blakesburg, was the oldest dog in the town. He was content now to lie by his master's side, and listen as well as he could when his master played the fiddle. Not only could Uncle Sweeter make the dogs and cats listen but he could play tunes, the old dance tunes and the old ballads that would start the young to dancing and make the old shed tears. Often, his yard in spring and summer would be filled with people to share with his dog, cats and chickens, his old-time fiddle music. They would come and listen for hours. Even the women from the old families would come, women who said they despised this old-time music, just because their fiddler was a direct descendant of Blakesburg's founding fathers.

When Uncle Sweeter walked over into the main part of the town each day to sit on one of Alex Scroggin's seats on the courthouse yard, whittle for the longest shavings and talk and argue with such young men as Charlie Allbright, Jeff Hargis and Bass Keaton, he would go dressed in his dirty rags. There would be dirt behind his ears and his frayed clothes would be spotted with grease where he had done his cooking and there might be a little yellow from the yolk of an egg in his long white beard that looked dirty with age. And there was always a little ambeer stain in the long fringes of his white handlebar mustache. Yet, there was no one who bothered to help tidy the old man, to look after his clothes, to wash and mend them and to help select his food and to cook it for him. There were guesses as to the last time he had taken a bath and Charlie Allbright said the last time he saw Uncle Sweeter in the river was in 1910. He fell off the ferryboat then. That was the last time anyone had seen him in the water.

But Uncle Sweeter was a part of the town, as much if not

more than any man in it. If there was ever a Blakesburg citizen who had the town at heart, who had seen it come of age, and who could talk for hours on its past history, it was he. His grandfather, Ezekiel Dabney, had told him the stories of the fights with the Indians and how they took the place, then a few wigwams, and how they had made a city of it. He had the history of the town in his head from its beginning, the history of all the old families, the houses and all the things that had taken place. But he was none too familiar with the Red Necks, whose family history he hadn't been curious to learn about. Many newspapermen on the local papers had from time to time gotten stories about the history of Blakesburg from Uncle Sweeter and published them.

Uncle Sweeter would have none of the Blakesburg churches as the years crept upon him and his hair grew whiter and whiter and his back bent a little each year with the weight of time. Many of the people thought this strange about him, for as he "neared the end of his travail upon God's footstool" in Blakesburg, it was contrary to human nature for him to get farther away from the church; had he been normal as other men, like Perry Denton for instance who was saved at eighty-two and was baptized in a running stream of water, he would have been "reborn again." But it was his fiddle that kept him out of the churches, his playing the old-time dance tunes for Blakesburg's young and old and the Red Necks who came to the Fourth of July and Labor Day celebrations and danced from the time they came to town until they left. They were great dancers and Uncle Sweeter admired them for this. He loved to fiddle for them and that is the reason why the "saved and sanctified" people in the town thought his fiddle was going to keep him from Heaven, because a fiddle could never belong to Jesus Christ like a guitar could; a fiddle was for dancing feet, dancing on the courthouse square on Saturdays, Salesdays and big celebrations. It was an instrument of the Devil.

Sallie Bain, a Red Neck who had been converted by Reverendess Spence, took it upon herself to look after the soul of this poor old white-haired and white-whiskered "Blue Blood" now bent by the weight of the years, living alone with his dog, cats and chickens. She had been very kind to him by talking to him on the streets, and even by flattering him about how any man could have so much knowledge in his head about the history of any town. Though she thought his fiddle was an instrument of the Devil, whom she so despised and fought on every occasion on the courthouse square and in the street, Uncle Sweeter was flattered by this woman. She had often told him, for a man of his age, he drew the smoothest fiddle bow across the strings of any man in the world and that he could out-fiddle any of the young bucks in the county. And when she got this close to him, he allowed her inside his house to cook for him when he was sick. She even washed his clothes on several occasions. Once she cut his hair, though it wasn't a good haircut, and trimmed his mustache and "cropped his whiskers."

And when she did these things the gossip went over the town she was trying to get the old Dabney home, that she had hopes he would leave it to her in his will. Such things had happened in Blakesburg when the last leaf of one family was ready to die, a stranger came in and took over and got the property plus a good bit of cash. And now this Sallie Bain, a Red Neck, was accused and stiff fingers were pointed at her in public. She was accused of "wrapping the old man around her finger" while her husband was an accessory to the fact. But Sallie came back at her accusers with her soft answers and not with stiff pointing fingers in their faces, because it took a soft answer to turn away wrath. She asked them if they knew God and if they didn't, it was about time; then she told them how she felt for Uncle Sweeter Dabney, "one of the sweetest old men" in the town, who was on the downward road and needed help to find his Savior. And when she was asked why she went after him instead of Tid Fortner, the biggest bootlegger in town, she answered that Uncle Sweeter would make a wonderful angel in Heaven with his long white hair, his long white beard, dressed in a long white robe. She said he would look like one of the patriarchs of old in Heaven. She said she believed he would look like Moses.

No one would believe Sallie Bain until on the night when the world was on fire from the north, the night when all signs pointed to the end of time, when there was great confusion among the citizens on the streets of Blakesburg. She left her husband, Ephriam Bain, alone with her four children while she took off for Uncle Sweeter's decaying ancestral home on the outskirts of Blakesburg.

When the people saw her running toward his home they wondered why she would be going back there now for even if she would get his property, and probably a little money and plenty of antique furniture, it wouldn't do her any good. She was just too late and all of her cunning conniving wouldn't do her any good. But she ran through the light of the wrath coming from the north, unmindful of the hisses and slurs of the people whom she passed on the way. And she knew that in a time like this, Uncle Sweeter would come to his senses and she thought he more than likely would be down on his knees praying. She knew that in a time like this he would put his fiddle away.

Before she reached the house she thought she heard sweet music on the slow-moving wind that rustled the leaves on the elms above her head. It was the music from the bands of angels, she thought. It was the sweetest music she had ever heard. And then she heard a livelier music, music for the steps of marching feet. Almost out of breath, she ran from the street, opened the rusty iron gate and ran upon his lawn.

"Uncle Sweeter," Sallie said, grunting for breath, "are you ready?"

There was Uncle Sweeter sitting in his straight-backed chair that was leaned against the slowly disintegrating brick wall of his house, with his fiddle against his soft white-bearded cheek, and his bony hand was drawing the bow softly across the strings making the music Sallie had thought was played by the angels.

And when Uncle Sweeter heard her, he didn't answer but went on playing while she stood looking at him with wild eyes bulging from her bewildered face. Uncle Sweeter didn't bother to look up but kept on playing until he had finished his tune while his old dog and his two cats sat around him listening to music as sweet as the angels sing.

"Am I ready?" Uncle Sweeter repeated, taking his fiddle down, holding its neck in one skinny hand and his bow in the other. "Ready for what?"

"The Judgment Day!" Sally asked.

"Who said it was the Judgment Day?" Uncle Sweeter said.

"Look at the sky, won't you?" Sallie said, pointing toward the north. "It's the end of the world!"

"Don't be skeered, Sallie," he said. "I've seen signs in the sky before. I've seen Halley's Comet. Hit skeered the wits outten a lot of people!"

"But this is not a comet!"

"I know hit ain't!"

"But aren't you afraid?"

"Afraid of what?"

"The end of the world and Judgment Day?"

"No!"

"What will you do if the world is just swallowed up and is no more?"

"What will you do? What will anybody do? I'll do just like the rest of you . . . nothing. I've lived too long to be skeered by any signs in the skies!"

Sallie Bain stood trembling as Uncle Sweeter stooped over and laid his fiddle and bow on the grass and then he picked up one of his cats and put her on his knee.

"Rosie, look at that sky, won't ye?" he said.

He turned the cat's face toward the great flashes of light and the cat seemed very unafraid and very satisfied to be on his lap.

"Rosie, what do you know about the infinite?" he asked.

The cat meowed to him as if she were telling him all she knew about the strange behavior of the skies.

"You know as much about it as I do, Rosie," he answered as if he understood what she had told him. "If I knew about it I'd know about everything! And so would Sallie! So would everybody!"

Then he rubbed his cat's back with his skinny hand while she continued meowing to him who played for cats, dogs, and people the sweetest fiddle music under Heaven.

"Yes, Rosie, you know as much about the infinite as anybody," Uncle Sweeter told his cat. . . .

And when he said this, Sallie who couldn't understand the strange actions of the old Uncle Sweeter whom she had so often befriended, suddenly about-faced and ran down the walk like a chicken. And while she ran toward her home where she could do more good helping to take care of her own family and her sinful neighbors, she heard again the sweet music like coming from the angels, floating on the wind that barely rustled the elm leaves above her head.

9

EVERYBODY IN Blakesburg knew Malinda Sprouse. Everybody had seen this big woman walking along the street carrying a basket of clean clothes to one of the Blakesburg homes. Everybody talked about her size. And they would guess at her weight. Many guessed her to weigh over three hundred pounds while a few guessed her to be as light as two hundred and fifty. Malinda had bright blue eyes that laughed when she did and she always had a smile on her face when she met a Red Neck, a Blue Blood or one of the colored people. She spoke kindly to everybody and she was nice to them. This was probably the result of her success of getting most of the business of washing and ironing clothes.

She had built up a big business in Blakesburg. She had competed with the colored women of the town and she was successful. And it was a general opinion among the women of Blakesburg that no one could wash clothes as white and iron them as smoothly as the colored women. But Malinda Sprouse, one of the Red Necks, exploded this accepted theory among the people. And the colored women soon found her to be dangerous competition, although many of the women among the older families would never let her have their trade. They wouldn't let any white woman do their wash. The colored women who worked for these families for their small pittance of livelihood were safe from Malinda's competition.

Malinda Sprouse didn't do her work for less. She didn't underbid any of the colored women. She stayed within the bounds of accepted pay. And that was two dollars for doing a family's wash for one week whether the bundle of clothes included a few garments or many. The wash usually included many garments. It all depended upon how many children the family had. Usually, Malinda got the wash from the big families since the old families would have none of her and they had the fewer children. However, Malinda managed to get some of the trade of these old families, that is when all their colored help had died or had moved away, something that seldom happened. But Malinda had a big trade among the Red Neck families, those who could afford the two dollars a week to have their washing and ironing done.

But one of the reasons Malinda could constantly keep cutting in on their trade, getting a few more families each year on her list was, she didn't have to have her money as soon as she delivered the wash. Many of the families, among the Blue Bloods as well as the Red Necks, didn't have the two dollars at the end of each week. And when one told Malinda she would pay her next week, or week after next, or even a month from that date, it was all right with her. She carried a little book along where she kept her accounts with her customers. The colored women couldn't do this; often they asked for their money in advance.

Another reason for Malinda's success was, that back in the early twenties when Blakesburg got its first electricity, salesmen flocked to this little town to sell electrical appliances. Among these newfangled things was a new creation known as the electric washing machine. Several of the women were afraid of it, especially the colored women, for one man of the town, a prominent citizen, who was rebellious to the new methods of indoor plumbing, went to his backyard in the dark and happened to hit a live wire that was blown down by a yard tree's falling on it in a windstorm. He wasn't electrocuted but he wasn't "manly" for the rest of his days. And everybody was familiar with his plight because of the gossip about him, and knew that water was a great conductor of electricity.

The women knew that these newfangled inventions were powered by electricity and they held water and if the electricity ever got to the water it was just too bad. As one woman said, "It makes me juberous to think about what one of the contraptions might do to a body." But this didn't bother Malinda. She took a chance and bought a machine. She realized its possibilities at once after the salesman had demonstrated it to her. And there wasn't any use to say the colored women couldn't have bought one on the EZ payment plan. Anybody could have bought one though he would have been a long time paying for it. Malinda didn't buy it on the EZ payment plan, for she saved dollars by paying for it with cash, which she did.

Then there was another thing that aided Malinda greatly in her business. No one knew exactly how much money she had. She didn't do any banking in Blakesburg. She took her money to three different banks, in towns not far away from Blakesburg. She bought discarded property, had it repaired and sold it for a good margin of profit. And she loaned money, to people in the town. Her loans were made secure by getting a mortgage on their property or by getting as many as five of the most well-to-do men in the town to sign the note. When anyone came to borrow money, she would tell whom she would take for security. If the loan were for twenty-five dollars or less, she would ask for only one signature. If it were for fifty she would have two; for a hundred, three; and anything from there up to five hundred she'd ask for as many as five endorsements of the note. She never lost. She made her loans a safe investment. And she made money by loaning money, for she charged ten percent interest. There was a law against it but she got by. She could only charge six percent but she collected the other four percent from the principal before she shelled the greenbacks over to the borrower. She was safe. Not only was she keen competition for the clothes washers of the town but she was keen competition for the Blakesburg Bank, the real estate dealers. . . . She was strong competition in any business she touched. She made money; how much she had was her business. No one knew. But she was rated by many to be the wealthiest person in Blakesburg. Many of the Blakesburg boys going to college had to borrow money from her, boys from both Red Neck, Blue Blood and colored families and these were the only ones she let have money for six percent. "It's for a worthy cause," she said.

By taking in wash from the families of Blakesburg, she knew the history of the town. She said she could judge the families, their wealth and their morals by the kind of clothes she gathered at their homes to wash. She said people's linens, table and bed, were the clues to their wealth and morals. But whatever discoveries she made, she kept them to herself. She never talked about anybody except to say something pretty nice for she was the biggest business woman, both in size and in money, in Blakesburg. She always had a pleasant smile and a pleasant word for everybody though she was none too sociable except in a business way. All her motives in life, her recreations, joys and happiness pointed to business and more business, and more wealth. And she lived alone in her own home and worked from morning until night. Sometimes her lights were on at midnight. Fridays she worked until late if she had a big wash to get out, for the deadline was always on Saturday because the Blakesburg citizens wanted clean clothes for the Sabbath.

Not anyone in Blakesburg would have thought Malinda Sprouse, who took a chance on the new electric washer, who was a business pioneer among the women in the town, who would buy property and farms and sell them at good profits, would have been afraid when she saw strange omens in the sky. She was at her ironing board when it happened, pushing her big electric iron up and down the board. Though she hadn't bothered to attend any of the churches in the town because "they criticized one another," she had prayed "fer her own salvation in her own home while she rested on the Sabbath." She unplugged her iron and waddled out the door as fast as she could go. When her neighbors saw her running from the wrath to come they wondered where she was going, and just how far she could get, since she was so large. And maybe, they thought she shouldn't be running because she was so fearless and so adventurous in the business world.

But Malinda wasn't fleeing from the wrath to come, she was in a hurry to collect the debts people owed her. This was a bad night to find her debtors, for many had left their homes and those who had remained were down on their knees praying. But this was a good time to collect old debts. Malinda knew her debtors would want their slates clean before they stood before the Judgment bar. She took her account book and walked all night collecting the back pay for her wash and collecting the interest long overdue on her notes. And when people wanted to pay the principal, for this was a night they wanted to wipe the slate clean, she collected.

All night long in the flare of the brilliant lights she went from house to house over Blakesburg, collecting interest and old wash debts. Many of the people who owed her debts she regarded risky and unsafe, paid her without question on this night. Many of the people regarded her a little off in the head to be out on a night like this collecting old debts, with the end of the world so near. They asked one another after she had collected from them and had gone to collect more if Malinda thought she could take it with her.

10

E DDIE BIRCHFIELD was one of the young progressives back in
the late teens when the horseless carriage came to Blakesburg. He saw great possibilities in this new invention and when
he told the people in Blakesburg that within ten years their
streets would be lined with them, they laughed at him. Eddie
prophesied the Blake County Red Necks would become less
afraid of the horseless carriage and would soon have improved
roads because of them and would be driving them to Blakesburg
and parking them along the streets at the places where they
used to park their teams. Eddie told the Mayor that it would
be better for Blakesburg for they would have less street cleaning to do. To prepare himself for the future, Eddie took a cor-
respondence course in automobile mechanics.

"Old Eddie's a nice boy," the people said. "But he's automobile looney."

But Eddie went ahead advancing his ideas about the future of
the automobile while the people laughed. They knew they
would never replace the teams of the Blake County farmers and
the pack mules for the moonshiners. They knew this could never
be done for how could one of these newfangled things go over
the muddy roads after the autumn, winter, and the spring rains!
And how could they go up the narrow-gauge hollows, beyond
the cliffs and bring to town the jugs of pure corn! It just
couldn't take the place of the sure-footed mule and they knew
it. Eddie was a nice boy but he was guessing wrong about the
future.

71

But like Marvin Clayton and Franklin Foster who had gotten the lead on one of the first business enterprises in the town, Eddie built the first garage in the town. He converted an old livery stable into a garage. It wasn't a big affair; just a small place. But the young people found it an interesting place to come to watch him work on these new horseless carriages. He tried to advance the coming popularity and necessity of these carriages to the young people since the old only laughed at him. And he probably learned to tell "tall tales" as well as become one of the best mechanics ever to work in Blakesburg. Eddie and his young wife were popular young Greenoughs of the old stock of the town. They liked the young people and the young were fond of them, especially the "big tales" Eddie told them about the things the automobile had done. The only thing it would never be able to do, he told them, was to climb a tree. But he prophesied that there would be contraptions built similar to the automobile, powered by gasoline engines, that would push a tree over. He said they'd use them to clear trees from the ground and lift up stumps that the old-fashioned stump pullers couldn't pull.

The children would relish these tales and would go home and tell their parents. Their parents would laugh at "old crazy Eddie" until they nearly went into hysterics. Eddie told so many of these wild tales about the automobiles, how he could look at the automobile and how it would start running, or how he could put his hand on the radiator and make it stop, that his garage became one of the loafing places in the town. It was where the young people went to be entertained. Whether the tales Eddie told them had a bit of truth or not and if they knew they were tall tales, the young people would come to listen. They loved to hear him talk.

Before 1930 the horseless carriage had replaced the buggy, surrey, hug-me-tight, jolt wagon and express. This was ahead of Eddie's prophecy. Bulldozers were used to clear the right-of-ways, uprooting trees and tearing out stumps. The world Eddie had prophesied in the late teens had come to pass and he had become somewhat of a prophet; yet the young people knew he told them many wild tales. They didn't believe he could look at an automobile and start the engine, lay his hand on the radiator and stop the engine. They knew he had some trick but he was sly with it. He kept his secrets to himself.

Not only did Eddie fix the automobiles, he could fix anything from one of the girl's vanity cases to an automobile. He made small steam engines that ran, took old pieces and put an automobile together, fixed sewing machines, radios, electric washers, telephones, and wagons. There wasn't anything this mechanical genius, prophet and teller of tales couldn't do. Once he demonstrated to the young people when the new theatre came to town and the young started going there and leaving his garage, how he could carry a suitcase, a guitar on his bicycle, ride alongside a freight train going at thirty miles an hour, catch the freight train from the bicycle and take his suitcase, guitar and bicycle all onto the train. He did it and not only the young people but the old saw him do it. The theatre couldn't take the young people from him. They'd been coming to him from the late teens and he wouldn't be content unless they continued to come to his garage which was not only a garage but a ketch-all for all the mechanical business in Blakesburg. There wasn't anything Eddie couldn't do and the Blakesburg people knew it. They trusted him now as much as they had once doubted him. He had won his way into the hearts of the people in Blakesburg through the succeeding generations of young. However, many an older citizen would shake his head when he heard Eddie's name and say, "Old Eddie's an awful liar at times, yet there's a lot of truth in some of the things he says."

The only business Eddie's competitors got was repairs he didn't have time to do. He had enough work for five men to do; he did as much as three men could do and let much of the work he couldn't stack up until the owners came and got it and passed it on to his competitors. But they didn't feel bad about it; they knew Eddie had to have a little recreation, a time to be with his family and they knew he would take time to entertain the young. He must have time to make little gadgets for the boys, steam engines, receiving sets, miniature radios, wagons, and kites, bracelets, rings and compacts for the girls. He would usually work on these things while he entertained them.

As the years passed and the young kept on coming to the garage, he had to change from telling his tales about the future of the automobile, for now men were soaring over Blakesburg in the "airyplane," a bird Eddie was as much against as the Red Neck teamsters had been against the automobiles. He was afraid this mechanical bird would replace his automobile. When the airplane stole the glamour of Eddie's automobile, he stopped telling tall tales about things mechanical. He switched to stories about his hunting escapades in the Blake County hills.

He immediately became a hunter and picked up the stray dogs in the town until he had himself at one time thirty-three. He would take this swarm of dogs and he would hunt at night in the Blake County hills. Many of his dogs were good dogs; he'd have a dog that would tree possums, one that would hunt skunks, a dozen that would run foxes, one to catch minks, weasels out of his thirty-three. The majority wouldn't be good for anything when Eddie first picked them up. But he could train dogs to hunt as he had trained children to listen to his tall tales. He even trained stray useless mongrels he had picked up on the Blakesburg streets to hunt rattlesnakes; he trained another group just to hunt the copperheads. He would bring to Blakesburg copperheads and rattlesnakes alive and put them in cages at his garage. He had dogs trained especially for wildcats and he caught many among the Blake County hills. He climbed a tree with a cage and put two wildcats in a cage, something many people in Blakesburg never believed, but he had wit-

nesses. He brought the wildcats back to his garage alive. At first
he told these hunting experiences to the Blakesburg young. He
aroused their interest until they wanted to hunt with him.

Eddie would take as many as fifty boys and girls, a pack of
thirty dogs of all breeds and he would start to the hills. Though
his having to take care of all his young followers slowed his
hunting progress, yet he brought back to Blakesburg wildcats,
rattlesnakes, copperheads, possums, coons, skunks, weasels, minks,
foxes, groundhogs, rabbits and squirrels. People could hear this
small army of hunters laughing, screaming, talking and the
barking of dogs and the blowing of horns for miles away. They
would know when Eddie was in their woods. Though Eddie
with all his pack of stray dogs, would sweep about all the game
there was before him, no one objected to his hunting on his
land. He was popular in Blake County as well as in Blakesburg.
After his young hunters had learned his secrets of hunting,
something they never grew tired of, Eddie had to find new
stories. The theatre was still in town and he had to compete
with it. This was in 1941 when he started telling his ghost
stories. He went "out of this world" for stories for he knew the
youth would never be let in on the secret. He had told stories
all his life, exhausting supply after supply, but this was a fresh
spring that never would run dry.

On the pleasant evening of September 18th there were fifteen to twenty-five boys and girls gathered in his garage, where
they had seated themselves on the automobiles, radios, sewing
machines, washing machines, stoves, bicycles and other things
mechanical that were awaiting the touch of Eddie's magic hand
to put them in use again. The crowd could have come every
night for a week and each one sat alone on a different object
each night, yet no one could have sat on all of them, for Eddie
still had the business in the town.

But on this night Eddie had told his eager listeners about a
haunted house while he made a box kite for one of the boys. He

told about a woman who had once lived there and had milked a cow so many times with a little shawl around her shoulders, and how he had seen her fifty years after her death with the same shawl around her shoulders at the spot where the milkgap used to be, milking an unseen cow, and he said he saw with his own eyes streams of milk going into her tin pail and he heard the stream zigzag across the bottom of the bucket with a strange sound. He said when he spoke to the woman she faded on the wind and was no more.

And while he fixed a compact for one of the girls he told how at this same house in Shinglemill Hollow a big red dog climbed upon the house and tore the shingles off with his mouth. Eddie told them he had seen the dog do it with his own eyes and when he called to the dog, he ran through the air like a dog runs on the ground. He said he could hear the dog's feet hitting the wind until the dog was out of sight. He had started to fix a bracelet for one of the girls and was telling about how a light fell beside a locust tree at this same house. He said the locust tree was behind the well and many of the youth had seen this tree. As he was describing this big light that came down from the sky and fell by this particular locust on many occasions (he had, he told them, seen it five different times himself), one of the boys looked out of the garage window and saw the flaming sky.

"Look, Eddie," the boy shouted, pointing to the window, "what's the matter with that sky?" Eddie started toward the window and all the young people got up from their mechanical seats and followed him toward the window. They couldn't all look through one window so they ran to the other windows.

"Just when I was tellin' you about lights," he said, his lips trembling, his face getting pale. "The world is on fire!"

"On fire?" one of the girls screamed.

"The world's on fire," the girls screamed in unison.

"But a rain will put the fire out," Eddie shouted to halt their mad stampeding in his garage. "It won't burn up! It won't burn up!"

"Burn up hell," one of the boys answered as he scrambled for the door. Eddie's words were too late. They ran for the door. Too many tried to go through the door. There was shoving and screaming, each trying to get out first. Many of the boys ran back to the windows and went out taking the windowpanes and whole window sashes with them.

"World's on fire," he heard them screaming down the street as he stood alone in his deserted garage, his body shaking like a "Holy Jumper" as he saw through one of his paneless windows, something more than a light falling by a locust tree.

11

NEVER HAD there been in Blakesburg's long history, a man with as much patriotism for his city as Bruce Livingstone. In his face he carried a burning fervor anyone could discern if he should look at Bruce twice. He was a nervous little man who worked constantly for Blakesburg more than he did for himself in his place of business which was a General Merchandise Store. He would let his business go or trust it in the hands of his clerks while he went on thankless errands for his city. And when anyone said anything against the city of Blakesburg, that person had "to swaller his words" or he would have Bruce to fight. During his forty years of living, he had fought over an average of three fights a year over insults people had given his Blakesburg. He had fought for Blakesburg since he had been big enough to use his fist.

By heritage he was the right man to take the destinies of Blakesburg to heart. He was half Red Neck and half Blue Blood. His father was a Blue Blood who had taken for himself a wife from a prominent Red Neck family. And from this inheritance, since his father was of the Dinwiddie political faith and his mother was of the Greenough political faith, he had a kindly feeling toward both political parties. He registered as an Independent voter and voted for the man he thought best to serve his city which came first, last and always; and second to his city was his county, then his state, and last came the Republic. He didn't go to any one church regularly but he attended all ten churches on different occasions. And he knew the history of Blakesburg from the days when it was a wigwamed village until the present. He had come under the influence of Uncle Sweeter Dabney when he had gone there to hear him play the fiddle. Uncle Sweeter had given him the history of Blakesburg to pass on to his own generation and those yet to come.

Many of Bruce's fellow Blakesburgians didn't like him for they thought he was a radical without any political faith. They said he tried to "carry water on both shoulders" by voting for men of both political faiths; they even said he was a man of Communistic leanings masking his face with Greenough and Dinwiddie political masks. It was true, he did have Communistic leanings . . . leanings for his Blakesburg community. . . . Not only did he lean for his community but he fell over backward and forward for it.

When modern luxuries came to Blakesburg the citizens were not too kindly disposed toward them. Mayor Charlie Collingsworth met with the city council in a special meeting to do something about this nuisance that was pestering their citizens, namely, automobiles speeding down the street and throwing up clouds of dust. They even had to buy oil to spread over their dusty streets after this strange vehicle arrived in Blakesburg. But the council did something about the clouds of dust. They put a speed limit of twelve miles an hour on the automobiles. Although the other cities had higher rates of speed, Blakesburg would never change theirs until Bruce Livingstone helped elect a council that would. For more people started buying these dust-raisers, even the Red Necks. And people kicked on this speed rate. The city had outgrown it.

Bruce Livingstone got electric lights for the town. And people at that time were very much frightened and bewildered by them, in the late Teens and early Twenties. And many of the people fussed about his getting them. Arch Saddler told him "they didn't have sicha confounded nuisance in Jesus Christ's day and time." And Bruce told Arch neither did they have kerosene lamps in His day. Then Bruce got a law through his city council to require everybody to pave his street and this brought on over a hundred lawsuits. But Bruce put it through anyway. After a series of typhoid fever epidemics, he finally persuaded the council to build a reservoir upon the mountain slope and have running water for the town, a sewerage disposal system and a telephone system. Bruce Livingstone did all this without pay; and each new thing he did he got plenty of criticism. Yet people knew when they criticized Bruce that not one of them had done more for Blakesburg. They knew his blood was in the city's concrete, stone and bricks and his sweat and tears were in each blade of grass and flower that grew from the very dirt the city rested upon.

Not anyone had done more when Blakesburg had her big holidays, Fourth of July and Labor Day, for the Red Necks who thronged to Blakesburg for a big day of fun and relaxation. Bruce would go over the town and collect from each merchant some small pittance for a prize. And with this money he would buy fowls to turn loose from the housetops, a greasy pig for the boys between eight and twelve to catch, and a greasy pole for the boys to climb for a five-dollar bill pinned on top of it. He bought lumber to build platforms for the Red Necks to dance upon. Bruce, who was half Red Neck, had these people at heart. He wanted to see them have a good time in his city and they did. Bruce would have the contributions from the Blakesburg merchants published in both local papers, the *Greenough Gazette* and *Dinwiddie News*, advertising what each was giving away, long before the holidays. It made the merchants feel good to see their names and contributions in the paper and it made the people in the hills feel good to know the merchants, with whom they had to trade anyway, were interested enough to give away something. Bruce Livingstone made everybody feel good unless it was some bit of progress for the town he wanted to put over. Then he would put it over if he could regardless of how anybody felt about it. He would ram it down their throats and make them like it. And that is why he was more unpopular in the city than he was in the country.

And when the Red Necks arrived in Blakesburg for their great days of celebration and all the merchants were busy feeding them, policing them, and selling them their wares, Bruce would go among them shaking more hands than Judge Allie Anderson. He knew hundreds of them by name and he would welcome them to the city. He was Blakesburg's goodwill ambassador to the Blake County Red Necks. And when Bruce went up through the highest building in Blakesburg, which was three stories high, and climbed out on the roof, the great multitude of people below, as many as three thousand, would stand and cheer. Then he would turn loose from the top of this high building as many as twelve hens and as many roosters for the people below to catch. He would turn loose as many ducks, guineas and turkeys. And from his perch he would watch the mad scramble below while the women, dressed in their best, would run to dodge the flying fowls that sometimes tried to alight on their heads. And it was always Bruce who turned the greasy pig loose; he was the man who pinned the five dollars on the greasy pole, started the sack races, the potato races and the foot races. It was he who always stood on the flag-draped platform and introduced Old Glory Gardner who made all the patriotic speeches on these occasions. When the dance platforms were filled with dancers and there were many more wanting to dance, Bruce would see they got a place to dance even if he had to shoo the people back and rope off the street and let them dance there. He often had done this. He was, as Charlie Allbright once said, the man who made Blakesburg tick. He was, as Eddie Birchfield said, the "spark plug of Blakesburg." He could get more publicity for the merchants in the city and more good will for its citizens among people in the county and in other

cities than all the rest of their public-spirited citizens put together. He was a combination of all churches, political factions
and people.

But with all his love for the city first, last and always and with
his great stamina for mental and physical work in trying to im-
prove his city, he had never taken time to read about the beginning and the ending of the world. He had a feeling perhaps that
the world would go on like it had before and after Christ. But
he hadn't given enough thought to such matters, not as much
as his neighbors had. He had heard a preacher say once the end
of the world would come by a sign in the sky, that it would come
in the twinkling of an eye and not anybody on earth nor the
angels in Heaven would know when the end was near. But he
couldn't conceive of Blakesburg's being included with the rest
of the world. And when Charlie Allbright prophesied the world
would end in 1930, Bruce only laughed at him. Bruce knew that
Charlie wasn't in the know when it came to the business of God
Almighty, who was over all things, including Blakesburg. But
Bruce wasn't as much concerned with where these Blakesburgians
had come from and where they were going as he was helping
them get along within the city limits.

On the evening of September 18, 1941, Bruce had visited a
councilman's home to suggest some street repairs for Blakesburg. He just walked outside the house and took one look at
the sky, and this liberal Bruce Livingstone, who was so often
called a Communist, had nervous tremors that first went up his
spine and then branched off into other parts of his body. His
body shook from head to toe. There wasn't any question about
it in his mind, this was the end of Blakesburg. No need to im-
prove the streets now, he thought. He had never seen anything
like this nor heard of it. He stood for a minute watching the
sky, his lips trembling and his teeth rattling until he couldn't
speak. But he could see his native Blakesburgians running in all
directions and hear prayers spouting from their lips as they ran.

He could hear their lamenting cries and wails all over Blakes-burg and it did something to him to hear his people in such distress.

Just as soon as the chills and tremors left his body, and he had gathered strength enough to run and scream, he took off among his people warning them to gather around the court square since the end of their beloved city was near.

"Everybody gather at the courthouse," he shouted to the people who were running in all directions. "Let us all go to meet our Savior in a body from Blakesburg. Let us not forsake one another at the ending of the world!"

12

WHEN "OLD GLORY" Gardner was a boy in Blakesburg, there wasn't anything to distinguish him from his generation, except that in school he had a love for history. He excelled in this subject in the primary school and in the high school. His history teacher Jolly Joe Wilkerson in Blakesburg High School had once patted him on the head and had said to him, "Son, there's something in that head of yours if you'll just go on to college. I'd love to live long enough to see what comes out of it!" And this boost coming from Jolly Joe was enough to send George Gardner to State University. He was one of the few sons from the old families that stuck with the school after he got there. So many of them had either failed in the University or had gotten homesick for their native Blakesburg. But George remembered the pat on his head and he knew something would come out of his head some day.

No one was prouder that George Gardner had gone to college, and that he was "a-stickin' to" his intellectual pursuits, than Bruce Livingstone. Even when he was in the primary school Bruce Livingstone had "taken a likin' to" this youngster because he had such a flair for history. Bruce was amazed how much history George knew. George was so thorough in Blakesburg's history he even knew the history of her dead. For many a summer day he had gone to the Lonesome Hill and had followed Uglybird as he used a scythe mowing over the graves. He listened to Uglybird tell the story of the person beneath each mound as his scythe ripped into the briars, sprouts and grass. When he wasn't with Uglybird or Bruce Livingstone he was sitting beside Uncle Sweeter Dabney's dog or holding one of his cats while he played his fiddle and told stories of the past.

Young George had all the local historians for his friends. He loved them and they loved him. But the one who influenced him most was Bruce Livingstone. George was a great imitator of this man. He tried to walk like him, talk like him, and he modeled his wearing apparel after the type Bruce wore. When the long necktie was the style for the young men in Blakesburg, George Gardner wore a smart Beau Brummel such as Bruce Livingstone wore. Probably a hundred people had heard Bruce say he wished he had a son he thought as much of as he did of George Gardner, a boy who was no kin to him, except "through mutual thoughts which were one and the same." Bruce not only imparted his local historical lore to George but he gave him lessons in zealous patriotism while his mind was young and plastic. First came Blakesburg, then Blake County, then the state, the Republic and the world. And when George was in his senior year at State University, Bruce Livingstone, who was the "spark plug" in Blakesburg, used all his dynamic force to oust white-haired Linn Gracey, with twenty years' experience behind him, as head of the Blakesburg City Schools and give George his position.

Since Blakesburg was a city of traditions many were opposed to this. George had never taught school a day in his life. People wondered if he could take over the school system and direct the destinies of their youth as well as the "venerable old Professor Linn Gracey" had. But when Bruce got behind George, his "favor-ite son of Blakesburg" as well as his protegé, he was a dynamic force. "This is a local boy," he told the leaders in the town. "Give him the job. What do you expect from your sons and daughters you send away to the University? No wonder they get homesick and return. What is there for them to work for if you are afraid to risk them in Blakesburg, their home city? It will be a lesson to the others who will go away to State! They will know we brought George Gardner back and made him Superintendent of Blakesburg's City Schools because he was a local boy that made good. If you turn him down and keep Linn Gracey who was born beyond the borders of Blake County, what hope will others have?"

Linn Gracey was a native of an adjoining county; therefore he was dismissed to make room for young George Gardner. Bruce Livingstone knew what to say to get close to "the people's heartstrings" when he was talking for young George Gardner, the Blakesburg "boy we are all proud of and have a right to be." George came home, a young college graduate, and a college graduate in Blakesburg in the middle Twenties was something. He was looked upon as someone to be proud of, one to respect, for his head was filled with superior knowledge.

When he took the school system into his own cultured hands all the teachers were older and each knew more about running it than he. George just didn't fill the old venerable Professor Linn Gracey's shoes. Not by a long shot and the people knew it. There was a lot of confusion at first but soon Bruce Livingstone came to George's rescue and helped him get started with his task.

But George did something his first year which had never been done before. He had the school board buy an eighty-foot flagpole and a flag that was twenty feet by ten. While the president of the Senior Class hoisted Old Glory each morning, the high school pupils had to stand at attention. This showed George Gardner's first buds of patriotism. And it wasn't long until George called a special chapel and made a thirty-minute talk just on the flag. He had a flag on his desk; he wore a miniature flag in his coat lapel instead of a flower. And such patriotism pleased the people at first.

During his first year as Superintendent of Blakesburg's Public Schools, he made a chapel talk each month. If his talk wasn't about the flag, he by some chance would draw "Old Glory" into his historical speech. He made speeches about the history of Blakesburg, Blake County, the state, the Republic and the world. And when he made so many speeches on patriotism and Old Glory, he would have the rostrum from where he spoke filled with flags. Here he would stand among them and drink water because he would get worked up in his speech and do a lot of sweating.

The parents of the high school pupils heard about his "great speeches" and they came and listened to them at first like the students but they soon grew tired of seeing the same decorated platform, seeing George there every time and hearing the same kind of speech. Unlike the high school pupils, they didn't have to come. The pupils had to sit and be bored with the patriotic speeches and George's flag-waving. For he would always lift one of the flags from the platform and wave it when he spoke of "Old Glory" in sentimental tones.

The high school pupils gave him the name of "Old Glory" Gardner. And soon the people in Blakesburg took it up. Everybody was calling George "Old Glory." But that didn't bother George as years went on; he held his position as head of the schools. And he wouldn't hire a teacher if he wasn't a patriot and a native. He still went down in Blakesburg with a miniature "Old Glory" in his coat lapel.

When Bruce Livingstone prepared for the big days of celebration in Blakesburg, he put Old Glory Gardner on the program to give a patriotic speech. Bruce would make a platform for George before each big celebration on the courthouse square and drape the platform with flags. He would put flags all around the speaker that would flutter in the wind while George gave one of his dramatic speeches, pounding his fists, waving Old Glory, sweating, spitting and drinking a pitcher of water. But if there were any of his high school pupils in the crowd they got away before George got started. The Blake Countians who had come to town to dance, drink and celebrate, would stand with their mouths open when they heard him for the first time. They thought George was a wonderful patriot and a great man. Many of the Blake Countians sent their boys and girls to Blakesburg High School because this "great patriot" was the head of the system. They "jist simply knowed" they would "git the right kind o' larnin' under George." And when their children went home and spoke ill of George, they couldn't understand.

George had a flagpole put on the courthouse square that was a hundred feet high. It was a hard pole to get up but the strong men struggled and raised the pole and an Old Glory twenty by forty feet was hoisted far above Blakesburg. This was all right and the citizens of Blakesburg thought it was their patriotic duty to put this tall pole and big flag above their city. They appreciated Old Glory's suggesting they should do it, but when he tried to make them salute it every time they passed the flag, no matter if they had a load in their arms, they didn't like it. And they told George they didn't. But George came back at them with speeches in the Blakesburg High School Chapel and he even made speeches on the courthouse square about the "unpatriotic people in Blakesburg." This was carrying it too far, they thought. And now they began to believe their children, pupils of the high school, when they came home complaining about him.

But George held on through the remaining Twenties, into the Thirties. Not only did he give longer speeches in the high school but he increased the number of them. Each April the students had a "tree-planting day." But now they had many tree-planting days and when they planted a tree Old Glory gave a long-winded patriotic speech waving his flag. They planted over two hundred maples on the two-acre school yard. It began to look like a young forest.

And if Esther Stableton couldn't conjugate her Latin verb, Old Glory would give her an A for her recitation if she would stand beside her desk and sing the Star-Spangled Banner. If

Mabel Cooley didn't have her assignment in English, something which was not very uncommon, she would rise from her seat, stand at attention while she would give the Pledge to the Flag. Then Old Glory would smile as he recorded an A for her in his grade book. If Fiddis Caudill couldn't prove his proposition in Geometry, all he had to do was recite, "Hats Off, the Flag is Passing By."

If any pupil who didn't know his lesson would rise and sing some patriotic song or recite some patriotic poetry he didn't have to worry about his getting a good grade. A poem about the flag would always get an A, a poem about the state was good for a B; and a poem about the Republic, such as "Sail on, O Ship of State," would pass for a C. At a teachers' meeting when Old Glory told his teachers to give the high school pupils grades if they didn't have their lessons but could substitute with something patriotic by singing a song or reciting a poem, his teachers rebelled.

The chapel periods became longer and while Old Glory waved his flag and spit patriotism to his pupils, they would sit silently or the boys would get close to the girls and hold hands and whisper their messages of love. The teachers kicked about the school and many resigned. It came to the place in the late Thirties something had to be done. But Old Glory held on through the influence of Bruce Livingstone until 1940. Stories were circulated that the pupils were behaving badly, if not indecently back in the chapel while Old Glory waved his flags. When these stories circulated over the town a petition was passed to get him out.

After a big school fight they ousted Old Glory. And they thought he would go someplace and get another school. But he didn't try. When Professor Daniel Marshall became Superintendent of Blakesburg's Public Schools, Old Glory wanted to go back to chapel "just to give one more talk." But Superintendent Marshall would have none of his patriotism.

Old Glory Gardner with all his college training drifted to the courthouse square where he sat with Bascom Keaton, Charlie Allbright, Uncle Sweeter Dabney and other philosophers. He would lecture on patriotism and the history of the city, county, state, Republic and the world. And it was here he got his listeners. They were more courteous to him than the high school pupils had been, for they were older men and women. They were more interested in the time, the trials and tribulations of man's life in this Republic. And they knew Old Glory was a "sharp" man and a great patriot. After he had gotten his jolt of being kicked out of his position, he lectured to the people that the country was becoming so unpatriotic that something would happen to this Republic and perhaps to the world. He was a student of history and he knew. Day after day he lectured the people about some colossal event that was to come and then he would end his lecture by telling them how he had been treated in Blakesburg.

On the night of September 18th when he was loafing with his philosopher friends on the courthouse square, he was one of the first to observe the coming of doom. And then he arose, climbed upon the seat where he was sitting as if it were one of the flag-draped platforms of old. He pulled the miniature flag from his buttonhole and he waved it as he began, "This is the last time I shall ever speak to you! This is the end of time! This is the end of Blakesburg! It is the end of Blake County, our State and our Republic! But I shall take," he paused, gripping the small handle in his hand, "the flag of this Republic with me and plant it in the Glory Land where it will bloom forever and forever."

13

WHEN WE entered World War I, Ronnie Roundtree, who was known as "some fighter," enlisted in the Army and went overseas where he had for his officer a man by the name of Douglas MacArthur. Ronnie distinguished himself as a member of the Rainbow Division. He was wounded and was decorated for bravery. But when he came back to the little town of Blakesburg, he was a little restless. He had taken to drink, something he seldom did before he went into Service, and now he consumed his part of the moonshine. There was plenty of bootleg and Ronnie drew a pension and he had a railroad job and the roaring Twenties were on in full swing. These were gay days in Blakesburg for the Red Necks came from the hills to spend their money there. And they had plenty of money now since everybody, almost to the man, was engaged in making moonshine. The country was bone dry and moonshine was in great demand, selling for as much as fifty dollars a gallon. This was the time for the Red Necks to cash in and they did.

Ronnie soon became dissatisfied with his beautiful Red Neck wife, Esther Blair, whom any man would look at twice when he met her on the street. "My wife don't appeal to me any more," Ronnie told Liam Winston, one of his best friends. "When I hug her it's just like puttin' my arms around a tree. And I don't git any thrill outten kissin' 'er. I'd as soon kiss a fence post!"

But there was Dixie Kimball, olive-complexioned, crow-wing-black straight hair and charcoal-black eyes, who walked the street wearing her tight-fitting skirt and her snug sweater. She was another girl in Blakesburg men looked at from two to three times when she passed them on the street. She was called by everybody "the sweater girl."

Ronnie not only looked at her twice; he stood on the street looking at her until she was out of sight. And then, it wasn't long until Ronnie was "a-steppin' out on Esther." As soon as Esther found out what was going on, she sued for a divorce and engaged the services of Joe Oliver to handle her suit. There was a big trial and everybody enjoyed it but Ronnie.

He didn't like the outcome of the trial, with all the alimony to pay, since he planned to marry Dixie Kimball and live on the same street where Esther lived in their little cottage with their two children. But this was the web of fate Ronnie had talked about. And as he later said, Dixie's snug-fitting sweater and her tight-fitting skirt had pulled him into the spider web of life. Charlie Allbright expounded his views to his faithful courthouse listeners by saying, "Hit never works when two blonds marry. Esther was a blond and Ronnie was a blond. Unlike objects attract. Now he will stick until Doom's Day with Dixie."

It did look as if Charlie Allbright were right. Willis Thompson, who was in love with Dixie before Ronnie took to her, made some bright remarks about Dixie after Ronnie had divorced Esther and married her. Ronnie didn't wait to let Willis tell him what he had said about Dixie's "honor." He brought his knife from his pocket, pushed an automatic button, springing a long sharp blade. Then he went to work on Willis, slashing him unmercifully before Liam Winston and Booge Didway could stop the fight. They kept Ronnie from stabbing Willis to death. Willis was sent to the Dartmouth Hospital where he spent nine months before he was released. One lung was stabbed so full of holes it was useless.

Then came another trial and Joe Oliver defended Ronnie because he had been defending the honor of his second wife. And this time the people, always on "old Joe's side" of the question, applauded Ronnie and made him feel better. People thought Ronnie would be sent to the Pen for "attempting to kill." They changed their minds when Joe Oliver took the case. They knew he wouldn't go. Ronnie was fined one thousand dollars and given a jail sentence of sixty days which was revoked when he paid his fine.

There was much gossip when people saw Ronnie standing on the street talking to Esther. Liam Winston said, "Somethin's a-eatin' on old Ronnie's mind." The religious people in the town said it was the spirit of the Lord reproaching Ronnie for his misdeeds. There were many discussions of Ronnie's personal life. People knew he was unhappy, that his former wife, Esther, was unhappy, and that his second wife, Dixie, was unhappy since they were living next door to Esther. And Ronnie, now without work, for the depression was on, walked the streets with a serious face. His blond hair became streaked with silver.

Willis Thompson, whom Ronnie had stabbed over Dixie, lived just across the street from them. He was in plain sight for Ronnie, Dixie and Esther to see, hobbling along on his crutches down the street when the days were fair, sitting under the elm shade in a lawn chair when the days were hot. Willis grew weaker day by day and finally had to give up his crutches and be wheeled down the street in a wheel chair. And maybe it was a relief to Ronnie when he died. But something else took hold of Ronnie. It was within his heart and brain. Ronnie went down to the church, a place he had shied from since he divorced Esther. And there he fell beside the mourner's bench and prayed for forgiveness of his sins.

"But how can Ronnie git right with the Lord?" people asked one another. "He has two livin' wives right down there together. He's a-livin' in adult'ry! He jist simply can't do anything like that in the eyes of the Lord!"

Maybe Ronnie was thinking the same thing. He couldn't stand up in the church choir and sing with the others; he couldn't get up to testify without looking at the floor. He couldn't face the people. Something was wrong and many people thought it was because of Willis Thompson's death. And yet, they reasoned, a murderer had the chance to repent and be saved. But an adulterer didn't have a right to put away a good decent wife like Esther just for another girl who was attractive to the eyes of men. And now they reasoned that the days of lusting for Ronnie, as the years were creeping upon him, were over. At least that's what the philosophers talked on the court-house square and the Blakesburg streets. They said he had put away the thoughts of lust for more spiritual things.

Ronnie went along with the church through the Thirties. He never missed going to church and Sunday school where he sat with his children by both wives, with Esther not far away from him and Dixie close beside him. At first this arrangement looked strange to everybody in the church, but as the weeks, months and years passed, the church people grew used to it. Even the aged Reverend Sykes accepted it as something for Ronnie him-self to work out with his God. But the trouble came when Rev-erend Sykes was retired and the new Pastor was attractive Miss Gertrude Spence.

When Reverendess Spence came to Blakesburg, she was filled with a burning fever. She was a go-getter. Her face was filled with fire and words flew from her mouth at the people like mis-siles. She was filled with fire and everlasting damnation. And the one thing she couldn't understand was Ronnie's being there, a church member with his name on the "Lamb's Book of Life," with his divorced Esther and two children, with his legally mar-ried wife Dixie and seven children. It just wouldn't work.

"You put away this good Sister Esther without a just cause," Reverendess Spence told Ronnie when she discussed with him his being trapped like a fly into the spider web of life. "You didn't have the right to do it! You weren't living in fornica-tion! It is your fault! You know it was! It was your lusting of the flesh! Esther has proven herself to be a lady! Look at these years without you!"

"Then what must I do?" Ronnie asked her.

"Go back to your first wife," she told him. "I've prayed over your plight! And this is the message I got! It's the only way you can become a saved man! You are not a saved man! You know you are not right with God! I don't have to tell you! You could testify and you could sing if you were! You would be a happy man! And you are not a happy man! I know you're not happy! Everybody knows you're not happy!"

"But if I go back to my first wife and begin life all over with her again," Ronnie said, after sitting in deep study thinking the matter over, "I would haf to put away my second wife and seven children!"

"But you married Esther first," Reverendess Spence flashed her words. "This Dixie didn't have any right to come betwixt you and your lawfully wedded wife! She sinned more than you sinned!"

"I'd never thought of it like that," Ronnie said.

"That's the answer to my prayer," Reverendess Spence came back. "Think it over! Go home and pray over it!"

"I'll do that, Sister Spence," Ronnie said. "And you pray for me too."

Ronnie got up from the chair where he was sitting in the Holy Room of her parsonage. He walked out into the street, his mind filled with trouble and indecisions. He had found himself drawn between two women, the one he loved and the one he had first taken to cherish and honor until death them did part. And he was faced with the problem of supporting both.

He remained on the brink of indecision and let the days, weeks, and months drag into years. He wondered if it were better to go back to his first wife and have a clear title to the Lamb's Book of Life, or to stay with the woman so hard to escape and with the bigger portion of his family and run the risk of the devil's hell. He had had enough hell on earth and he didn't want an eternity of endless hell and torture! Yet he couldn't leave Dixie and their children and go to Esther and their children until . . .

The evening of September 18th when the great lights flamed across the northern skies. And he had just heard Sister Spence preach a roaring sermon on the end of time less than a week before. Now he knew she was in on the Know, for it had come to pass. As good a soldier as he had been when he fought for Douglas MacArthur, he was a troubled man! He could face machine-gun fire and Germans behind barbed wire! He could go over the top and get them! But he weakened now! He was no longer a soldier and he was no longer brave! Not in this time of breaking up the world!

"O Jesus!" he screamed, "I will go back to Esther!"

When he went through the front door, Dixie was holding to his coat but he slipped himself from the coat. Dixie stood with Ronnie's coat in her hand, her body trembling like a winter leaf under the light from the fiery sky. She watched him run madly down the street where Esther opened the door and greeted him on both cheeks with showers of kisses that were softer than drops of April rain.

14

NELLIE BLAKE was the last living member of her family. She had descended from Blakesburg's fathers. And it was for her early ancestors the city had been named. If she had wanted to boast about her predecessors, she could have done so. For one of her ancestors back about 1820 when the state was still a wilderness, introduced a bill at the state capitol for free education for the children of the state. Her people had been pioneers in education. They had been teachers and musicians and they had amassed considerable wealth. Much of this was in large landholdings her ancestors had acquired in the early days and passed down through succeeding generations.

But Nellie Blake, like Uncle Sweeter Dabney, was the last leaf on her tree. And that is why many Blakesburgians had whispered to each other that Miss Nellie should marry Uncle Sweeter Dabney although he was thirty years older. This would be taking a last leaf from each tree and putting them on one tree so they wouldn't be lonesome. But the question here was, which tree should hold the leaves. Each leaf wanted to cling to its own family tree until the end. Neither wanted a change now. And neither would have been happy away from his native tree.

Miss Nellie had never married. And this was what the Red Necks called "the seed a-runnin' out." Miss Nellie's two old maid sisters and two bachelor brothers lived in the old home after their parents had died. Miss Nellie had seen them go one by one until she was the last one left. Maybe she lived alone with her dreams of the former days when Blakesburg was different. She had often spoken of the old days and how good they were. Those were the days when she was very young.

A few of the old people could recall when Miss Nellie was the belle of Blakesburg. She rode in a rubber-tired surrey behind one of the best pair of horses ever seen in the town. And never had Marvin Clayton had finer harness on his draft horses that pulled the first hearses in Blakesburg. The horses she rode behind were not only sleeked and groomed but their long black tails were done in perfect little knots on rainy days so they wouldn't be splashed with mud from the town's dirty streets. Not only did her horses have red tassels to decorate their harness but they had bells to jingle. And when she drove up Main Street a couple of times each week, everybody walking along the street craned his neck to watch her surrey pass. In those days her sisters would be with her and they would all be dressed fit "for the eyes of a King." Often she and her sisters rode through the town with the top of their carriage down; they would be holding fancy umbrellas over them whether there was a sun in the sky or not. They would be wearing white gloves, white shirtwaists with leg-of-mutton sleeves, skirts that fitted tightly around their wasp waists and bulged around their hoops just a little beneath. They wore shining combs in their hair, rings on their fingers, bracelets on their arms and lockets around their necks. They were the belles of Blakesburg; not another family of girls could touch their standing in Blakesburg society in the early days.

Gossip lived from generation to generation that Miss Nellie was once to marry a man beyond the borders of Blake County. It was rumored she had her trousseau ready and her Prince Charming failed to show up. She hadn't found a young man in Blakesburg that she would marry. And she had been criticized for going beyond the borders trying to find herself a husband. And people didn't sympathize with her because she had been jilted. They thought the people of their city were among the finest in the world and that "is jist what she got for a-trying to find someone a little better." They didn't believe her courtship was one of love; they thought she was trying to climb above her station in life which was the highest in Blakesburg, for her accusers were jealous though they wouldn't admit it.

But all of this was society history in Blakesburg and there wasn't any way of turning to the old files of the *Greenough Gazette* to check upon Miss Nellie now. A rapidly rising flood had once cleaned both newspapers of their files of old papers. There were many girls in the 1920's and 1930's who would have liked to have checked up on her past, now that she was living alone and there was much talk about her. For the years had crept upon her and this little woman could be seen on Saturdays at the stores buying her groceries among the masses of people from the county and town who took her for just another old woman without a history in the past. Her past belonged to her and she knew it and that was all.

But everybody knew when she left the old home, after her last sister had died, "because the place was too lonesome." She went into another one of the many pieces of property she owned. This one was down in the town near the river where she would have next-door neighbors. She hadn't had neighbors near her in the old home for there was "a small farm" around this big house. She hadn't more than moved into her house in the downtown section before the big flood came; she lost her furniture and her house was wrecked. She had to be taken from the upstairs window in a rowboat, and paddled across the town to her old home which was on high ground.

The following spring some farmer burning a tobacco bed let the fire out and it burned over the Blake timberlands, destroying almost all of her virgin timber. She had to sell it in a hurry for a greatly reduced price. Then she talked about a careless Red Neck's ruining her by letting out this fire. But one night, when only she was in it, her big house caught fire and burned to the ashes. All that was saved was an old stable where they had once kept the gay horses that pulled the surreys, buggies, and the hug-me-tights. But she wouldn't leave these grounds. She had a carpenter to fix up the stable and she moved into it. That spot of earth was still her home despite the fact that all the precious possessions her family had handed down to her were a pile of gray ash in sight of the stable.

No one knew about her financial affairs. But everybody in Blakesburg guessed her to be "hard up." For the flood had destroyed her downtown properties and the forest fires had ravaged her virgin timber. And it was rumored she owed Malinda Sprouse a big wash bill. Some said it was for six months; others guessed it to be a year. But on the night of September 18, 1941, when the great lights came and Malinda was out collecting, she waddled up the hill to Miss Nellie's stable and knocked on her door.

"Howdy, Malinda," Miss Nellie said when she opened the door never bothering to look at the sky and the world of strange glittering light around her.

"Miss Nellie," Malinda said, "don't you know?"

"Know what?"

"Everybody thinks the world's a-comin' to an end."

"They do?" Miss Nellie spoke calmly.

"I'm just out collectin' my debts." Malinda spoke rapidly for she was in a hurry with her collections.

"Well, if the world is a-coming to an end you won't need it," she said.

"But I want to git all my business squared away."

"All right, Malinda," she said, walking back into the house. "I'll pay you."

Malinda waited a few minutes and Miss Nellie came with the exact amount she owed Malinda and put it in her hand.

"Now I'll have my money and you'll have everything squared away with the Lord."

Miss Nellie laughed louder than Malinda had ever heard her.

"It's no laughin' matter, Miss Nellie," Malinda said. "You'd better get outten here!"

"Where'll I go?" she said. "I've moved from a flood; I've been burned out by fire, and I'm not moving again. Let the world end!"

She closed the door on Malinda's back and went into her stable.

15

BILL SIMPSON gave Blakesburg more publicity for a while than any one of its two thousand citizens. Simp's father died when he was twelve and he hired out to anybody who would give him a day's work to help his mother, who was trying to support his five sisters. Simp was her only son and at the age of twelve he tried to assume the duties of his father to help provide a livelihood for his mother and sisters. His mother also competed in the washing and ironing industry of Blakesburg. Lillie Simpson's and her son's earnings were barely enough to support the family.

But one day when Simp was chopping old, sun-dried, seasoned crossties, discarded by the railroad line that ran through Blakesburg, into stovewood for Leander Fitch, he was angered the way Leander bullied him. Leander called him a lying Red Neck. This was more than Simp could take. He dropped his ax and flew into Leander, who was a muscular two-hundred-pounder about thirty years old, and gave him a good mauling. Jeff Anglin, one of the many spectators who gathered to enjoy the fight, told Simp he would be a greater prize fighter than Jack Dempsey and that he would buy him a pair of gloves and a punching bag if he would take up fighting. To this, Bill Simpson agreed and Jeff Anglin, eager and anxious for fame and fortune, asked to be his manager. Bill Simpson not only agreed but was delighted.

This young woodchopper, good with a double-bitted ax, a spade and pick, was just as good with the boxing gloves. He was matched with Dartmouth's Pete "Mauler" Mennix, a man of twenty-two and a seasoned fighter. Jeff Anglin had given in Simp's age as nineteen since he looked much older than his sixteen years. Simp got through with "Mauler" Mennix in eight rounds. He knocked him out. And from this time on, Bill Simpson was called "Simp the Slugger." After this fight, his cutting crossties into stovewood for the people in Blakesburg was over. This fighting money was good money. It was easy-made money that just fell from the skies.

Simp's mother stopped taking in washings and left that competition to Malinda Sprouse and the colored women. She dressed her daughters and herself better and had enough food to go on their table for the first time since her husband, Dexter Simpson, had died. For Jeff Anglin, who had a love for money equal to Malinda Sprouse's and was a publicity man second to Franklin Foster, was the right combination for Simp's promotion. He got the fights for Simp and the cash rolled to them in a steady stream. By the time Simp the Slugger was eighteen he had won thirty fights, had two draws and had lost two by close decisions. He was known well in fighting circles in three states. The two local papers played "Simp the Slugger" up as their wood-chopping native son. And to prove his ability to chop, when a great celebration was held for Bill Simpson, they gave him a sharp ax and let him demonstrate to his city and county admirers how he could use an ax by chopping down one of the fine elm shade trees on the courthouse square. Charlie Allbright had been against his cutting this tree but there wasn't a lot he could say when a poor boy who had risen to fame and fortune, like Bill Simpson, wanted to demonstrate his power with a double-bitted ax. His reputation had been spread far and near with his picture in all the papers, which was good for Blakesburg, for Simp was rated to become another immortal Jack Dempsey. And the signs of the wealth he was accumulating were shown in his sisters' and his mother's clothes, their buying a fine old home in one of the better sections of Blakesburg, furnishing it clumsily with Horse's antiques, and buying an expensive limousine.

But at the age of nineteen a strange thing occurred to Simp. He had dates with a girl who was large, robust and mature for her fourteen years. His mother and sisters protested his going with this Red Neck girl, whose reputation couldn't be questioned, for they wanted him to stay with his own family and keep on with his boxing career until he had attained the heights to which the immortal Dempsey had risen. People in the town, jealous of the Simpsons' rapid rise in the city, which they called the rise of the Red Necks, spread gossip about Mrs. Simpson and her daughters just wanting poor old Bill to fight for them the rest of his days so they could have the comforts of a luxurious living. And when it was rumored young Dollie Keene was going to have a baby, it was hard to believe. It was one of the biggest scandals in the town. Jeff Anglin did his best to keep it out of the papers and it was he, not Bill Simpson's mother, who encouraged Simp to marry Dollie and to give her child its father's name. Simp and Dollie were married while his mother bemoaned her and his sisters' fate as well as her son's career and the money he was making.

Bill and Dollie went to housekeeping in the town. And from this time on things were not the same. Everybody knew it would have been a shotgun wedding if Jeff Anglin hadn't got his protegé married to her. They knew Alec Keene was a man who'd a-taken a double-barrel shotgun and would have gone after Simp if he hadn't married Dollie.

"Simp will go down the ladder as fast as he went up," Charlie Allbright said.

Dollie went with her fighter husband on several road trips after her baby was born. But she didn't like fighting; she didn't like to see men stand in a ring and beat each other up. And she told Simp she didn't. He told her that after all he was making a living for her and she would either like his work or leave him,

which she did after two years of marriage. This hurt Simp and
caused him to lose two fights in a row. At least Jeff thought this
was what caused him to lose them. But there was a weakness
about Simp found out by the first old veteran fighter who beat
him. He passed the word on to other fighters. "Simp the Slugger can't take beatin' in the belly. Hit 'im in thar and he'll
vomit purt nigh every time." And this was true of this young
fighter who was thought to be the second Dempsey. At twenty-
one, he was not only through with his wife, but he was through
as a fighter. He had fought eighty-six fights, had won seventy-
one, had reached a draw on nine and had lost six. Never was he
knocked out.

And now to make a living he had to do something and he
didn't want to go back to chopping wood. He knew that the
meager pittance he had saved wouldn't last long. His mother
had gotten most of his "take," and she wouldn't give it up to
him now nor anything she had bought with his money. He
bought a small restaurant and called it "Simp the Slugger's
Place."

It was more than a place. Simp was a little enterprising for
the town. He built a row of cozy booths where the young people
came to love. He had a six-piece hillbilly orchestra to play for
the young to dance. Simp took part in these frolics and left the
running of the restaurant in the hands of incompetent help. And
when the restaurant started going under, Simp thought of something that would pull him out of the red. He started selling
moonshine whiskey. Now his place became, as Sallie Bain said,
the hellhole of Blakesburg. When "Revenooers" were tipped
off to raid his place, there was never anything they could find;
yet a dozen or more men would be sitting inside his place too
drunk to move. The Law that failed to go after Mary Blanton,
who had never given Blakesburg anything but bad publicity,
went after Simp as Blakesburg's Number One Enemy. But Simp
was as smart as the Law.

He had behind his restaurant a little chicken house. And here he spent much of his time raising chickens. He would call his friends back and show them the young chickens he would one day be frying in his restaurant. He told them chicken-raising was his hobby. And everybody he called back noticed a stepladder behind his place of business but no one thought about what it was used for. If they had even thought about the stepladder they would have thought he used it around his chicken house, which was under a giant elm tree. But the truth about the step-ladder was, Simp used it to climb up into the elm where he could step off onto its branches. And it was in this tree he had a very fine saloon. He tied jugs and bottles by their necks to each limb and twig. And when a customer wanted a drink, he would go to his hen house, pretend to be working around with the chickens while he put his stepladder in place and ran up into the tree like a squirrel and cut his whiskey down from a limb.

When the strange lights flashed, Simp was up in the tree getting Tomas Fiddler, Blakesburg's stuttering barber, a quart. Simp, who had fought many a fight and had feared not man nor the devil, almost fell out of the tree when he stood for a minute watching this light. Then, with his quart in his hand, his legs trembling beneath him, he came down out of the tree and took the quart inside the restaurant.

"It's on me tonight, Tom," he said. "You've been a good customer."

Tom hadn't been outside and he hadn't seen the sky. That was one reason he couldn't understand why Simp, whom Blakesburgians had denounced, was so generous to one of its citizens. But he knew that he had always been a friend to Simp. He had held up for him in the face of bitter criticism. And now Simp was showing his token of friendship. While Tom sat brooding over his bottle, he saw Bill Simpson jump up on one of his tables. And when he did a thing like this, the eyes from his crowded restaurant were turned upon him.

"Blakesburg will be no more by mornin'," Simp screamed and then he gave a wild laugh. "And no one will be prouder than I am to see this goddamn place knocked out fer the last count! If you don't believe me, go outside and look at the sky! God ain't a-foolin'. He aims to destroy this place! I ain't a religious man but I know when His signs are here! Go see fer yourselves!"

Simp watched the people leave their tables like wild birds leaving their nest and stampede toward the door, jumping over top of one another like hornets leaving their disturbed nest. And their loud, panicky screams seemed to rip the air as they poured like water from the door into the street and beheld the spectacle which held their doom.

16

NOT ANY woman in Blakesburg had a reputation like Mary Blanton. She was called "a weaked and sinful woman" by most everyone who knew her. Not only was she well known among the inhabitants of Blakesburg but she was well known over Blake County. Her reputation had spread far and near among people she had never seen.

Even when her husband, Sid Blanton, was still living with her, she had lovers. They didn't meet her away from her home. They didn't hide from Sid. They went to the house to see her when Sid was there. They came when he wasn't there. It didn't make any difference. She didn't have one lover but she had as many as five and six. And if her husband did or didn't like it, there wasn't much he could do about it.

At first he fought against his wife's dating other men. He said it was bad for his children to grow up under such circumstances. And every time he fought one of her lovers, she would help the lover and the two of them would give Sid a good beating. After a few of these beatings he gave up, packed his clothes and went home to his mother. But he wept so much for his Mary that he came back to her. He just "couldn't stay away from his youngins," he told the people, and they wouldn't leave her to go with him.

A fight occurred on an average of once a week at the Blanton home. They got to be a common thing and no one, not even the one-armed cop, would pay any attention to the fights. People in Blanton's neighborhood protested but their protests were never heard. The fights usually occurred when Mary invited to her home a new lover. A new lover was always fussy until he was acclimated by the older ones. It was surprising how well her old lovers got along. They seemed to understand each other perfectly and to understand her. Sid told many of his friends that as soon as his children grew up, he thought they could help him remedy the situation. Sid said he lived on with Mary in hopes that someday after the children grew up, they would talk to their mother and change her way of living. And he said he would be perfectly willing to settle down to a quiet life with Mary in the latter part of their married life and forget the first half of it which had been stormy indeed. There was not another couple in Blakesburg or in Blake County who had lived as they. And everybody hoped Sid would have luck, for Mary's house was a sore spot in Blakesburg. People just didn't talk about it. And the Law didn't do anything about it. It was rumored the city and county officials were afraid.

When Sid and Mary's oldest boy, Delmar, was sixteen he left home. Their oldest daughter, Roxie, ran away to Sid's relatives when she was fifteen. Later, the two younger daughters, Grace and Essie, followed, and the youngest child, Adger, stayed at home longer than any of the children. He was eighteen before he left. After the children had run away, Sid's hopes vanished. His children not only ran away but stayed away. To "stay away from Mary" was something Sid hadn't been able to do. He tried living on with her after his children had gone. When the last child left, Sid thought she might change. And the neighbors hoped she would change. But even losing her family didn't change her. When one of her many suitors left her, she would get another to take his place. And it didn't matter whether he was married or single. Yet the majority of her lovers were married men.

One man was killed, another was shot, while a third was knifed at her house, as she brought in new lovers to take the places of those who deserted her because of their age or jealousy or because of their wives. Sid, fighting her and one of her new lovers one night, was badly beaten and injured, so he packed up and went to his children, this time for good, leaving the house to Mary. The deed was in her name although Sid had worked and paid for the property. This was a great disappointment to the people in Blakesburg, especially her lovers' wives. Many of them went to see Malinda Sprouse, for they knew she had the money, to encourage her to "buy Mary out and git rid of that weaked woman." And Malinda Sprouse, since these women were her customers, made three attempts, each time offering her a little more than before. But Malinda didn't offer so much she couldn't break even on the property if she bought and resold. For Malinda didn't have a husband and she didn't understand the problems some of the Blakesburg women had with their husbands. She didn't intend to put too much of her hard-earned cash into an old house to save their skins. That wasn't good business. But she could pretend she was trying to buy the place and keep them for her wash customers.

As the years passed women were surprised that big ugly Mary Blanton could have so many lovers. They couldn't understand how she could take husbands from their good-looking wives. But she did. As the women described her she didn't have a good-looking feature. She would weigh nearly two hundred pounds. She was a "big raw-boned woman who could knock a man down with her fist." They knew she cooked big dinners for the men but the men bought the grub. And she had drinks and smokes for them. And often she would have as many as four of her lovers sitting around the table at the same time eating with her, flattering her, speaking of her mysterious beauty the Blakesburg women failed to see. If ever there was a woman in Blakesburg the other women wished would get old, it was Mary Blanton. They wished time upon her to gray her hair and to age her body, to make her grow so feeble she would walk with a cane.

Then they knew she wouldn't be the lover that she had been. They wanted her to grow too old for love, to grow so old she couldn't capture their husbands and "lead the single boys astray." But Mary Blanton, their problem in the town, didn't take to age like a duck takes to water. Age didn't gray her hair or wrinkle her skin as it did so many people's. As the years passed, she seemed to grow younger. And as the years passed her old lovers died or went away and the new lovers came, leaving behind a trail of broken hearts, fights, knifings, and broken families.

But Sallie Bain had an idea. She was more adventurous than all the women in the town. She was the only one who would visit Mary Blanton in her home and discuss the possibilities of saving her soul with her. She thought this was one way to solve the problem since the Law hadn't been able to do it and since other women just talked and didn't do anything. And if Sallie Bain had solved it, she would have been one of the most popular women in Blakesburg. When she went inside the house and stated her business and told Mary Blanton she had a soul and that she would be accepted into the Kingdom of God if she would only lay her sins upon the altar, Mary showed her the door. Maybe Sallie had gone at the wrong time, for Mary had two lovers in the house at that particular moment. And when Mary slammed the door behind Sallie, she told her when she wanted her soul saved she would go about getting it saved and wouldn't ask Sallie for any help.

There wasn't anything more the people in Blakesburg knew to do—only to leave Mary Blanton alone. They had done everything they knew to do; they had tried everything. And they resigned her to her fate, all except the women whose husbands she loved; they ranted and raved but it was all in vain. Cora Madden, whose husband, Denver, was Mary's lover, carried a pistol for Mary. When Mary met Cora, whom she had heard was carrying the "difference" for her, she walked up and talked kindly while she frisked Cora's clothing for the pistol.

Mary couldn't find it about the clothing so she opened Cora's pocketbook and relieved her of a .25-calibre pearl-handle automatic.

But there came a night when Mary had five of her lovers seated around her table. She had cooked them a mutton supper. And she had on the table plenty to drink. This was a big night for Mary who was without fear of man or woman or her soul; Mary, the woman who was unafraid of time creeping upon her, for it was a little thing and she was younger than ever and certainly more fearless.

On this night she drank and ate with her five lovers. There was one who had come to see her for the past twenty years. Denver Madden, the senior of them all, had a wife and family of nine children only six miles away. Even his three grown sons couldn't keep him from going to see Mary. And his wife, Cora, had nagged at him for nineteen years over his helping buy Mary's clothes, food, coal, whiskey, and paying her light bills. There was Rodney Gantz, living only a few doors down the street, who had a wife and three children. There was Elmo Chadswick, whose two orphan children were with his mother, for his wife was dead. And Lister Starks, a man under thirty with a wife and six children who lived less than a mile up one of the dark hollows from the town. And there was young Denbo Wainwright, somewhere under twenty, who lived in Blakesburg.

Denbo it was who first observed strange lights in the sky, for he was sitting at this table of love where he faced the dining-room window on the north. When he stopped eating suddenly, then got up from his feasting and ran to the window, Mary and her laughing happy lovers stopped talking and turned their eyes upon Denbo's strange actions. But when he screamed the world was on fire, they jumped up from their love feasting and merry-making and ran to the window. Many of them still had their mouths filled with mutton but they either got it out or swallowed it whole when they got a glimpse of the sky. Mary Blanton shook like one having chills before fever. Maybe at this moment she remembered Sallie Bain.

Denbo was the first to grab his hat and take off like a greyhound out at the door and down the street. He acted like one running from Sodom or Gomorrah in the day when they were smote by the hand of the Lord for their wickedness. Suddenly, Rodney Gantz followed and then Lester Starks ran toward the door and fairly flew up the well lighted hollow as fast as his legs would take him to his wife and six children. Elmo Chadswick observed the sky a few minutes longer and then took off, leaving his hat in the house, almost turning the table over getting out.

Denver Madden stood beside Mary a few minutes. He would look at her and then at the sky. And for the first time in his life, he watched her face grow white from fear. He had seen her in many fights. He had seen her knock her man Sid down faster than he could get up, in their younger days. But now, as she and he faced a great catastrophe together, one the Lord had sent upon Blakesburg to destroy it and the wickedness of the people therein, he watched her weaken. He saw her fall to her knees on the floor. Then Denver knew it was time for him to go.

Denver couldn't run like the younger fellows but he went as fast as weakened legs would carry him. He butted into the table as he ran and then bounced over and hit a door-facing. But he ran, with his hat in his hand, through the house where all doors were left opened by "the boys" who had preceded him in flight. And he didn't take time to close a door behind him. He ran out into the light and hit the homeward road as fast as his legs and breath would allow.

"Sweet Jesus, I turn to Thee who will not forsake me in this hour of need," were the last words he heard of Mary's prayer as the distance was increasing rapidly between them.

17

WHEN HORSEFLY SALYERS walked away from the supper table in his father's house, he stepped out on the back porch to roll himself a cigarette. As he was pouring the Bull Durham from the little sack onto a piece of brown sugar-sack paper, he noticed the light was unusually bright for a back-porch electric light. Then he took one look at the rolling seas of liquid fire over his head and his body froze stiff as a corpse. His fingers stuck to the cigarette like a fly to flypaper. It was more than a minute before he could overcome the spell to get action into his body again. He had had this same powerless feeling many times before when he had been drunk. But he was not drunk now; he had only had a few drinks. If he were a little drunk, what he had seen in the sky sobered him. For he ran like a gray game rooster into the house and grabbed one of his girl babies up under each arm.

"What's the matter, Horsefly?" Mrs. Salyers asked him.

"My God, Ma!" Horsefly said, his face white as a sheet and his lips trembling. "Go out on the back porch and look at the sky! The world's a-comin' to an end! My God. . . ."

"Where ye a-takin' yer little youngins this time o' evenin', Horsefly?" his father asked.

"Back to Sue, Pap," he said.

"What's come over ye, Horsefly?" his father asked.

"Go to the door and see fer yourself, Pap," he said.

"Are ye a-goin' to take the cow?" his mother asked.

"How can I take a cow and my three little girls?"

"But ye must come back and git 'er," his mother said as she walked over to lift a window shade.

114

Horsefly didn't take time to answer her as he left the house with a little girl in each arm and one following at his heels.

"Dad, it's the end of times," Horsefly heard his mother tell his father as he hurried out of the house.

Horsefly didn't hear any more for he was running down the back road as fast as he could run. Overhead the great arms, darts and tentacles of light crisscrossed on the sky. People running across this back road toward the mountains, screaming and praying and calling the names of their loved ones as they ran, put more fear in Horsefly. His heart pounded like a triphammer and he got his breath like a winded horse for he wasn't in good physical condition. He had drunk too much "herbs" and he hadn't done a day's work since he had parted with Sue.

Sue'll tell me the truth now, Horsefly thought as he ran on long weakened legs, struggling for more much needed breath.

As much as the people in Blakesburg had loved gossip, it was hard for them to believe what they had heard about Horsefly's wife, Sue. Many people couldn't believe a mother of seven daughters could be meeting Speedo Traylor in Dartmouth on Saturdays when she went there to shop for her children. Though, they did wonder why she hadn't done her shopping in Blakesburg. Speedo was a married man with a wife "as fine as women come" and six children. They just couldn't understand why she would want to leave her children to meet this Speedo.

It wasn't until this gossip went over the air lines that people began to investigate Speedo's reputation. Everyone in Blakesburg knew he wasn't one of their people for he had come from a "furrin county" of their state years ago. They didn't know he had left a wife and six children "back in the mountains." But now that he was supposed to be having a love affair with Horsefly Salyer's wife, this gossip about his former wife and six children had been unearthed.

"Just to look at Speedo ye wouldn't think he's a great lover," Mary Blanton said when she heard the news. "But ye can never tell about a man!"

But Horsefly was going about telling his friends a man never could tell about a woman. And while he was discussing his unfortunate situation, he didn't fail to show his friends the two loaded pistols he was toting for Speedo. "Just as soon as I lay eyes on 'im," Horsefly would tell them, "one of us will be a hurt man. I'm shore hit aint a-goin' to be me." And he enlightened the people who loved to stand to listen to this interesting news, that his wife had not only met Speedo in Dartmouth but she had met him many times on a greenbriar-covered hill near Blakesburg. He said he had heard about it, although not another person had heard this.

Horsefly was on his way to work the day he got this news. But he didn't go to work. He went home, blacked his wife's eyes, and took his three youngest girls and his cow home to his parents. He left Sue with the four older children at the shack. He told her he was leaving her forever. Sue cried not only because he had nearly beaten her to death but because, as she told him, she hadn't had anything to do with Speedo. When Speedo ran in a Greenough Primary election, she admitted she had voted for him and had ridden to the election with him in his car. Horsefly, who was a Dinwiddie, didn't like his wife's politics and he certainly didn't like the man she had voted for.

Though many people sympathized with Horsefly, there were twice as many who did not. They remembered Sue Bellamy when she was a pretty little girl, with peaches-and-cream complexion and two large braids of hair down her shoulders and a bow of ribbon on each braid. She was in the seventh grade then and the little boys in her class "claimed" her. She was thirteen years old but she was big and robust for her age. And no one could understand why Horsefly Salyers, a young man of twenty-three, had married this little girl. But her father was dead and her mother worked in the homes around Blakesburg to support a family of six.

Blakesburg women, who hadn't any sympathy for Horsefly,

remembered that at fourteen she became a mother. At fifteen she had her second daughter. At sixteen she had her third daughter. Each year she bore a daughter for Horsefly with the exception of one year. And that year she had lost twin daughters. Had they lived she would have had nine daughters before she was twenty-two. She was still beautiful, one of the prettiest young women in Blakesburg.

"That Horsefly married Sue when she was in the cradle," the women who sympathized with Sue would say. "She never had youth like the other girls. She never had any good times. All she's known has been child-bearing for a worthless man. It serves him right if she looked at another man."

After Horsefly had married Sue, he would go places but he never took her. He left her at home to "look after the youngins" while he went down the street and loafed with the boys. Often he would get drunk, go home, beat her and scare his little girls. Many times there was not food in the house and his parents would bring them food. But in 1940 when manpower became scarce, he was offered an easy job with good pay and he accepted it.

It was the first time in his life he had ever worked.

"I got the best job I ever had in my life," Horsefly went about telling his friends, "and then my home was broken up by that Speedo. I had just worked long enough to get my youngins clothed and shod, a good supply of provisions stocked in the house and my winter coal. And now I've lost my job; I've lost my home. I've lost my faith in women; I've lost everything."

Horsefly's parents wanted him and Sue to "git back together" so they would take the three younger children back home. They admitted they were getting tired of keeping them, clothing them and feeding them as well as Horsefly. They told their neighbors they had raised one family of eleven children and they didn't want to start all over again with a family of three. They said Horsefly was still in love with Sue regardless of how he had talked about her and that he had occasionally gotten drunk from the time he was fifteen but now he was getting drunk every day and was becoming a sot.

But from 1940 until 1941 Horsefly's parents had to keep him and the three children at their home while he ran about drinking and talking about his troubles. He had seen Speedo Traylor, whom he had threatened to kill on many occasions, but he would run like a turkey at the sight of him. Speedo had also denied Horsefly's charges that he was guilty of fornication with Sue. On the nights Horsefly said Speedo had met Sue on the greenbriar-covered hill, Essie Traylor claimed she was with her husband. But after Horsefly had advertised his unvirtuous wife to everyone that would listen, he put his divorce suit in Attorney Joe Oliver's hands. The trial was scheduled for October.

"It's in good hands," Horsefly said. "Joe Oliver will show her what it means to be untrue."

But Horsefly's sister Sadie Salyers had married Hank Redfern, who had recently been "saved" and had "got the word" and started preaching. After Hank started preaching, his first convert was his wife Sadie. They "were full of the fire" and were trying to "spread the gospel flames" everywhere. It didn't take Sadie and Hank long to think they should start spreading the flames at home. They would try religion on Sue. If she were converted, she would confess the truth. It would be better than swearing her before Attorney Joe Oliver. They didn't want this thing in court. And if both Horsefly and Sue would get religion the "Devil's sins couldn't keep 'em apart any longer."

Sue knew her brother-in-law Hank Redfern hadn't been an angel. She knew her sister-in-law Sadie had "lived in sin" as much as her husband. She knew how they had "fit like dogs and cats" and now since they had "got religion they lived like two love birds." She knew their getting religious had done wonders for them. And when they went to her shack and prayed for Sue, she became a saved woman. When she made her confession she confessed she had been a virtuous woman.

And now Hank and Sadie turned their attention toward Horsefly. Night after night they went to his parents' home and prayed for Horsefly. While they were praying for him, not Horsefly but his parents came under "the spell" and became saved and baptized in their early seventies. Hank's and Sadie's influence made a great change in Horsefly. Their preaching hell's fire and damnation had stopped him from "a-rippin' out a big oath every time he spoke." But when he learned that Sue didn't confess fornication, he said, "Sue's not a saved woman. She didn't confess everything."

When Horsefly reached his home, the shades were pulled down. The windows, mirroring the lights, were shining balls of shifting fire. He set the little girls down from his tired arms. He tried to open the door but it was locked. Then he put his ear against the keyhole and above the sound of his three little girls' crying, he heard Sue praying as he had never heard a woman pray before.

"Sue," Horsefly said, pounding on the door.

His pounding was not much louder than his heart beats.

"Sue, it's Horsefly," he shouted as he pounded again.

But Sue was too busy praying to hear his knocking.

"It's Horsefly back home, Sue," he screamed as he kicked the door. "Open the door! The world's endin'. . . ."

"I know it," Sue said as the door opened wide and she and Horsefly stood face to face. "I'll tell you in the face of death, I had nothin' to do with Speedo Traylor!"

In a split second they raised their arms and rushed toward each other to embrace while their daughters were reunited. The younger ones stopped crying and went into the house with the older ones while Horsefly and Sue were silent in embrace. The multi-colored lights played on their happy faces and closed eyes but not their lips that were pressed as close as if they had been welded together.

18

ONE OF THE greatest rivalries in Blakesburg was undertaking. Each undertaker tried to take care of his "side" and keep his rival from encroachment.

Marvin Clayton was by inheritance of blood, political and religious faiths a Greenough and it was he who was supposed to get the Greenough Blue Blood and Red Neck dead. Franklin Foster was by inheritance of blood, political and religious faiths a Dinwiddie and it was he who was supposed to get Dinwiddie Blue Blood and Red Neck dead. And since this newfangled idea of making an industry of burying the dead in Blakesburg had gotten underway in about 1911, Marvin Clayton and Franklin Foster had been bitter rivals each trying to hold and care for his own people.

When Dink Clayton, Marvin's father, got the idea that this was a coming industry, sometime before 1910, he immediately shipped his son away to an embalming school. At the same time Archie Foster got the idea to send his son away to return and rival the son of his old political and religious rival. They went to the same embalming school where they were rival students. Never could these two political factions meet, not even when it came to putting their deceased away. For there was not one of Greenough religious and political faith who would want his kin put away by one of the Dinwiddie religious and political faith. This wouldn't work when the old family groups would not be planted in the end on the "Lonesome Hill" overlooking Blakesburg side by side. They had been rivals for more than a century and a half and they couldn't see any need to be buried side by side in the end. And they weren't buried side by side.

When Marvin Clayton and Franklin Foster returned to Blakesburg and hung their shingles above the doors of their undertaking parlors, which were on the same street, their bitter rivalry continued. Each, in those days, tried to get the finest pair of horses to pull his hearse. Each tried to get the nicest and most expensive hearse with the most fringe on it. And each soon developed the idea of hauling the relatives of the deceased to the funeral which was not a sad occasion like in most places, but a rare occasion of mirth and fun and someplace to go. Only the deceased's close relatives ever did much weeping in these days.

And for all the luxuries that each undertaker was adding year by year, his paper in the town carried the news in the form of advertising. In those days they had rubber-tired surreys to haul the deceased relatives to the funeral. At one time Marvin Clayton boasted in an advertisement in the *Greenough Gazette* he could put six rubber-tired surreys behind his hearse. That meant he had to keep seven spans of big horses and the barn behind his undertaking parlor where he kept his horses looked like a livery stable. But Marvin Clayton would outdo his rival, Franklin Foster, or he would know the reason. The Greenough dead must be properly put away; there must be more fanfare, more services and more beauty to a Greenough funeral than Franklin Foster could possibly do for his Dinwiddie dead. Franklin Foster, in the early days, never could advertise more than four rubber-tired surreys for his funeral processions. Besides, Franklin Foster's horses were never as well groomed, nor did they wear silver and brass buckles on their harness nor the decorations of many red tassels on their bridles nor the silver rings for the driver to slip his checklines through.

But Franklin Foster had pride for himself and the people on his side. He not only had pride but he had business sense. He wouldn't let his rival put anything over on him. He started

advertising in the *Dinwiddie News* how one of his embalmers
had slept in one of his coffins and had found it feathery soft,
luxurious, and comfortable. And above this advertisement was
the picture of an opened coffin, showing the lacy trimming, the
fancy handles and the streamlined contours. Not any of its points
of beauty were left out by Franklin Foster who had a flare for
writing ads with flowery language. He was as gifted along these
lines as his rival Marvin Clayton was for picking spans of handsome horses to pull his rubber-tired surreys and the big dapple-
gray draft horses to pull his hearse. In addition to all the beauty
and luxuries he had described in his ads of his coffins, he went so
far as to list twenty-six additional services. And he listed them
in order. He showed Marvin Clayton and his Greenough kind,
that he and his Dinwiddie clan would not be outdone.

Not only was this rivalry manifested in hearses, horses, beauty
of coffins and additional services but it was shown in their undertaking parlors as well. Each got a new coat of paint each spring
with their borders done up in fancy trimmings. Each had a nice
lawn with flowering shrubs. And any stranger coming to this
town immediately pointed out that these undertaking parlors
were two of the most beautiful houses in Blakesburg. Not a
dwelling house in Blakesburg was half so beautiful nor was any
yard a fourth so well kept. Even the people in Blakesburg
argued over whose undertaking parlor was the nicer. That was
a question for speculation and people just didn't agree on it for
the people of Greenough political and religious faith whether
they be Blue Blood or Red Neck stood for their side and the
same was true for the Dinwiddies. But anyone would have to
agree that this was a case where independent, unobstructed rivalry in business paid the deceased dividends. Although it was
a bad time to pay them when they knew nothing about it.

When the roaring Twenties rolled in there was a great change
in these businesses. Each started expansion since the Red Necks
back through the county were getting sold on this undertaker

idea. And when these two men got all the county's trade it meant bigger and better business. Not any business, up until this time, had taken on a greater expansion in Blakesburg than the undertaking business. This just went to show how a business could grow in a few years even if it was the business of planting the dead. It wasn't exactly a pleasant business but it had been made into one with all the extra services and the grandeur of the materials used for their last cocoons.

And when Marvin Clayton, who was falling a little behind Franklin Foster in "beauty and splendor," got the idea to build him a new undertaker's parlor since his business had increased tenfold, he immediately started to build one of bricks, mortar and stone. It was rumored that he got Malinda Sprouse to assist him financially. And at this same time Franklin Foster made plans to erect him a parlor similar to Marvin Clayton's parlor, only a much larger one. He waited to start his after he had seen the foundation of Marvin Clayton's parlor. But Marvin waited until Franklin bought him a newfangled automobile hearse and then he bought him a larger one; yet both undertakers still had to keep their horses, team-pulled hearses and rubber-tired surreys for the country roads. Automobiles still bogged down on these impossible wagon-rutted roads. And many Red Necks were still afraid of the automobile back in the far parts of Blake County.

Their rivalry roared as the Twenties roared and it expanded as everything else expanded in the Twenties. Each man hired young embalmers and had as many as a dozen and a half people working for him, caring for the horses, repairing the carriages, driving the automobiles, embalming, conducting funerals, keeping the parlors clean and their lawns in tiptop condition. Neither destroyed his old frame-house undertaking parlors due to senti-mental values of themselves and their followers. Nor did they keep them for a relic of the past. Business was still carried on in the old parlors as well as the new ones, which were monuments to Blakesburg. These industries thrived and expanded through the Twenties with each undertaker buying the best new automobiles of both popular makes and sport models.

And when the depression came, everybody thought the undertaking business would fold up like the wash industry and the railroads which had laid off nearly all their men and every other small industry in the town where people earned the small pittances of their very existence, but the undertaking industry didn't fold up. It kept on going, for the people still died. And people looked upon Marvin Clayton and Franklin Foster as business men with plenty of foresight to start the undertaking business in the town and their advertising it with such pleasant aggressiveness they got the people used to it. Their businesses marched right on through the depression with a few cuts in salaries which their workers didn't mind accepting since they realized hard times were on them. They were glad to take anything.

Into the Thirties Marvin Clayton and Franklin Foster went. Each was trying to hold his own. They didn't have the fear of any more competition in business. A third undertaker wouldn't have had a chance. These two men had the county and town sewed up. Would a member of the Dinwiddie clan have anybody but Franklin Foster in the end? Would a member of the Greenough clan have anybody but Marvin Clayton in the end? Anybody living in Blakesburg or Blake County in the early Thirties would have said "no." They would have told you the lines would not break for another century.

But as Franklin and Marvin grew older, and as their businesses kept expanding, they had to hire more help. Just about all each did as the Thirties rolled along was to be the titular head of his thriving business. Each tried to hire young men who were bright, young, eager and ambitious. And it later turned out to be that Marvin Clayton got a genius in the undertaking world. He was not only one to "undertake" but he was one to fulfill . . . and to dent if not to break the old lines of religious and political faith. His name was Archibald Troxler. He was called "Poodi" Troxler for short.

When Poodi Troxler came to Blakesburg to get a position of embalming, he first tried to get with Franklin Foster's undertaking establishment. But Franklin Foster after interviewing Poodi Troxler wouldn't hire him. He didn't listen to the youth's ambitions nor did he give his grades consideration. He had graduated with the best grades in his class. Many thought the reason Franklin Foster let this young genius escape was because of his eyes which were badly crossed although he wore thick-lensed black-celluloid-framed glasses that partly hid his eyes and they didn't look bad until he removed his glasses. But Franklin Foster's loss was Marvin Clayton's gain.

The only thing he couldn't do well when it came to the undertaking business was, Poodi told Marvin Clayton when he interviewed him, he couldn't drive a hearse very well but yet he could drive one. But he preferred not to drive one when there were so many other things he could do. Then he showed Marvin Clayton his grades and no one knew better than Marvin that Poodi was his man for he had never made grades like these when he was a student. This boy must have something on the ball for he was so sincere and honest and right with the Marvin Clayton undertaking establishment he went to work that very day, despite the fact Franklin Foster had turned him down and Marvin knew it. But Marvin was not to be fooled. He knew that such a slap in the face would give Poodi an impetus unrivaled among his help, to help him not only keep his Greenough following in line but also to cut in on Franklin Foster's Dinwiddie following.

Not only was Poodi Troxler an undertaker but he was "a great mixer." And maybe he could be called a kind of a psychologist. He would spend his day working in the parlor where he proved himself to be one of the best embalmers and at night he would go searching for some old people of the Dinwiddie political and religious faith. He would never cross them on their religious or political beliefs for Poodi had come from an adjoining county and he wasn't Greenough or Dinwiddie in faith. He was neutral. He was an undertaker above everything else. He would talk to these old people and get acquainted. And when he left he would be invited back again. He would never tell them where he worked until they were interested enough in him to ask him and then he spoke of his work casually. They to him were of first importance, his work came second. And when he went back to see them he would take them a basket of fresh fruit. Often he would take them groceries.

He never visited the aged among the people of Greenough religious and political faith. He knew his firm had them. He worked on the Dinwiddies. He would go visit someone he thought didn't have much longer for this world, and he would do them favors. He would go see one aged person or an aged couple every night. The firm furnished him a car. It wasn't long until he had a whole host of friends among the aged. And he had a considerable grocery and fresh fruit bill at DeWit Addington's store. But as he told Marvin Clayton he would break the line for him and get the business and he did. He told Marvin his idea would pay dividends, an idea aggressive Marvin Clayton was a little leery of at first but accepted joyfully after he had seen it work. He was so jubilant over the idea, he gave Poodi a slap on the back and a raise in salary.

Not only was Poodi valuable for hocking trade from the Dinwiddies but when somebody had died, who had no blood kin to weep for him, Poodi went to the services to do the mourning. He would take on so that he would get others to weeping for this sad occasion and before the services were over and the corpse laid to rest, people would get to weeping until they jerked and many of the women would faint. There was no question of Poodi's genius in his field and Marvin Clayton knew it. In order to hold him to his establishment he sold him a few shares in his business and made him sort of a lesser partner with a promise that he should assist his son to carry on the business when he was departed from it. As Marvin said, he wanted somebody who could subdue the Dinwiddie crowd, to steal Franklin Foster's business and to hold the Greenough business to the end of time.

Dave "Daddy" Claxton was ninety-two years old when Poodi made his acquaintance a couple of years before. He was one of the first of the aged Poodi had gotten acquainted with. And no one knew better than Poodi that this man of Dinwiddie faith should have Greenough funeral services. About once a month he had gone to visit Daddy, had taken him baskets of soft fresh fruit, for the old man didn't have any teeth, had taken him to-bacco and baskets of groceries. And it was a long time before Daddy asked him what he did. When Poodi told him what he did, how he was a stranger in Blake County and how he had tried to get a place at first with Franklin Foster and how he had turned him down when he'd worked his way through the em-balming school and had made the best grades in his class, the old man, like many previous ones, immediately began to think about his dying, his death and who should bury him. And his re-quest was to have Poodi do it. Poodi pretended to be very reluc-tant about it since they were such close friends but he agreed finally to do it according to the old man's written specifications.

At ninety-four Daddy Claxton passed away and when Frank-lin Foster learned Marvin Clayton had one of Franklin's very own, who was deep in his heart's core of Dinwiddie political and religious faith, he was very much upset. Now it was an estab-lished fact to Franklin Foster that Marvin Clayton, who had hired young Poodi Troxler, an undertaking genius, on whom they had had first refusal, was cutting deeply into his business. Marvin Clayton was really working on him. It wasn't Marvin doing it . . . but it was this young Poodi Troxler whose name had become a household word in Blake County. Poodi was in-

different to Greenough or Dinwiddie faith and people of both
groups, except some of the old diehards. Dinwiddie Blue Bloods
were fond of him. For he had not only been friendly with them
but he had put up some powerful weeping for their dead which
they hadn't forgotten nor would they ever forget. His interests
were in them.

But when Daddy Claxton died on the morning of September
18, 1941, Poodi was busy embalming and didn't go with Fid
Sperry who took the horses and the wagon-ambulance to get
him. For this was Daddy Claxton's request to Poodi that he
wasn't to be hauled to the undertaker's parlor in an automobile
hearse nor was he to go to the graveyard in one. He had told
Poodi he had always loved horses and he had hated automobiles.
Poodi had agreed with him that the horse-drawn hearses were
surer, safer and certainly better riding. Daddy Claxton would
be safe with Fid Sperry, Poodi thought, and it was all right for
him to stay at the parlor and do a special job embalming one of
his deceased friends since this was his last request that he should
embalm him.

But Franklin Foster, who had been alerted to his rival's possibilities among his own Dinwiddie Clan, knew when Fid Sperry
took a younger span of big dapple grays hitched to the horse-
hearse out on Buck Run, eight miles back in the county to get
Daddy Claxton. It was late in the afternoon when he started.
And he regretted very much to lose a body that belonged to him
and should be put away with pomp and ceremony by "their
side."

He was willing to lose Daddy Claxton until he saw the first
great flashes of the lights. And like other citizens of the town,
Franklin Foster knew the end of time was at hand. His mind
went back to this deceased patriarch of his clan whom his rival
in business had sent a slow-going team to get.

Franklin Foster put Dock Taylor in his best and fastest ambulance and gave him instructions to go get Daddy Claxton. He

told him to pay no attention to the abuse of his new ambulance but to shoot it over the rough country roads now that they were dry.

"What ever you do, Dock," he said, "beat Marvin Clayton's team to him. In the end of time, we want our own. Go get 'im, Dock."

And Dock did.

19

Not many men outside the Blakesburg City limits, who had found employment in the city, were able to take unto themselves brides from the native population. And not many of the young women had gone away and found husbands for themselves. It was a rare occasion when one did. And there were many reasons for this. But the main reason was, both the Dinwiddies and the Greenoughs were not only suspicious of marriage into each other's clans but they were both very suspicious of the people beyond their city limits and they were even afraid of people beyond the Blake County borders.

The Blake County Red Necks, whether they were Greenough or Dinwiddie, would come nearer marrying someone beyond their borders. But even they were suspicious and reluctant to do so. However, there were a few who advocated marriage beyond the boundary lines. Bruce Livingstone went so far as to say. "We need some fresh blood amongst our people," and Charlie Allbright had remarked many times in his philosophic discussions at the courthouse square that he couldn't see "no harm in a Blakesburg boy or girl a-takin' a mate beyond the border." But Charlie Allbright and Bruce Livingstone were criticized by both factions of the townspeople for their views.

When Poodi Troxler, a native of an adjoining county, had been given employment by the Marvin Clayton Undertaking Establishment, he became a citizen of Blakesburg. At least he thought he had become a citizen of Blakesburg. And he had a right to be sure when Marvin Clayton had sold him shares in the establishment and had given him promises of a permanent future for his good work. Now that Poodi Troxler thought he was getting himself well established in Blakesburg, he began to look around for a prospective bride. Like all other young men he was looking for himself a helpmate to help him face the future, to share his joys, his business successes and his little worries. Little did Poodi dream there would be trouble ahead for him since he had made such rapid strides in the beginning of his career.

But he did need a wife to share life with him. Suddenly this became his ambition as much as to get a start in the world had been his ambition when he first hit the town. So he knew what he wanted and he set out to get her. As he told his boss Marvin Clayton once, he "wanted to do a little shopping before he finally invested." And that is what he did. He did plenty of shopping before he finally invested.

Poodi thought he knew the Blakesburg people and he did know them in a business way. Not any stranger who had ever come to Blakesburg had done as well. Not any had ever made more friends. But when it came to marriage to a daughter of one of these families he found it quite a different matter and it wasn't just because he was cross-eyed. Many of the Blakesburg women had married cross-eyed men before who didn't have as good clothes as Poodi and who weren't making as much money as he nor were as well established in a permanent business future. There was a saying in Blakesburg, "Clothes don't make the man but man makes the clothes." Poodi just wasn't of their people. "He aint rooted among us on either side. His roots aint here." Nor did they make any overtures to cultivate his roots so he would grow permanently in their soil.

Poodi made many overtures to many girls, both Greenoughs and Dinwiddies. It didn't make any difference to him just so he took unto himself a bride. And from a financial standpoint it would work all right either way, he reasoned. If he married a Dinwiddie he would cut in on their business more than he already had; if he married a Greenough he was showing his loyalty to his boss and his firm. But this wasn't the question. Girls just didn't take to him.

Blakesburg citizens still have memories of Poodi in April when all the city's flowers and shrubbery were at their peak of blossom, how he would stroll down the street with one of their native daughters of one of the clans and how they would sit under a flowering shrub and how he strummed his guitar and sang for her. He was not only an accomplished man in the trade he was engaged in, but he was excellent with the Spanish and Hawaiian guitars and he could sing like a lark. Not only would the girl he was singing to sit and listen to him for hours but other girls would come and bring their beaus and listen to Poodi. And they would make much over Poodi and his music. He was even invited to the homes to play for them. But that was all. When he put the marriage proposition to one she "crawdaded backwards." Though he was popular among the younger set, the young women's instincts came to life when he proposed marriage. There was that reawakening in the young woman that he wasn't her people.

And for two years in Blakesburg and in Blake County young Poodi Troxler tried to get himself a bride. No one knew exactly how many girls he had asked to marry him but Mister Pat Greenough said he had heard it rumored that he had proposed to over a score. And he had played his guitar and sung to more than a hundred.

Poodi even made such an overture to the townspeople to declare himself one of their own and his intentions of staying as long as he lived and becoming a part of the town, that he bought himself a fine home near his work. He furnished it with the best of furniture that money could buy in Dartmouth. And he went to live in his home alone. Since he hadn't a helpmate he ate his meals at the Winston Boarding House. His home was an invitation to marriage. He had the cage but he didn't have the bird not until . . .

Bill Simpson's divorced wife, Dollie Keene, sent for him to come and "pick his guitar and sing for her." This invitation resulted in love. And there was much gossip since Dollie Simpson was used to plenty of money when Simp was in his fighting prime. And now here was a young man with a well furnished home, owing no man a cent, and one who gave good promise in the future. Everybody said Dollie was "money hungry" and that she would marry Poodi if he would have her, but they wondered if he would since she had a son by Simp the Slugger. But he did. They were married and moved to his furnished home.

And the difficulties of her former marriage and her son by Simp didn't stand in the way. For the people soon were aware Poodi was a better stepfather to her son than Simp had been a father. Each evening when he was free from work, he would take the little boy by the hand and walk proudly down the street with him and buy him ice cream at the Drug Store or he would go to DeWit Addington's store and buy him candy. He was as proud of his stepson as if the boy were his own. Dollie's son, whom the people gossiped would be a stumbling block in her marriage, turned out to be an asset.

Poodi showed the people in Blakesburg he had no inhibitions about marriage, any more than he had about entrenching himself with the Dinwiddies or the Greenoughs. His wife was a Dinwiddie Red Neck and he worked for a Greenough Blue Blood. But Dollie Keene Simpson was an attractive girl, much younger than Poodi, and he was devoted enough to her to play his guitar and sing for her any time she was willing to listen. He bought her anything she desired and the first thing was a brand-new automobile, a high-priced and swanky model.

But with all the affection he bestowed upon her, the people whispered that something would happen to the marriage. They said it wouldn't last because Poodi was still a stranger in their midst, that he wasn't rooted in either the Greenough or the Din-widdie clans, that he wasn't rooted any place not even in Blakes-burg or in Blake County and that he wasn't their people. They even went so far as to pity Dollie Keene for marrying him since she was one of their own. Franklin Foster even went so far as to call Poodi a "spy." Franklin said he'd come into their place of business so much that he ordered him to stay out. He said Poodi was going back to Marvin Clayton and telling what he had in his place of business. Said he caught him going over his books checking on his profits. But Marvin Clayton said this was propaganda put out by his rival to hurt his business.

If it hadn't been for what happened on Thursday night, September 18th, when the sky warned everybody in Blakesburg, including the undertakers, this fight about propaganda might have gone on and the Marvin Clayton Undertaking Establishment might have kept on rolling over their rival house through the genius of Poodi Troxler. And Poodi Troxler might have shown the people they were wrong when they said "something would show 'im up yet." Poodi might have become the city's wealthiest man. His fortune might have gone beyond that of Malinda Sprouse. But when he took one look at the rolling mountains of fire in the sky, he wilted like a stalk of corn beneath an agate July sun.

"Lordy-lord," Poodi shouted, running from his front porch into his living room and over the ankle-deep plush on his floor.

"What's the matter, Poodi?" Dollie asked, jumping from her luxurious antique base rocker where she was comfortably sitting smoking a cigarette.

"Make ready, darlin'," Poodi gasped. "The time has come."

"What do you mean, honey?" Dollie asked. "I don't understand!"

"Look at that sky and you'll understand what I mean," Poodi warned. "It's the end of time! It's here, darlin'!"

"I'll go see," Dollie said, walking reluctantly toward the porch.

"I'm not a-kiddin' you, lambie pie," Poodi moaned as he stood in the middle of the living room, trembling from fright.

When Dollie saw the lights she let out a hysterical scream and made a wild leap for the door. She slammed it shut and ran toward Poodi screaming with her arms over her head. Poodi grabbed her and they embraced in this final hour as they never had before, while their son lay asleep unmindful of the world's ending.

"Do you love me, darling?" Dollie wept.

"I love you better than life itself, sweetheart," Poodi said.

They put their lips together and held their breaths.

"Do you have any confessions to make, sweetheart?" Poodi asked Dollie as soon as they breathed after the long kiss.

"I'm on the right side," Dollie said. "I'm on the side of Jesus!"

Then Dollie felt Poodi's body shake with a chill as they were locked in close embrace. And she saw the tears stream from his eyes.

"What's the matter, honey?" Dollie said sweetly. "Do you have a confession to make?"

"I'm afraid I have," he wept on her shoulder.

"Just so it's not a woman," she said, her face changing expression. "I hope you've never knowed another woman but me."

"But don't fergit you've known another man, sweetheart," he said.

"Yes, but that was legal," Dollie came back. "I was married to Simp. It was lawful under the eyes of God and man!"

"Hit's not a woman," Poodi confessed slowly.

"Then what is hit?" she asked him after she'd waited in silence for a minute. "Confess before it is too late!"

"O Jesus," Poodi said looking up toward the ceiling, "be

merciful to me, a thief! That's all I've done, honest, hit is!"

"What've you stole, honey?" Dollie asked, pleased that his confession wasn't another woman.

"I've been a-stealin' tools from Franklin Foster," Poodi wept.

"Then Franklin Foster was right!"

"Sure he's right," Poodi said, holding Dollie closer.

"But you can make that right before hit's too late," Dollie said.

"And I will make it right," Poodi said. "If only God lets me live long enough until I can!"

"Oh, how I love you, darlin'," Dollie said.

"And how I love you, sweetie pie," Poodi whispered, getting a firmer grip around her soft warm body in their embrace, squeezing her until he heard something pop like a broken twig.

20

WHEN ANYONE died in Blakesburg, the whole population became jittery. There was a reason for this. Since the latter part of the eighteenth century, when Death called a Blakesburg citizen, he always came back and got two more within a week. Uncle Sweeter Dabney said it happened as far back as he could remember. He said his father and his grandfather told him this tradition Death wielded over the city went back to its beginning. After the first death everybody became jittery, thinking it might be his time next.

The week Uncle Jarvis Stevenson, a patriarch among the colored populace of Blakesburg, went, Death came the following day and called Murtie Downs, a Dinwiddie Blue Blood, and the following day he took Cyrus Whittinghill, a Greenough Red Neck. Now he had taken his three and it might be some time before he would visit the city again. But these three deaths would give the people in Blakesburg something to talk about and some place to go. The funerals would give the women a chance to show their new clothes and the undertakers a chance to demonstrate a competitive spirit with their new methods and the conducting of funerals with all their extra services.

Franklin Foster naturally got Murtie Downs. But Marvin Clayton got Cyrus Whittinghill and Uncle Jarvis Stevenson, who was a colored man of long undisputed Greenough political and religious faith. And his funeral would be one of the big events for the colored populace of Blakesburg.

For Uncle Jarvis Stevenson was one of the best-known citizens

137

in Blakesburg or Blake County. He was the last of his race to die who had been born in slavery. He didn't know his age exactly since the state where he was born, though it was one of the earliest states to be admitted into the Union, didn't start keeping birth records until as late as 1912. But he often told the Greenough and Dinwiddie Red Necks when they gathered around him to hear him talk of "the olden days" that he was a young man wanting to marry when he regained his freedom from Doctor Elijah Stevenson, whose horses he fed, shod and groomed, whose saddles he kept polished and whose bridles he kept repaired and decorated with tassels. He said his days in slavery with Master Doc were easy days and that he was lucky to have a master as good to him as Doctor Stevenson. He said he couldn't remember any members of his race in the days of slavery who fared as well as he.

People would guess Uncle Jarvis's age. Everybody guessed him to be well into his nineties, and many took him to be over a hundred. Only in the last couple of years had he started walking with a cane. Less than five years ago he was able to run and leap onto the saddle on a trotting horse. He had been one of the best horseback riders in Blake County. Ten years ago he had ridden at the Blake County fairs where he had shown the young bucks how to run alongside a horse and mount him when he was in full gallop. He was well past eighty then.

And when Uncle Jarvis told the crowds that thronged about him how he used to win all the foot races in Blake County they believed him. He told them that after he regained his freedom he went to work in one of the Blake County iron furnaces in the days when they cut cordwood for fuel. He told about the foot races at the furnaces, how they would see who could win a race to the top of the steepest cliff-scarred hill. One day after he had won one of these races he told how he had returned jubilant to the furnace because the white men who had bet on him had won their money. And he spoke sadly when he said that on this par-

ticular day, he and his race received the biggest insult he had
ever heard up to that time come from a member of the white
race. He told about some man losing his lunch and how he said,
"Some goddamn nigger stole it!" He said that made his blood
curdle and how pleased he was afterward when it was learned a
white man had stolen the lunch.

He would sit for hours on one of the Alex Scroggins seats
with Charlie Allbright, Bass Keaton and other Blakesburg philosophers, whittling and talking with them while the eager crowd
would gather to listen to his magic stories of the early days. He
would tell of hillsides that were once cleared away, "down to
every stick big enough for cordwood" and how fire had been set
to the remaining twigs and leaves, leaving the land burned
cleaner than any backyard in Blakesburg. Then the land would
be sown in wheat, set in tobacco or planted in corn. And now on
the same hill slopes there was another crop of trees that the
present-day generation thought was virgin timber. But Uncle
Jarvis remembered another day, another world, which sounded
strange to his eager listeners, even to Charlie Allbright and Bass
Keaton. He remembered all the old families who owned slaves
and he would tell any colored person in the town about the family who owned his ancestors and from whom he had gotten his
name.

But where Uncle Jarvis told his best stories was when he sat
on a stool in the yard or on a· doorstep in front of one of the
shacks in the colored section of Blakesburg. Not always did he
talk about what a long way it was back to slavery, the hard
thorny uphill road he had been over, but he told animal stories
to the children. This small man would sit and fumble the handle
of his cane while the wind played with his long curly locks of
hair, white as clean sheep wool, telling without end about the
days when the wild pigeons were so thick they broke the limbs
from the trees when they gathered to roost at night. All one had
to do to kill himself a mess of forty or fifty was to slip into the

woods and shoot once into the roost with a double-barrel shotgun.

He remembered where the last otter was killed. It was killed in a little valley, not more than three miles from Blakesburg when they were clearing the right-of-way for the Old Line Special. Then he told a favorite story about a panther that had escaped from a show and had lived in the cliffs of Artner Ridge not far from Blakesburg. He told how Sarah Jane Spencer, a white woman who had been in her grave more than eighty years, was walking out the Artner Ridge road home with two pairs of shoes and some clothes she had just bought in Blakesburg. When the panther saw her, it ran after her screaming. It was about to catch her and she turned and threw a pair of shoes at it. The hungry panther tore open the box, chewed a minute on each shoe while she ran; then it learned the shoes were not good to eat and that Sarah Jane would be better so it took after her again. When it got close she threw it the second pair of shoes. While it opened the box she ran farther. She threw every package she had to the panther and while it opened them, she ran a bit farther. After she threw the last package she made it to the house. Bill Spencer shot the panther when it came toward the house screaming after his wife who had fallen exhausted on the front doorstep.

Then he told the young boys about Bigfoot. He told this story over and over again. Bigfoot was a fox that outran any fox in Blake County. Fox hunters had seen his tracks along the ridges and in the river bottoms. They were bigger than any hound dog's tracks and they named him Bigfoot. Hunters hated this fox because he would circle farther than any fox was ever known to circle. He had been known to circle as far as fifty miles. And on such circuits he lost many of the hunters' hounds. He led them out of the county and they never returned. That is why they wanted to kill this fox. For twenty years hunters tried to kill him. Then one day a pack of hounds ran him a sight chase to a split in a rock or they would have caught him. The hunters hur-

ried to where their hounds were baying and here was old Bigfoot, trapped at last, his red hair now turned gray, not a tooth in
his head. He was the biggest fox ever caught and killed in
Blake County.

Uncle Jarvis's death, though many people had long expected
it, came as a shock to everybody. He was the greatest storyteller
ever to live in Blake County. He was loved by everyone, his own
people, the Red Necks and the Blue Bloods and the Dinwiddies
and the Greenoughs. His word was law among his people and
they looked up to him as their patriarch. His death severed the
last living source of information they had from the days of
slavery to the present. His going had ended an era. Marvin
Clayton took personal charge of this funeral and took with him
Poodi Troxler.

One of the traditions that had been handed down in Blakesburg since the automobile had replaced the rubber-tired surreys
for hauling the funeral crowd to see the bodies interred on "that
Lonesome Hill" was, when a Greenough colored person died,
the white Greenoughs loaned them their automobiles to haul their
populace, with the exception of children too young to enjoy the
event. The same was true when a Dinwiddie colored person
died. The white Dinwiddies furnished them with automobiles.
Neither undertaker had enough automobiles to supply his side
for this occasion and the white people on his side backed up their
business leader with anything they could do. This tradition
started in the early roaring Twenties when competition boomed
at its highest mark and when the automobile replaced the horse-
drawn vehicles. At this particular time, Marvin and Franklin
were trying to outdo each other with modern transportation.
They didn't know they were starting a tradition they would continue throughout the years. It continued through the Thirties,
down to the Forties. . . .

For on that afternoon of September 18, 1941, when Uncle
Jarvis Stevenson was hauled from the colored church to the

Greenough Colored Division on "that Lonesome Hill," none other than Marvin Clayton remarked he had never seen a more magnificent spectacle than this funeral procession hauling Blakesburg's colored population, plus many white Greenoughs and a few white Dinwiddies. The procession was more than a half mile in length. It was the biggest funeral the colored people had ever had, as it was for their most distinguished citizen. It was a procession of the finest automobiles in the city. For the colored people on this occasion were loaned the very best automobiles. They had been washed and simonized and the tanks had been filled with gas by their white owners. For this, too, was part of the tradition. Even the colored people who owned automobiles, usually not the newest and best, left their cars parked and borrowed better ones for this occasion which was always something magnificent and wonderful to them. Though the whites enjoyed funerals and put on a show, the colored people could outdo them when it came to the sheer enjoyment of a funeral and of putting on a better show. Everybody knew this. There wasn't any question about it. It was never disputed by either colored or white. It was an accepted fact.

And after the body at a colored funeral was laid to rest, the drivers of these borrowed automobiles could drive them for the rest of the afternoon and into the night if they wished, and they always did. The return of the cars was midnight or before. This was in keeping with the old tradition started by Marvin Clayton and Franklin Foster in their earlier days of competitive spirit.

And on this particular occasion, after Uncle Jarvis Stevenson was laid to rest, the funeral crowd could hardly wait to get started on their drive in their big fancy automobiles, clean and shiny and with full tanks of gas. The day had been one of grief for a few, excitement and joy for many. The colored people knew Marvin Clayton had gone the limit to make this day a success by coming in person and bringing with him his young and well-known Poodi Troxler. It was a fine overture to make toward the colored people and they were as appreciative of this as they were of the Greenough limousines in which they were riding.

And when the dirt started falling onto Uncle Jarvis Stevenson's grave, they hurried to their automobiles for an afternoon and night of fulfillment and enjoyment. This was one of the rare occasions when no one worked but everybody took the day off dressed in his best. Marvin Clayton and Poodi Troxler who remained to supervise the grave watched the procession of cars go down the Lonesome Hill much faster than they had come up. It was a magnificent exodus of speed, power, and beauty, and little soupbean-colored clouds of dust trailed them down the Lonesome Hill until they reached the back road, all heading for cities beyond. There were only two ways they could go, east and west, for the hills were a barrier to the south and the river was a barrier to the north. Here they parted in two directions and lined each road with cars.

Little did these people dream they were leaving their homes before a disaster which would come on this night. They left with the best of intentions. And like the whites, not one of them had received a secret warning. They were leaving their native Blakesburg, of which they were a part, on a trip of pleasure and enjoyment. They went away laughing, smoking and talking. Never had they laughed more than now, for they loved leisure as no other race had ever loved it. If ever a race of people should have been born for leisure, it was theirs. Instead, they found everywhere they had lived, tasks of menial drudgery. They should have been directors and overseers. Then life for everybody would have been much easier and less serious.

But Uncle Jarvis Stevenson, who had lived approximately one century, had died one day too soon. This trip should have been conducted before the great lights started flashing in the north and caught them on roads and in cities far from Blakesburg. For when these lights flashed, no one knew better than they that these were the signs of the earth's finish. Time would be no more. And from their car windows they looked to see if they could see the White Messiah coming in the clouds. But they didn't look for long. They started stepping on the gas. The road was as bright as day and they forgot to turn on their lights until they hit a place in the road like a cut between bluffs or behind an embankment where there were shadows. And this caused several collisions and prayers beside the highway. For not a car returned that didn't bring a carload of praying people who had gone away laughing for an afternoon and evening of traditional happiness.

When they raced their cars back to Blakesburg they brought the smell of burning rubber tires, hot engines with radiators boiling over. There were prayers, songs and lamentations coming from their lips as they tried to get the cars back to the rightful owners before the town was wiped away. They didn't want to be accountable for borrowed property. And all who hadn't gotten lost or wrecked on the highways hunted for the car owners on the Blakesburg streets.

Their hurrying home to go into eternity from their native city was a touching scene to the white citizens, who faced with them for the first time, equality of Death and impartiality in the last and final judgment.

21

H E WAS CALLED Uglybird by everybody because he wore a
long sad face. Even the school children called him Mister
Uglybird. That was the only name they ever heard him called
around Blakesburg. And every child had heard his parents talk
about Mister Uglybird from the time he could remember because Uglybird was as much a part of Blakesburg as one of the
twisted gnarled-rooted elm trees that shaded the streets or the
old courthouse that was built before the nineteenth century.
Uglybird didn't have the most pleasant job in Blakesburg but
he had a permanent job. Like his father "Sweetbird" Skelton
before him, he was the "Lonesome Hill" Sexton.

The long apprenticeship he had served with his father digging
graves and mowing the grass from the graves during the spring
and summer months was, the people in Blakesburg thought, the
reason for his long sad face. It didn't make any difference to the
Blakesburg people whether he had a pleasant or a sad face since
he was one of their people. And there wasn't any denying this.
Like Uncle Sweeter Dabney, Uglybird was steeped in the town's
traditions. He could tell any visitors who came back to the Lonesome Hill looking up the unmarked graves of their dead, where
they were buried. There were more people sleeping on Lonesome Hill than there were living people in Blakesburg, since the
town was very old and had grown so slowly. Many of the graves
were unmarked but Sweetbird Skelton had schooled his son,
Uglybird, about the history of each grave before he turned his
duties over to him.

And now Uglybird was getting old, and he was teaching his oldest son Kirby all the history he knew about the Blakesburg dead. By knowing the history of all Blakesburg's dead, Uglybird knew more of the intimate stories of the families dead and gone than Uncle Sweeter Dabney knew. And he knew plenty about the living families in Blakesburg . . . things he never cared to tell. Uglybird knew of some event that had happened on each day of the year. When he got up in the morning and started to work, he would always say something like this to his son Kirby: "Well, hit's March the 4th. On this day in 1911 old Kim McGinnis was swung up to the old hang tree at the lower end of Blakesburg fer stabbing his wife." Or, "Well, hit's March 5th. On this day in 1889 Fid Higgins was hung fer getting old Dan Billup's gal, Biddie Billups, with child. Old Dan wouldn't have a shotgun weddin'. He wouldn't let 'im off that easy atter he'd disgraced Biddie." "Hit's March 6th. On this day in 1882 Ephriam Wheeler died with the fever." "Hit's March 7th. On this day in 1905 Bill Kalup's house burnt down when him and Callie's out a-milkin' the cow and burnt up a couple of thar little youngins. The ashes are buried right over thar." "Hit's March 8th. On this day in 1922, Houndshell Pennix was shot in Tim Spriggs' hen house."

Uglybird knew where everybody was buried, what had caused his death, what he did in life, what he ate for breakfast, the kind of clothes he wore, whether he drank whiskey and whether he was loyal to his wife or not. And he knew the women who had died in childbirth out of wedlock, women who had been faithful to their husbands, the old maids, the young women and the little girls and boys. He knew about all of them for his father had lived to be ninety-five and he had imparted all his knowledge of Lonesome Hill to his son before he retired at eighty-five.

Since Uglybird had seen his domain expand as the years had passed slowly at Blakesburg, it kept him and his son pretty busy, especially in the summer time, to keep the grass and bushes mowed down and to dig the graves. Yet Uglybird found a little time on the side to supplement his salary. Usually he supplemented his salary in the winter time when there weren't any bushes and grass to cut on Lonesome Hill. For during the winter and sometimes in the summer he would find veins of water beneath the ground for people living on the outskirts of the town and the nearby farmers who were having wells dug. Many of the people living in the town had their own water supply from wells for they didn't believe in having water piped into their houses from a common reservoir.

Uglybird was a water witch who claimed he never had failed to find underground veins of water with his peach-tree fork. He disputed with anyone who used the willow fork. He claimed it had failed for him but the peach-tree fork had never. He would break a forked branch from a peach tree and hold one of the forks in each hand letting the main branch be before him. He would walk along and wherever the main fork bent groundward was where he would say there was a vein of water. If it dropped suddenly downward, it was a big vein and not very far down. If it was slow to drop it was a small vein. He had it all figured out in his head—from the time the fork started dropping to the place it dropped, was the way he judged the number of feet the diggers would have to go to hit the vein of water. He charged people for his services though he didn't dig their wells. And he was much in demand just to find the veins of water for the people, for his reputation had spread among them as one of the best water witches in the county.

Uglybird wasn't afraid of anything. There wasn't a child in Blakesburg but knew the stories his parents had told about how bad Uglybird had been in his younger days to drink moonshine whiskey. He went up Cowpath Hollow on the southwest border of Lonesome Hill and there he got his moonshine from Dennis Marcum. He never had to pay more than two dollars a gallon. Though nearly all the people in Blakesburg were afraid of Dennis' whiskey since Noonie Griffee went blind three months from drinking a gallon of it, the whiskey never bothered Uglybird. As he said, he had "drinked hundreds o' gallons of hit and he had eyes that saw in the daytime as good as a chicken hawk's and as good at night as a hoot owl's."

But one night he was drinking Dennis Marcum's sugar moonshine and playing poker by the railroad tracks. And it was on this night that the Devil appeared to Uglybird and scared him sober. A lot of people said it was Dennis Marcum's rotgut that made Uglybird see the Devil. But from this time on, Uglybird went a little slower on his drinks. He said his seeing the Devil was some sort of a "token" but he hadn't been able to figure what kind.

Uglybird had seen stars fall at night when he was doing a rush order of three graves. The night of Halley's Comet he was working on Lonesome Hill. He said it made the cold chills run through him when he saw this monster flash through the sky but that he "wuzn't skeered." Everybody knew he had seen so much death, had heard so much weeping on Lonesome Hill, he had become used to it and it took something unusual to scare Uglybird. Halley's Comet and the Devil hadn't been able to do it. Stars falling at night and working among the white monuments was just another night to him. It may have saddened his face a little throughout the years but he could still laugh and joke. He could tell jokes about the strange things that had happened on Lonesome Hill, how he had kept a sheet to wrap around him and scare people who had passed that way at night. He would laugh when he told how the people would tear out screaming and jumping over the tombstones as they left the hill. One of his favorite jokes was how he scared Noah Billups and his wife Bertha when he caught them on Lonesome Hill one night praying to the Devil. He slipped up on them shrouded in his sheet and stood silently before them. Uglybird said Noah took the lead and ran off and left Bertha. Both screamed as they ran.

But when Death came to Blakesburg, Uglybird had a rush order of graves to do. Due to his father, Sweetbird's, past experience, Uglybird dug the graves in order as Death called them. In this week of September 14–21, 1941, he dug Uncle Jarvis Stevenson's grave first since he was the first called by Death. Then Murtie Downs was called the following day and Cyrus Whittinghill was called the next day. After he had dug Uncle Jarvis' grave and had seen, which was part of his job, that he was properly buried and a good mound placed over him, he went to work that afternoon on a grave for Murtie Downs. He and Kirby worked that afternoon and that evening while it was cool, they took their lanterns and went back to finish the grave. It was never an uncommon sight to see Uglybird's lantern on Lonesome Hill at night.

Little did this fearless man know when he and his son walked up the Lonesome Hill after supper, to complete Murtie's grave since they would have to dig one for Cyrus Whittinghill next day, that he and Kirby would see something that would shake them from the hair on their heads to their toenails. They walked casually up the hill with a lantern unlit for it wasn't good dark. But they knew they would need the lantern to shape the grave up properly, for Uglybird was an artist on digging graves.

They had gotten back to their work and had lighted the lantern for they needed light down in the shadows to finish their artistic piece of work. Kirby would hold the lantern while Uglybird got down and worked until he was "winded." Then Uglybird would sit upon the brink and hold the lantern while Kirby went down and "hit it a spell." When a strange kind of light coming from the north lit up the Lonesome Hill, Uglybird was sitting on the brink holding the lantern while Kirby was down trimming the walls with a broadax.

"Hold that light steady, Pap," Kirby said. "Ye've made me dent the wall!"

But Uglybird was watching the light from the north. He was

sitting in a strange light while he held the lantern down among the shadows with his long arm. Uglybird knew this wasn't a natural light. He suddenly realized it wasn't anything like Halley's Comet. And he had been to church and had heard the sermon preached many times about when the earth would end. He didn't pay any attention to that for he had thought the world would go on as long as he lived.

"What's the matter with ye, Pap?" Kirby asked. "Have ye got the fidgets? Why can't ye hold the light steady? Ye've made me about ruin the wall of this grave!"

"Steady hell," Uglybird shouted as he jumped down into the grave. "Thar's too much light!"

"What's the matter, Pap?" Kirby asked. "Ye aint had no moonshine, have ye?"

"Stick yer head above this grave and see what I see!" Uglybird told Kirby. "Then ye'll see plenty of light!"

When Kirby caught on the brink of the grave with his hands and pulled himself up where he could see, he dropped back quicker than he had jumped up.

"My Lord, Pap," he said, "what is it?"

"As near as I can figure, hit's the end of time," Uglybird said. "I remember hearin' hit said the end of time would come in the twinklin' of an eye!"

"And us here in a grave," Kirby said, his voice trembling.

"Hit's the right place, aint hit?" Uglybird said. "We've dug hit ourselves and hit's a good grave."

"Maybe ye're right, Pap," Kirby said thoughtfully.

Then Uglybird blew out the lighted lantern and he and his son lay down side by side lengthwise of the long grave. The light was too bright for their eyes. They turned over in their grave with their faces against the cool earth, waiting.

22

Bascom Keaton was a direct descendant on both sides of the house of Blakesburg's founding fathers. His mother, Effie Dabney, was a great-niece of Uncle Sweeter Dabney; his father, Battle Keaton, was a great-great-grandson of old Duvall Dinwiddie, who with his flintrock rifle and his hunting knife, helped to drive the Indians from the wigwamed village now known as Blakesburg. Duvall Dinwiddie had said, and it was passed down through his family, "Thar won't be any hoss swappers amongst my people. But they will be rulers and warriors!"

Old Duvall had prophesied too far into the future. He didn't know what there would be among the future generations of his posterity. He didn't know there would be a boy named Bascom Keaton, born in Blakesburg seventy-five years later with Dinwiddie blood in his veins, who would be one of the greatest horse traders Blakesburg had ever seen. Horse trading was not keeping in the Dinwiddie-Keaton-Dabney tradition, for they were rulers, politicians and warriors but young Bass was a form of mutation from these inherited professions. Maybe it was his environment that caused him to break away from his people's professions to the more lucrative and enjoyable one of horse trading. "Hoss swappin' " wasn't considered an ethical occupation by the early dignitaries of Blakesburg. It was something a son of one of the respected families shouldn't do. It just wasn't nice. But Bass Keaton came along and changed all of that.

When he was a very small boy, the world of Blakesburg to him was an interesting place to live. Men rode horseback and muleback and came with buggies, surreys, hug-me-tights, jolt wagons and expresses from all parts of Blake County and brought their products to barter for city products. Young Bass would get out on the streets and walk around among these county Red Necks. They were tall lanky men with bony sunburnt faces when they weren't covered by long beards. They cussed, drank and smoked and chawed and carried long mule whips over their shoulders. They would bring their wares to Blakesburg and barter with the merchants for their necessities and then they would start swapping horses, mules, wagons and teams. There would be trade after trade and it was on one of these days that Bass heard the word "boot" used for the first time in his life. And right there he learned that "boot" was money.

Bascom Keaton's parents were embarrassed at their son's inclinations to follow the trading Red Necks. But he was born at the right time to be a trader. Blakesburg was a trading town. It was the mecca for the Red Necks since all roads from Blake County pointed to Blakesburg, the county's Capital City.

At this time Blakesburgians feared the Red Necks most. They regarded them as "furriners in the flesh." Because, after they had finished bartering their produce for city wares and swapping horses five or six times each before they left town, they would get drunk and pull their pistols and start shooting. People would run in the houses and close the doors; merchants would have to close their stores and women would leave the streets. This was an everyday occurrence in Blakesburg. But Bass would never leave the street when they started shooting. He would watch them leave the town, riding hard as their horses would take them, emptying their pistols as they left. He loved to watch wisps of smoke leave their long, hot pistols. This was the Blakesburg Bass Keaton knew as a child and loved.

But to stop so much trouble the merchants of Blakesburg got together and banned hoss swapping except on Saturdays and the first Monday in each month. This would give the people of

Blakesburg five days of terror instead of thirty and by doing this they would keep the goodwill of the Red Necks with whom they had to trade.

Bass went to the trading grounds bright and early each Saturday morning and the first Monday in the month, when the school was in session, Bass always skipped school. He knew what his education was to be. He wanted to know how to trade horses. He wanted to make a lot of boot. And before his schooldays were over, and the fifth grade was as high as a boy could go in Blakesburg at that time, he bought a plug horse for a dollar he'd saved from pennies and nickels and he was off to his fortune. He bought his plug in the morning and traded all day and by sunset he had "ten dollars boot" in his pocket and one of the finest saddle mares in Blake County. That afternoon, Tommie Alexander, a Red Neck, was riding the plug Bass had swapped him when it fell dead on the road and nearly killed Tommie. It took four men to roll the horse off of Tommie. It had broken a panel of his ribs.

Before Bass was old enough to think of taking a bride he had accumulated much "boot" and he was one of the most influential men in the city. He owned several pieces of property, a half-dozen farms and he dressed in style except when he was among the Red Necks on the trading ground. There he became a poor man, riding with a quirt in his hand and unshined spurs on his briar-scratched boots. The Red Necks all over Blake County knew him, respected his judgment of horses and yet they feared him. They knew he was one of the gifted traders who could look at a nag one time and tell what he was worth. Bass would trade sight unseen. Ask the man what he had and Bass would describe what he had and the two would trade right there and then go look at their bargains. He would buy farms and never go look at them. In a short time he would sell these farms at a big profit. Money came his way.

Then Bass married a Red Neck wife, and this too was as much

against the tradition of his forebears as "hoss swapping." By her he had four children. His children grew up, not interested even in "hoss swapping," and they helped Bass spend some of the money he had made. They didn't work at anything except spending money and they became geniuses at this. Bass, discouraged with family life since he found it not half as interesting as hoss swapping, finally took to drink. And he drank as he had traded horses. The people of Blakesburg watched this man and his family quickly disintegrate. His children married off; his wife died. And he spent day after day sitting on the courthouse square trying to whittle the longest shaving. Often he was so drunk he couldn't see the shaving.

Bascom Keaton who had let a small fortune slip through his hands, would often not have a place to sleep. And he'd sleep on one of the political seats on the courthouse square. He let his beard grow long; he seldom had a haircut and his clothes were soiled rags. Many of the people who knew him in his younger days couldn't believe he had come to this. But he had. Often a few of the traders of a new generation would go broke. And when they tried to start again, they would hire Bass, if they could catch him when he was sober, give him five or ten dollars to go with them to judge the livestock they bought. This was about all the money he ever made in his old days. He didn't have any ambitions except the horsequart of pure corn. He had gotten fat and people wondered how he had since he never knew where the next meal was coming from. But he wouldn't lay down his horsequart, not as long as he was able to buy one, bum one or "git it on tick."

Though people wondered how he had managed to cling to life and grow old and live as he lived, sleeping on the streets on winter nights, going without food and warm clothes, Bass kept on living. Although he got to the place he did have to walk with a cane. He drank and bummed through the Thirties and into the Forties. On the evening of September 18, 1941, he was sitting with Charlie Allbright arguing for the Dinwiddies while Charlie upheld the faith of the Greenoughs. He had his cane and Charlie had his crutches leaned against the seat and they were whittling as they argued. And while they sat there they noticed a great light appearing in the north. Charlie got his crutches and hobbled off to be sure that "this token in the sky" was the real McCoy he'd been expecting for some time while old Bass sat silently looking at the flashing lights and their great reflections in the river.

"What is hit, Charlie?" Bass asked, spitting a bright sluice of ambeer.

"I'm not sure what it is yet, Bass," Charlie spoke prophetically.

And it was about this time the people started stirring over Blakesburg.

"But I see somethin', Charlie," Bass said, pointing his cane at the sky.

"What do you see, Bass?" Charlie asked.

"It's the Savior, I do believe," he said solemnly.

When Bass said these words many who had gathered on the courthouse yard took off without looking to see if they could see the Savior coming in the clouds.

"But I don't see Him, Bass," Charlie said.

"But I do," Bass said, pointing again with his cane. "I'm sure hit's Him. My eyes aint a-foolin' me that much."

"I can see something," Charlie said, looking the way Bass had pointed his cane.

"And I'm not ready to meet Him," Bass said, getting up, grabbing his cane. "He won't have any use for me, a hoss swapper and a sot!"

Bass limped off in the direction away from the lights while Charlie stood looking with his prophetic eyes trying to see Christ coming to Blakesburg on a cloud.

23

NOAH BILLUPS was once considered the meanest man in Blakesburg. He wouldn't fight any man fair. He would gouge, bite, cut and shoot in a fight. Once, in a fight with Liam Winston, he got Liam by the ear with his teeth and bit a half-circle from his ear clean as a whistle. It was a funny-looking ear that he had left Liam. And he had cut Ephriam Sparks to the hollow with a long-bladed knife and Ephriam was left in the Dartmouth Hospital three months before he pulled through. He slashed Sid McCallister across the stomach with a knife and laid it open. But Sid held his intestines in his hands and walked nearly a half mile to Dr. Hinton's office and had them put back and his stomach sewed up without much trouble.

Noah Billups was also a heavy drinker. He could put more fishbowls of beer down his gullet than any man in the town. He would bet that he could drink more beer than any man in the crowd. And he would bet with drinking men that he who drank the least had to pay. That was the way he got his beer free until people learned his capacity. He could kill a pint of Tid Fortner's pure corn without taking it from his lips or batting an eye. And for years he had drunk his quart of sugar moonshine a day until something got wrong with his stomach. Noah said the lining in his stomach must be burnt out for he got powerful hot every time he took a drink and he felt an awful burning in his gullet.

The good women in the town said his wife, Bertha, drank with him. Many times they had been seen at midnight staggering up the street with their arms around each other trying to

hold each other. They would be going home to their three children they left alone in the house while they were out drinking.
His oldest child, Bruce, a boy of nine, cared for a sister six and
a brother three. Everybody talked about it but no one did anything about it. He dared the one-armed marshal to stick his nose
into his private affairs. The people were afraid of Noah. They
were game men in the town who would fight for their honor
but they didn't mess with Noah. But everybody prophesied, especially Charlie Allbright, that Noah would come to a bad end.

Everybody thought Charlie was right when Noah lost his
job on the railroad section. People were sorry to see him lose it,
not so much because of his wife, who would stoop to get drunk
with him, but because of their three children. After he lost his
job, Noah got to be the biggest bum in Blakesburg. He would
stand on the street, so drunk he could hardly see, and ask men
for a quarter. He would try all the strangers, especially the
young men coming to Blakesburg to get married, and if he
had luck with them he wouldn't bother his friends. But if he
didn't have luck with the strangers he would go after his friends.
And they were afraid not to shell out a little change to Noah.
Liam Winston told Noah once when he asked Liam for a quarter that he would give it to him, even though he had taken most
of one ear, but warned Noah that he made more money begging
than Liam's mother paid him for working at the Winston Boarding House.

And everybody in Blakesburg was of the opinion that Noah
made more money begging than he had ever made on the railroad section. They could tell by the way Noah dressed his wife
and children and bought himself a new suit. And he didn't have
a charge account at the stores any more. He bought everything
with cash. And, Noah even quit drinking moonshine. He started
buying "Govern-mint" whiskey.

Everything seemed to be going all right for Noah until Bertha
had her fourth baby. Noah didn't have Doc Hinton with Ber-

tha but he had Jinnie Slemp because she had a good reputation "ketchin'" babies and she didn't cost "too damned" much. She had hurt Doc Hinton's practice badly because she had never charged over five dollars. As prosperous as Noah was, he didn't get Doc Hinton but he got Jinnie who had successfully delivered three babies for them.

And it was through Jinnie Slemp and two neighbor women there the night their child was born, the story got out that the baby was marked with the Devil. Vennie Didmore, Vera Pratt and midwife Jinnie Slemp all told the same story to the women in Blakesburg. They said the baby was born dead and that it was well and good it was born dead. Said it was born with a long tail and on its forehead were two little horns like born to a young calf. And that very night Noah put the dead baby in a box and carried it somewhere upon the mountain and buried it. He wouldn't let anybody see it. But these women had already seen it and they spread the news how it was marked with the Devil. But everybody agreed that it should be marked with the Devil the way Bertha and Noah had lived since Noah was a son of Satan and Bertha was Satan's daughter. Charlie Allbright said he had heard from reliable sources that both Noah and Bertha had gone out on the dark mountaintop away from the town at night and had prayed to the Devil. Uglybird Skelton had told Charlie Allbright that he was digging a grave one night when Noah and Bertha came to pray to the Devil and that he ran them off Lonesome Hill with a mattock. And now the Devil had betrayed Noah and Bertha and no wonder they had paid the price by Bertha's having a marked baby for their getting mixed up with such company.

Reece Nimrod had once taken a party of six boys and they went upon the mountain, shortly after the child was buried, to hunt for its grave. They knew they would see the signs of fresh dirt if they went soon enough. They found the signs of fresh dirt which had been packed down by a recent rain. But they dug through the packed dirt with their mattocks, shoveled it away with their spades and had the top of the box off where they could peep in when out of a clear sky the clouds begin boiling up like giant thunderheads. Then it started thundering and lightening and the rain poured so they threw dirt back onto the grave and took off through the rain down the mountain side with their mattocks and shovels. But they said the rain was the work of the Devil for they hadn't run a quarter of a mile until they reached sunshine and dry earth. Anybody in Blakesburg will tell you if you go into the patch of woods where this devil-marked baby is buried that it will start thundering and lightening and the rain will start pouring. Many people have tried it and they will tell you that Reece Nimrod, who made the discovery, told the townspeople the truth.

But the Devil's sending this baby to Bertha and Noah changed their whole lives. Just as soon as a tent meeting came to Blakesburg where the Holiness Preacher spoke through a loudspeaker not just to the tent packed with people, but to the people all over the town, it put Bertha and Noah on the Lord's side. They were sitting on the porch of their shack near the railroad tracks listening to the good guitar music and the singing by the Gospel Singers and the words of the Little Preacher when they got the call and ran to the tent. There they threw themselves upon the altar and they had some confession to make. They confessed to their allegiance with the Devil, how they said they had thought he was being mistreated because they had only heard God's story and not the Devil's story; they told how they had gotten all lickered up on the Devil's medicine and went to the mountain top together and had prayed to the Devil; they told about how their child had been conceived after one of these meetings on the mountaintop when they were under the influence of the Devil. Before the tent packed with people they made all these confessions and warned the people to beware of the Devil for he would in the end betray them.

It was such a good message that the Little Preacher wanted to get it over to his people in the town. He had them to make another confession through the loudspeaker so all the people in the town would hear. And then came the payoff for the tent meeting when a man and a woman as wicked as Noah and Bertha Billups could get saved and redeemed by the blood. There was a chance for everybody, no matter how wicked, no matter what he had done. And people fell to their knees until the confession altar was packed and the floor of the tent was full. There had never been such revival and soul warming as this tent meeting with the Little Preacher, the good guitar music and the Gospel Singers. That was why Noah and Bertha were ready when they saw the signs in the skies.

"Bertha, the time has come," Noah said, as they stood side by side on their front porch looking toward the north with light in their eyes. "Christ is a-coming!"

Bertha put her arm around Noah and hugged close to him while he beamed with happiness and lifted his face toward the great panorama of light.

"Honey, I'm glad," Bertha said. "I'm glad we saw the Light two years ago!"

"Glory be to God," Noah said joyously, waving his hands above his head, "Glory be to God! Christ's a-comin'! Look fer Him in the clouds!"

When their children heard Noah shouting, they ran out on the porch to see what was going on.

"What caused that light, Papa?" asked the oldest one.

"Christ is comin', Herbie," Noah said. "We're a-goin' to leave Blakesburg!"

"Where we a-goin', Papa?" the little girl asked.

"To Heaven, Daisy!" Bertha said.

"Not in these clothes, Mama?" Herbie said while the little one tagged at Bertha's dress frightened until he screamed at the electric streamers of light.

"What are we a-goin' to do with the house?" Daisy asked.

"Leave it," Bertha said. "We won't need it any longer, honey, we'll have a nicer home than this'n!"

The children stood looking thoughtfully at the lights and then at their father as he clapped his hands and shouted, "Glory be to God, the time has come!"

"Noah, we'd better git dressed and git the youngins dressed," Bertha said, after they had searched for Christ among the clouds until they'd strained their eyes. "The time is gettin' shorter every minute! We'll soon haf to be a goin'!"

"What am I a-goin' to wear, Mama?" Daisy asked.

"A white dress," Bertha said. "We'll all go dressed in white."

"Can I take old Bob, Mama?" Herbie asked.

"No, you'll haf to leave 'im."

"Won't they have dogs in Heaven?"

"No."

"Then I don't want to go," Herbie began crying.

"You'll live forever in Heaven, son," Noah said. "You'll be happy ferever and ferever!"

"Not without my dog," Herbie cried.

"Come on, Noah," Bertha said as she carried the smaller boy into the house, "fetch Herbie and Daisy. Let's git dressed!"

"But I don't wanta go," Herbie wailed. "I don't want to go without old Bob!"

24

FELIX HARKREADER was born on the head of Hog Branch which was "back in the sticks" of Blake County. As a young man he lived with his parents who cared for him more than they did for any other of their eleven. They were partial to Felix, "becaze he wuzn't sharp as a tack." He had managed to get to the second grade in school.

That was why Sarah Harkreader would save back an extra piece of pie or cake for him after she had fed her flock. She was always making him an extra shirt, or buying him an extra little present. And when her sons and daughters grew up and "flew from thar nest like young birds over the land," Felix remained in the nest for his parents to care for.

When he was a small boy he was afraid at night. If he saw a shooting star he would run home screaming unless there was someone with him to keep him quiet. He was always seeing angels or devils in the dark. If he was walking along the road and darkness overtook him, he would stop at the first house and spend the night with the people whether they invited him or not.

After John Harkreader had died, Felix lived on with his mother as she ripened with old age. Sarah Harkreader said the only reason the Maker hadn't called her was because of Felix. She said Felix was all she had to live for and to leave him was the only reason she hated to die. She hated to leave him alone in the world for she didn't know who would take care of him since his brothers and sisters had moved away and not one of them wanted him.

But Sarah Harkreader did die and leave her son. And for a while, though scared almost to death at night, he lived alone in their shack at the head of Hog Branch. For this creek was the domain of earth that belonged to him; it was all of the world he knew. It was a good world to him even if others didn't think the place was good and moved away from the steep slopes and high walled cliffs to greener pastures. Felix had never been farther away from Hog Branch than Blakesburg and he hadn't been there more than a dozen times in his life.

But something got into his head after his mother had died. Maybe it was because he didn't like to live alone like a stray dog left behind when its owner moved away. Maybe, Felix had a struggle trying to live from the worn-out tobacco bluffs around him. And maybe he remembered the times when he went beyond his little world to Blakesburg, the big city, where there were many well-dressed people and cars drawn without horses that ran up and down the streets and lamps that didn't use oil or have wicks. It was a strange world indeed, this Blakesburg beyond the hills. And maybe it was that he remembered this city and started out in 1938 to find it.

When Felix left home, he closed the doors, tied up a few of his belongings in a dirty sheet and tied the sheet on the end of a stick which he put across his shoulder. With his turkey across his shoulder and a large stick in his hand, he left home on an April afternoon. When darkness came, he had walked six or seven miles and he dropped in at a farmhouse to spend the night. He didn't ask to stay with Herbert Greene. But Herbert kept him the night and the next morning he asked him to chop stovewood to pay for his night's lodging. Herb Greene knew a good wood chopper and a good worker so he asked Felix about himself and where he was going. And it wasn't long before he knew here was a bargain for some extra good help and the pay would only be keeps and clothes. Herb was a big tobacco grower so he kept Felix in bondage for clothes and keeps until Felix ran away in June 1939 when a thunder and lightning storm scared him in the tobacco field.

Again he ran away in search of this beautiful city, Blakesburg, he had dreamed so much about. But there was night and falling stars between him and his city. And since he had started late in the afternoon, he had only gone five or six miles into another hollow when night overtook him. And he dropped in to spend the night with strangers to him but people who knew about Felix.

Now he was with Tom Fiddler who saw good prospects in Felix. Next morning Felix wanted to go on his journey but Tom wouldn't let him. He had captured Felix and he intended to keep him which he did, although Herb Greene heard about where he was and came to take him back. But Tom let Herb Greene know that from this time on Felix belonged to him.

Felix stayed with Tom Fiddler until August in 1940. And one Sunday when they thought it safe to leave Felix as they thought it safe to leave one of their dogs at the house, the Fiddler family walked across the mountain to visit a neighboring family. Tom Fiddler was fooled for Felix still dreamed of the beautiful city beyond the hills. He gathered his few belongings into one of Martie Fiddler's sheets and hurried down the road. When night came on he was captured again for his reputation as a good worker had spread among the farmers. Everybody who tilled tobacco was waiting for him to pass his way. This time he was captured by Dannie Middleton where he stayed only two months and made his escape. But he was a few miles closer to Blakesburg.

He was captured by Finse Gilbert and Milo Higgins before he finally reached Blakesburg in June 1941. But now he had reached his beautiful city, nearly three and a half years after he had started from his home on Hog Branch. And his heart was filled with both delight and fear. Here were the fine houses, much better than the shacks on Hog Branch. But the horseless carts kept him jumping especially when he tried to cross the streets. With his turkey on the end of a stick across his shoulders, well-dressed people stopped on the street and stared at him.

But one big fat red jolly-faced man recognized him. He had seen this man before too and remembered him. He had come to his home on Hog Branch and had spent the night when he was running for the office of Blake County Judge. He didn't remember his name but he remembered how the man had bragged on the good people of Hog Branch and how it had pleased his mother. And then he had handed her one of his little cards. And this man knew Felix and invited him to his home.

Modock Dudley didn't let a bargain pass by. He had ideas. He needed somebody at his place to mow his big yard, to split the kindling, tend his garden, milk and feed his cows, and keep their stables cleaned and bedded. It kept one man busy around his big home which was one of the best in Blakesburg. And besides, he had a little building near the stables with a bed and stove in it. Felix could live here, eat his meals and Modock wouldn't have to be bothered with him in his home. Modock knew that Felix wouldn't feel at home in his house anyway and he knew he needed this man. He would save him money.

He not only gave Felix quarters in "the little house behind" where he took his meals to him, but he had his hair cut, his beard trimmed and he bought him new work clothes. Then he worked hard to get Felix acclimated to his new abode, teaching him how to turn on the new lights, to use the indoor privy and flush the commode. He gave him an advanced course when he taught him how to turn on the shower and take a bath. But he knew that all this work and expense would pay him dividends on his investment.

Modock had heard that Felix was afraid at night but he knew Felix would have nothing to worry about in Blakesburg. He would hardly notice a falling star among all the bright lights. Besides, Modock knew, he would have enough work to do to keep him looking at the ground instead of the sky. And he wouldn't be seeing any devils here because they'd been taken care of by the good people of Blakesburg. There wouldn't be anything to upset Felix in Blakesburg.

But on the night of September 18th when Felix had just begun to pay Modock dividends on his investment, there came that strange warning in the sky. Felix had retired to his "little house in the back," when the sky became a mass of seething flame. It was more than a shooting star to Felix or the Halley's Comet that had scared him into hysterics when he had seen it from his shack on Hog Branch. When he had seen it he had run under the floor of their shack. But here he didn't have a floor to run under.

Felix didn't look at the sky but once, when he ran from his quarters up the back street to Master Modock's big house with all the glass doors. He pounded frantically on the locked door and no one answered! They were gone! Hysterically he rammed through the glass door into the house screaming for Mister Modock. But no one answered. He couldn't escape the lights in this house for there was too much glass. Any way he looked toward the north there was a big window or a glass door. And now it wasn't a question of gathering up his clothes into a sheet; he didn't have time. Something was happening but Felix didn't know what!

He ran through the lonely house over the plush rugs to the front door. He didn't take time to open it for it didn't look like it was closed. He didn't see the glass. He ran through it, out onto the porch, jumped the full length of the steps down onto the yard and took off down the street with his hat in his hand.

"I know where I'm a-goin'," he screamed as he headed out a street toward the hills. "And I won't be as long a-gittin' back as I wuz a-comin'!"

25

LITTLE WAS SAID about what Justin Whitt had done for Blakes- burg High School. He had gotten only small notices in the Blakesburg papers for his scholastic achievements. Reece Nimrod had received more publicity for his athletic achieve- ments for he had given the Blakesburg spectators "thrills that jist make goose pimples break out all over ye." Justin wasn't an athlete because he had a lame foot. He hadn't been able to take a part in sports as the other boys had. But what he had lacked in sports he had made up in his scholastic achievements. Many of the larger papers in the state had carried his name for win- ning high scholastic honors. He had, without question, the high- est scholastic record ever made by a pupil in Blakesburg High School. And he didn't like "Old Glory" Gardner.

Before Justin's father, a Red Neck Greenough from Blake County, was elected to a county office, the native Blue Bloods of Blakesburg had spoken of the Red Necks as having a lot of brawn "but not much above the ears." But Fiddis Whitt's elec- tion to office and his moving to Blakesburg and bringing his pre- cocious son soon disproved this theory that was norated as the Greenough Red Necks rapidly rose to power through the in- fluence of their Judge Allie Anderson. Judge Allie was backed to the man by the members of his religious faith who were as powerful in politics as they were influential with the Lord.

People questioned where this boy got his knowledge. He had only attended a few rural schools six months out of the year and not all of that. His inheritance on both sides of the house was

Red Neck, his people were uneducated. And as soon as he was turned loose in the Blakesburg High School, he not only led his classes but he "stumped" his teachers. He was envied by students from the Blue Blood families. High school pupils from the Red Neck families were proud of him.

In his first year of high school he was entered in four subjects in the state scholastic contests and he won first place in each subject. In his second year in Blakesburg High School, he was entered in four scholastic contests and won four first places. Maybe it was because the state wanted someone else to win a few honors besides a Blake County Red Neck that they changed the rule and would only let one of the state participants enter in two subjects. Justin won in the two subjects in his junior year and two subjects in his senior year, giving him twelve first places in the state. He had won four honors in English, three in history, three in math, and two in Science. In addition to his being a good student, he was a good musician. He was self-taught but he played the flute exceedingly well; he played the violin very well, and played any of the wind instruments in the local band. He wrote poetry that had been accepted by many small magazines and he did many black-and-white drawings and many water colors said by art teachers to be the work of genius.

With all of his achievements it couldn't be said that he was a softie. Had it not been for his physical handicap he would have made any of the athletic teams; however, he would not have made another Reece Nimrod. Nor would he have been the type to domineer the coach and his teammates as Reece had been. Nor would he have had the glamour to give the spectators thrills such as Reece had. No one could say Justin was afraid. For he always figured everything out for himself as he had figured music for himself and drawing from "ten E-Z lessons." But maybe he hadn't figured the signs in the skies although he had heard all his life in the Blake County rural revivals that there would be signs in the sky when the time had come that earth would be no more. And he knew the end of time would be kept a secret even from the trusted angels, that only God in Heaven knew when this memorable time would be. There was no need for him to question nor to try to figure it. He never thought of trying to figure it anyway and never dreamed that the end of the world would come in his lifetime.

He never thought about such serious matters when he lay sprawled on the floor after he had eaten his supper reading a book. He did this each evening all through his high school days and after he had finished high school and was helping his father in his office. For his father had barely enough education to manage his office. And he had given his son an "eddication so he could hep 'im with writin' and figures" in his office. But Justin didn't like his father's office. His supreme delight was to get his book and sprawl on the floor after each evening meal. He had done this for so many years it had become habitual for him and his mother wouldn't let him be disturbed in his evenings of mental recreation and enjoyment.

On the evening of September 18th, after he had worked for his father in the office, he came home as usual, ate his supper, then ran for Plato. He was reading Plato's story of a sunken continent. And while he read from this favorite author his mind was filled with the thoughts of destruction of our own North American continent. What if it should sink? Justin thought. Such thoughts ran through his mind as he read the words from one of his long departed friends he knew so well. He was wading through the account of a Plato civilization and the sins of the people. And he thought about the people of Blakesburg, Franklin Foster, Marvin Clayton and Poodi Troxler, Bruce Livingstone, and the fight among the ministers of the town over the marriage industry, how they had cut in on the Justice of the Peace.

When he thought of sin he thought of Blakesburg and Blake County for it was his world. Beyond his own borders he had not been and all he knew was what he had read in books of the big world beyond. Now he was in Plato's World and it revived his imagination. For here the people were sinful back thousands of years ago as they were now. Suddenly Plato cut into destruction and there Plato stopped for Justin stopped. His mother had been across the street talking to a neighbor and after she had stood for a minute observing the strange lights in the sky, she made for her home screaming. When Justin heard her he dropped his book, jumped up from the floor and ran to the door.

"Look, Justin," she screamed.

When Justin looked at the sky, he knew what it meant. "Another sunken continent!" he screamed. "This time it will be the North American continent!"

"What are you talking about, Justin?" his mother screamed louder.

"Plato," he said. "Plato had it!"

"Plato! Who's he?"

"My friend!"

"What's he got to do with the world's end?"

"Don't ask me, Mom. I don't know! I just know he was a wise understanding man and he had the answers!"

"Forget about Plato and get ready, Justin," she screamed.

"I'll be ready in a minute, Mom," Justin said. He picked up his Plato from the floor and walked out into the bright light holding it in his hand as he watched the signs before the continent on which he was a small living atom should soon disappear from all time and space.

26

WILLIE DEAVERS was born of highly respected Blue Blood stock on both sides of the house. His mother, Arabella Dabney, was the great-niece of Uncle Sweeter Dabney; and his father, Thomas Deavers, was a great-great-great-grandson of old Tom Deavers, one of Blakesburg's founding fathers. By intermarriage of these pioneer families, young Willie had Greenough and Dinwiddie blood mixed in his veins. Though he had but little Dinwiddie blood, much less than a gill, he was proud of it. But he was of Greenough political faith. He would talk for hours about his ancestry if he could find anyone who would listen to him. And often he told people of his "famous ancestry" when they didn't want to listen.

Since Willie was an only child, life was very easy for him. His father was a merchant who "just ran his business" and hired all the work done. He made a comfortable living. "I don't want Willie to work like I've had to work," he said to many people. But none of Blakesburg's citizens had ever seen Tom Deavers do any manual labor. They had never seen him mow his own lawn, carry a box of groceries or a sack of feed into his store. He had hired help to do all these things. The only work he ever did was to see that his hired help worked. And he saw to this. He had a domineering way, when it came to getting work done and to "a-gettin' ahead." His wife Arabella never cooked a meal, swept a floor or washed a dish. She "couldn't be bothered with a lot of drudgery work" when she could "afford to have hired help to do it."

This may account for the reason Willie would never work. He never was taught to work; he never saw his parents work since his father was too busy running his business and his mother was too engaged in the Social Life of Blakesburg. All young Willie wanted to do was ride his bicycle or swim in the river. He didn't care anything about school; he didn't like any of his teachers except Old Glory Gardner. He had a fondness for this patriotic man who was interested in the history of Blakesburg first. He had heard his parents say this was the way it should be and he grew up to believe them. And like his parents he had faith in his native Blakesburg.

Although his parents hoped he would want a higher education than just a Blakesburg High School diploma, which he got after much finagling, Willie said he didn't have any desire to leave Blakesburg. Old Glory encouraged him to go to "State" but he would have none of this higher education. His parents had plenty of money to send him; he could have worn the best clothes and joined the most expensive fraternity. But he wouldn't be coaxed to do something against his will by all these promises. His parents had enough money for him to spend and he was going to stay with them and help spend it.

In the late Twenties when his father was most successful in business, he bought Willie an expensive automobile. Willie would ride all day in his automobile, now that he was too old for a bicycle, and he would come home at the end of the day dog-tired. He would lie stretched on the divan and smoke a cigarette. His mother would carry him a drink of water if some of the help wasn't there to do it. When many a Blakesburg father chastised his son, he would say, "Don't be a Willie Deavers."

And when the depression came and Blakesburg Citizen's Bank crashed with Thomas Deaver's savings and his investments in "furrin bonds" went down to "almost nothing," Thomas Deavers couldn't take it. With all his life's savings wiped out, and the dwindling trade he got all "on tick," time had come for Thomas Deavers to leave this world which he promptly did, of his own accord.

"I'll never start a business in another world," were his last words to Arabella.

Since young Willie said he would have nothing to do with his father's business which was in the red, Arabella Deavers sold it for a small sum. That left them their home, car and a little money. But in two years Arabella died and left Willie alone in the big house. He slept in his old bed, had help to clean his house and cook his meals and to wait on him in general. But while the depression was still on and Willie was living alone, a strange thing happened that shocked the town. A daughter of one of the well-known Red Neck families, who was a Blakesburg High School graduate, came to Willie and applied for a "position" to run his house. Though Willie may not have known it, she had previously tried many places to find something to do. She couldn't find anything to do and she had heard of Willie's plight; she had heard he was one man in Blakesburg with a little money left. When Willie took one look at attractive Sylvia Moore, he told her "yes." Right then she was hired. He was amazed that such a beautiful and physically attractive girl would want to work for him. He fell in love with her and was married to her in less than a week.

Everyone in Blakesburg knew what his people had thought of the Red Necks. In fact, the Red Necks were Willie's pet hate. He had denounced them for their taking over both the Dinwiddie and the Greenough Parties. He had talked with "Old Glory" about their rapid rise in the city and the county. He pointed out Judge Allie Anderson, how he had taken over his own party. Then he spoke of how Tid Fortner had worked himself into power with the big "moonshine block" and how Bruce Livingstone, whom he didn't like, was the "spark plug" of Blakesburg and he was a half Red Neck.

Willie prophesied the Red Necks would eventually get control of all the businesses, the political offices in Blakesburg and Blake County and the churches. As he said, he had seen their faces and their long Red Necks and he knew them. He knew they would not only have the businesses but they would eventually own all the property in Blakesburg. They would finally establish undertaking parlors and run out such well-established men as Marvin Clayton and Franklin Foster. The time was near, he prophesied, when the old families would be swallowed by these hard-working, hard-fighting, heavy drinking, fanatically praying Red Necks. They not only had red necks but they had red blood and it was really dangerous as far as blue blood was concerned. And now, Willie had married one with red blood in her veins. Would he go over to her people and become a son by adoption or would he persuade beautiful Sylvia Moore to become a "blue blood" by adoption? People waited to see which way the pendulum would swing. They didn't have long to wait.

Willie's wife fitted too well in the old society in Blakesburg. She was a "natural" for adoption. And she loved the idea of their society, something she had never known before. She became one of them. She had, by marriage, inherited a beautiful home with antique furnishings. She could entertain lavishly here, and maybe she had in mind that money grew on trees for the Deavers and that Willie had much of this easy growing fruit stored away. But here is where she was fooled. Willie didn't have much money and he spent it lavishly with his beautiful Sylvia until it was gone. Although they had the well-feathered nest, they couldn't eat the wind and Willie had never worked. There wasn't anything he could do. He'd never been trained to work. But she had. She had taken typing and shorthand in high school and she could be a secretary to someone. But to whom?

Willie was lying on the bed when the idea came to him. He was a Greenough politically and his people had been for generations before him. Though Willie had never worked for his party, his people before him had worked many long and faithful years. Now why not let the party work for me, Willie thought. He could get Sylvia a job as a secretary. And he coolly calculated where he would find her a place. He didn't like Judge Allie Anderson, who was a crude Red Neck judge with a hogpen in his backyard, but here was the place to get his wife a job. They had come to the place they were buying their groceries "on tick" and his wife had to have work. It would work with Judge Allie too; it would have to work for he was one of the influential Greenoughs and Judge Allie had to have their vote if he continued in office. He had the connecting link to tie the Blue Bloods with the Red Neck Greenoughs. That link was— and he could soon explain it to the Judge at his hogpen that evening—to give Sylvia a job as his secretary. And he got up from the divan with light in his eyes, ran to the rendezvous, got the position as he had calculated he would.

Sylvia was glad to have the place. She would do anything for this Blue Blood who had stooped to marry her, to give her this magnificent home with antique furnishings, and to give her an enviable place in the society of Blakesburg. Yes, she would work for him and make their bread. The Blue Bloods in Blakesburg wouldn't criticize her but the Red Necks would. They would criticize her for working when her husband didn't work. And they did.

Sylvia would spend a hard day in Judge Allie's office and then she would come home and cook Willie a hot supper. On her small wage they couldn't hire help to clean the house. Sylvia did well to make enough to buy their food, his beer and tobacco and his Wild West magazines. Though she had to pay the price to get Willie and all the prestige and social standing he had given her, she didn't mind. She was young, strong, beautiful and she could do it. She didn't mind to get up first in the morning and light the fires and get Willie's breakfast. She even went over

part of her house after she'd gotten breakfast and washed the
dishes before time to go to the office. At noon she met Willie
at the Winston Boarding House where she bought their dinners.
In the afternoon, after her day was done at the office, she went
home and got Willie a hot supper and worked with her house
until bedtime.

In addition to her doing this she made life comfortable for
her husband. When he wanted his house slippers or his bathrobe
she got them for him. All he had to do was call her from the
kitchen to reach him his pack of cigarettes that was lying upon
the mantelpiece. She not only came running to get them but she
took one from the pack for him, struck a match and lit his cigarette and put him an ash tray in a handy place so he wouldn't
have to move. If he wanted a drink of ice water she brought
him one in a crystal tumbler. If he wanted beer, candy, or Wild
West magazines she ran an errand over in town to get them for
him. Anything he wanted, she got it for him if it was in her
power. She thought a wife as lucky as she was should be dutiful
to her husband's wishes. She even fixed the water for his bath,
laid out his socks, underclothes, shirts and ties. She kept his
shaving utensils in place. Willie was not going to change from
the old life; he was going to keep on living as he had always
lived.

Many of the Red Neck parents warned their sons and daughters about marrying into one of these Blue Blood families. "You
see what happened to poor Sylvia Moore when she married that
thing. She's become a slave to 'im. That aint marriage. No man
is worth that much. That Willie's not worth powder and lead
to blow his brains out. He's a nogood and he's our enemy." And
while Judge Allie Anderson gained votes one way he lost votes
another. The Blake County Red Necks were all of the same
mind. "It's all right to let Sylvia work but not to keep that
pretty thing who laughs at our religion and is afraid of our

people. Let him get out and dirty his hands once! It will be good for him to work and sweat!"

But Willie didn't work and he didn't sweat. He never put a callus on one of his hands. He had never worked and he never intended to. Not when he could make a living without work. Now that he had a beautiful wife to do it for him, life was good and sweet and kind. And the Thirties were good years. One thing he boasted that no one would ever be able to accuse him of trying to oust any man from any job. Another thing, Willie had often told his friends, that he and Sylvia would never have any children. He said they didn't want any while Sylvia was working and everyone knew they didn't want a child at all because Sylvia would be working as long as she could have and hold a job.

But in the summer of 1941 Sylvia couldn't hide it any longer. She was pregnant. People wondered what Willie would do now. She would have to quit work. Willie wouldn't have her pay check coming in nor would he have her to work and wait on him. Each morning and afternoon when she walked across town, heavy with child, people wondered when she was going to stop work. But Sylvia didn't stop. She didn't do as many little things as she had done for Willie but she still waited on him and cooked for him and did her housework. He did go over town and buy his cigarettes, beer and magazines.

On the afternoon of September 18th, Sylvia came home from Judge Allie's office a little early because she was "feelin' bad." Willie had taken a drive, had come home a little tired from riding and he stretched out on his favorite resting place to read, relax and smoke. Sylvia, though in much misery, got up and got him a cigarette and put an ash tray handy for him. She also brought him a bottle of beer to sup as he smoked, read and relaxed.

"I think I'm going to have to have the doctor, Willie," she said.

"Well," Willie said, thumbing the pages in his Wild West magazine to the last one to see how the story ended. "A bad endin'! I don't like it!"

Willie grabbed his hat and ran out at the door into something, the like of which he'd never seen before.

He looked at the sky that was a rolling mountain of fire. He watched the long projected rays of light flash this way and that across the sky and crisscross each other. And there were so many different shades of light. But he took off as fast as his weak legs would carry him. When he got downtown on his way to get the doctor, he saw people running everyway. They were screaming and taking on. And he heard the shouts that the end of time was at hand. He saw tough men, he knew they were tough sinners, running to the courthouse square where Sister Spence, whom he had laughed at many times, was inviting them to come to get prepared to meet their Maker. But he hurried after Dr. Hinton for his wife.

"Doc," he gasped as soon as he reached Doc Hinton's office.

"What're you after, Willie?" Doc asked. "Don't you see I'm busy? Look at the people here!"

"Yep, he run in ahead of us," a beardy-faced man said who was embracing his trembling wife to keep her from falling.

"But my wife's a-havin' a baby," Willie said.

"And my wife's about to die," the beardy-faced man said.

"I'm a-tryin' to save these already in the world, Willie," Doc said.

"But I gotta have you, Doc," Willie said.

"Just the right night for a baby to be born," Doc said. "They arrive at the most unexpected times!"

"Are ye a-comin', Doc?" Willie asked.

"I can't go, Willie," Doc said, getting his needle ready to give another hypodermic.

"I'll remember ye, Doc," Willie said, pushing his way among Doc's patients until he reached the door.

Willie slammed the door and ran across Blakesburg through the brilliant light to get Jinnie who was a midwife.

"Child, I'd a-never thought ye'd a-wanted me," Jinnie told Willie.

"But you're my people," Willie said. "And ye will be from now on!"

"Child, what's come over ye?" Jinnie asked him as she grabbed a shawl to put around her shoulders.

"I've had a change of heart, Jinnie," he said.

"Hit's time fer ye to have a change of heart," Jinnie said when she left her little shack and stepped out into the light. "Life a-comin' into a world that's a-goin' out!"

"Yes," Willie said as he ran in front with Jinnie Slemp stepping on his heels.

"But don't tell Sylvia about this night!"

"I won't," Jinnie muttered with a short breath.

When they reached Willie's mansion, Sylvia was in much pain.

"Where's Doc Hinton, Willie?" Sylvia asked.

"I don't know," Willie said. "I fetched Jinnie Slemp!"

"Why?"

"Because she's one of my people!"

"Willie!" Sylvia said.

"From now on, your people are my people," he said.

"Oh, Willie, darlin'," Sylvia said.

"And for every pain you have I'll do something kind for you," Willie said, standing by the bed holding her hand. "So help me God, I will!"

"I'm so glad ye got me instead o' old Doc Hinton," Jinnie Slemp said as she hurried for the coming event. "He can't do this kind o' work like I can! He aint had as much experience!"

"Oh honey, you talk wonderful," Sylvia said as she writhed in pain.

"And from now on I'll be Judge Allie's secretary," Willie said.

"Oh, you will?" Sylvia moaned.

"I'll do the work and you can stay at home," Willie said.

"Oh, you do love me, Willie!"

"More than my own life," he said softly to her.

"It won't be long," Jinnie said.

"We should have done this long ago, darling," Sylvia said.

"Yes, sweetheart," Willie said.

"Shore ye should," Jinnie laughed. "A boy as fine as this'n ties any two people together."

"O God," Willie said. "O God! How wonderful!"

"O darling," Sylvia said weakly, "you're so wonderful!"

"O God, if you'll just let us live," Willie prayed, "I'll be a changed man the rest of my days. I'm already a changed man! I'll never be the same again!"

27

Reverend Perry Rhoden had come to his small pastorate in Blakesburg from beyond Blake County's borders. He wasn't one of their people in the flesh but he was one in spirit. For he had his church and a devoted following. And he often told them from the pulpit he had been chosen by the Savior for this little church in Blakesburg. And since he was chosen by the Savior to preach at this little church to a congregation of his religious faith, he never "had a desire in his heart to leave Blakesburg."

However, there were many dissenters among his following. They said they didn't believe what he had preached to his congregation about his being sent to Blakesburg. And they didn't believe he should stay in Blakesburg until the Lord called him to another place as he had often told them the Lord would do when He needed him for another sinful congregation. He had preached that he was one of the shock-troops chosen by the Lord to clean "filthy messes of corruption and sin."

When Reverend Rhoden got wind of one of these rumors, he would defend himself from the pulpit. He would come back at his critics by saying that shrouds were pocketless and that he couldn't take money to Glory with him for it wouldn't have any value there. All he wanted was life's subsistence for his family and himself while he was fighting "vile and filthy messes of corruption and sin" on God's footstool which was Blakesburg.

This, his dissenters didn't deny. And when he was given pound parties where members of his faithful followers each took him a pound of coffee or a pound of sugar, loaf of bread, sack of meal, even the dissenters did their part; yet each dissenter felt that he should be changed to another church. But Reverend Rhoden didn't think so. And he told them he didn't think so and didn't have any intention of going. Reverend Rhoden was in love with Blakesburg and its people; they had gotten under his skin and no doubt he planned to remain here the rest of his days preaching in the old church that was considered a firetrap and unsafe. In fact, it had been an old store building converted into a church years ago by a handful of people of Reverend Rhoden's religious faith.

While Reverend Rhoden managed to hold on to his church, a strange thing happened in Blakesburg. One of the greatest industries yet to come to the city was beginning to take hold. There had been a Justice of Peace race between the Greenoughs and Dinwiddies and each ticket was headed by a young man. No one had paid any attention to this race; not many would care to have it. Heretofore some older man would ask for it and get the position without opposition. But when young Frank Seagraves, a Dinwiddie, was elected to this office, Dick Nolan, a Greenough, whom he had defeated by six or seven votes, shook hands and wished him well with his office.

But Franklin Foster, who had a flair for publicity, asked Frank to bring his first young out-of-town couple to his undertaker's parlor to be married. And Frank brought the couple to the Foster Undertaking Parlor, married them there. Franklin Foster gave the story to the local *Dinwiddie News* and from there it spread into other papers like wildfire. A thriving business was started. Couples came from everywhere to be married in Blakesburg. As many as a hundred couples a day came to Blakesburg which became known as the Gretna Green. When a couple got married the least the groom ever paid the Justice of the Peace was two dollars, usually he threw down a five, ten or twenty dollar bill and often he gave fifty and sometimes a hundred. Frank Seagraves was in the money. The old philosophers who sat on the courthouse square and whittled sat watching the steady stream of couples with out-of-county and out-of-state licenses on their cars drive to the Justice of the Peace's swank office in a steady stream. They realized what they had missed and so did Dick Nolan. No one knew the thing would turn out "to be a gold mine" just because a publicity-minded undertaker like Franklin Foster had suggested that Frank marry his first couple over in his parlor. People yet couldn't understand why "sicha doins had started a marriage boom" in Blakesburg.

No one knew how much money Frank Seagraves was making. But they knew he was making plenty. Not anyone guessed him to be making less than a thousand dollars a week and many guessed that he was making two thousand, a few calculated by counting the couples that he was making three or four thousand dollars a week. And they had ideas that this money since it came as gifts would be free of all taxes. What a gold mine! What a lucky boy was Frank to strike this gold mine. But when a man does strike a gold mine there is much jealousy among the men who cannot get a chip of the precious stuff, who must sit by and see the other fellow get it all! This was the way the people looked at it in Blakesburg.

The ministers preached that a marriage should be performed by a "minister of the gospel" and not by a Justice of the Peace. This was the work of God and why should a Justice of the Peace start taking over God's work of making the twain as one? Reverend Rhoden didn't say as much as other ministers in Blakesburg who immediately refreshened the signs on their pastorate doors, added new and large ones in their yard with arrows directing the loving lovebirds, after they had obtained their license, to a place where God's marriages were performed. They were fighting the Justice of the Peace. And the citizens of Blakesburg watched eagerly the progress of their greatest industry which brought more money into the town than anything else.

The Blakesburg Drug Store saw their business increase by leaps and bounds. They put in a line of jewelry, new brands of cosmetics and a line of gifts and they prospered by leaps and bounds; the clothing business increased in this "quaint little old town" and the county court clerk who issued the license had to hire extra help; the Winston Boarding House got more people to feed and bed than they could possibly take care of and their old boarders, who had been with them for years, were beginning to be worried; even Bill Simpson said his business had doubled; Tid Fortner, Blakesburg's pure corn bootlegger, was seen walking around with many of the prospective grooms. The sugar moonshine business had increased among sixty-eight bootleggers. Everybody in Blakesburg was sharing directly or indirectly from this promising industry. For more people were married in Blakesburg than in any town in America in proportion to its population with the exception of Reno and Las Vegas.

Young lovebirds riding in their swank automobiles with "furrin" license plates were very reluctant to see the signs before the ministers' homes. If they saw them they didn't pay them any mind. They would as soon have a Justice of the Peace to marry them as a minister. Usually they were in a hurry to get married. And these signs didn't influence the Justice of the Peace's business one way or the other until. . . .

Several boys in the town riding down the shady streets on bicycles watching for cars with "furrin" licenses would catch the cars as they came into Blakesburg for not one of the two roads or any of the byways were left unguarded for marriage prospects, and they would direct the couples to the courthouse to get their license and then they would take them to a minister, or to the Justice of the Peace. He had to resort to the same tactics as were used against him. These young boys were given a cut of the proceeds by the minister or the Justice of the Peace and the one who forked over the biggest cut got the business. In addition to the boys' cut they were usually tipped well for directing the couples to the courthouse and then to the right place for the twain to become as one. Soon, young men and married men with families were out riding bicycles to solicit marriages for their men. The attendance officer couldn't keep boys in school any longer; the lure of money was too great. And they made it.

Among these bicycle riders was Mace Rhoden, son of Reverend Perry Rhoden. When the Attendance Officer went to Reverend Rhoden to see why his son hadn't been in school all week, Reverend Rhoden replied, "I'm not keeping him out. I'm sending him to school. I'll see tonight why he hasn't been in school."

Reverend Rhoden was as good as his word. When Mace came home on his bicycle as he had been accustomed to on days when he went to school, the Reverend met him at the door.

"Come into my study, son," he said. "I want to have a talk with you!"

Mace followed him into his study. Reverend Rhoden closed the door behind them.

"What do you want to see me about?" Mace asked.

"Why aren't you in school?" he asked.

The boy didn't answer his father; he stood looking at the floor.

"Answer me!" his father commanded.

"Who told you I was out of school?" he asked.

"The Attendance Officer said you hadn't been in school all week. Where have you been?"

"Working," he said softly.

"What kind of work have you been doing?"

"Taking couples to Reverend Horsely to be married," he said.

"To Reverend Horsely!" Reverend Rhoden repeated. "Don't you know your father marries couples too! Have you forgotten your father is a minister? Have you forgotten your own church!"

"But I didn't know. . . ."

"That's right, I'm not into this racket," Reverend Rhoden broke in before the boy had time to finish his sentence. "I don't believe in it!"

"But, Father," Mace said, coming back at his father, "I'm making money. Others are making it! I'd just as well make it as the other boys!"

"How much chicken feed do you make a week?" Reverend Rhoden asked his son.

"From fifty to seventy-five dollars," Mace said. "You wouldn't call that chicken feed, would you?"

"Are you telling me the truth, Mace?"

"I'm telling you the truth."

"Where is your money?"

"Upstairs in a pencil box," he said. "I have over four hundred dollars saved and I've bought myself some clothes! I'm tired of taking these old second-hand suits given to us! I'm tired of other boys' castoff rags!"

"More money than I make in a year," Reverend Rhoden said, solemnly looking down at the floor with puzzled eyes. "And I preach them sermons three times a week; I bury their dead and I marry. . . ."

But Reverend Rhoden stopped. He knew he hadn't had a couple to marry since Frank Seagraves married the couple in Franklin Foster's Undertaking Parlor.

"Father, all the ministers around here are getting a good business but you," Mace said. "Their children are wearing good clothes to school. And they have money to buy ice cream and sodas! But look at us!"

"But you are doing all right, son," he said.

"I know it, Father," Mace said. "I don't like other people's castoff rags and pound parties! I'd rather make my own money than to have to depend on the charity of others!"

"You may go, Mace," Reverend Rhoden said.

Mace ran out at the door and on into the yard where he

climbed on his bicycle and fairly flew toward the bridge on the far end of town the way the couples came who brought the money. And the most couples came that way too. He wanted to get back into the competition that he loved so well. This was after school hours now and he wanted to take Reverend Horsely couples before night; and if he was lucky he might get as many as four. This would net him with his cut and tips, ten or fifteen dollars.

When he left, his father remained inside his study. He had something to study about. He had to think the thing through. The idea had flashed in his mind when he had talked to his son. Why shouldn't he have these marriages? Why should his son work for Reverend Horsely and make money for him and the Horsely family who were of a faith foreign to his belief? But deep within him, he reasoned honestly with himself and in the presence of his God, he didn't think it was right. But he thought of the words his son had said to him about "wearing somebody else's scraps" and the pound parties and their living on charity. It was hard for him to deny these facts. Far into the night, after he had had his supper, he pondered over this grave question. What would he do? He had a son who could compete with any of the boys and bring him the business. Mace was a go-getter. He knew that. Not any other minister in Blakesburg had a son as big and as old as Mace. There was not a boy with the pep and the personality in the whole town. He had seen them riding bicycles down the streets hunting for couples but strange he had never seen his own son. He was smart enough to dodge his father. He knew his hours of study, of meditation and prayer. And he knew the times he went down the street. He reasoned things. He would be a good partner. He could pay him something and the two of them could make the money. Yet, he reasoned it wasn't right. . . .

But while he reasoned another thought occurred to him. He was preaching in a firetrap, in an old store. And this wasn't a good tabernacle in which to worship God. God should have a fine temple where his people could worship Him. And then it occurred to him to tithe and to build a Temple for the Lord if he could make enough money! When he thought of this he prayed over the situation with the Lord and in his prayer he promised God, "I will build You the nicest temple in Blakesburg if You will permit me to accept this business." His prayer, so he said, was answered. And that the Lord was pleased.

The next day Mace had taken a new hold on life. He worked as he had never worked before bringing his father the couples to be married. Reverend Rhoden had to break his schedule of meditation, prayer and study now; he didn't even have time for his walks down the street. Mace brought him the couples until all competitors in the town were aware of what was happening. A new business had opened in the town. And it was a hard one to rival. Reverend Rhoden's critics now pointed out that he didn't give enough of his time to the church. But he told them in one of his brief Sunday morning sermons that he was working to build a fine temple for the Lord wherein they may come to worship. He told them God would have the finest temple in Blakesburg. He told them he was tithing twenty-five percent instead of ten. Everybody was pleased. They knew what an old flimsy church house they had in comparison with the other churches of Blakesburg. Now they would step up and take their place, probably head the list of beautiful churches in Blakesburg.

For months Reverend Rhoden married the couples. He wondered why he hadn't thought of it before, why he had to be influenced by his son. For why shouldn't the young couples be married by a Minister of God instead of a Justice of Peace, who would take a drink of whiskey, who cussed and smoked?

People from the other churches knocked and condemned Reverend Rhoden and his church but he went ahead with his congregation's blessing. And he drove ahead with a clear conscience before his God. He'd prayed it over; he'd gotten an answer and knew he was right. Let the public rave and rant. Let other ministers condemn him for he knew they were trying to do the same as he but he was getting the business. And he was making the money. No more pound parties for his family; no more left-over scraps of clothes thrown on his front porch for himself and his family. He was wearing new clothes; his seven children were as well dressed as any children in the town. He didn't have to worry when he was going to have another pound party for he was buying at the stores, all he wanted, steaks and anything he wanted. It was a new life and a better life and the money rolled in and it wasn't chicken feed either. It wasn't pennies, nickels, dimes, quarters and half dollars, occasionally the smallest denomination of folding money! He was getting big denominations. He had for the first time seen a hundred dollar bill. And it was his. Put in his hand by an elderly man marrying an elderly woman. Both for the first time after years of courtship.

He was marrying a couple in his study when he happened to hear the screams outside. He pushed back a window curtain to look. It was then he saw the light in the northern skies. And no one knew better than he there would be signs in the sky when this sinful footstool of the Lord's was swallowed into oblivion. And right there in the midst of his marriage ceremony, he dropped to the floor and said, "Let us pray." Maybe the couple thought the way he was marrying them was a strange way, the prayer he was praying was a strange prayer, for he not only promised the Lord that if He would let him live through this night he would start the new temple tomorrow and that he would give more than twenty-five percent. He promised he would give all of his money to build a finer tabernacle than originally planned for his Prince of Peace if He would only stay His Hand of Destruction until his dream was accomplished.

28

JEFF HARGIS wasn't a native of Blakesburg or of Blake County.
He was really a "furriner in the flesh" who had migrated
from an adjoining county in a strange way. Back in the old
country, as Jeff referred to his home county, he had been in his
younger days a prosperous farmer. He had married at nineteen,
a girl of seventeen; and they both worked hard and saved
enough money to buy a farm. Then he went in debt for a sawmill, sawed his timber on this farm and paid for his sawmill and
bought another timbered farm. He cut the timber on this farm
and bought another. He kept on doing this until he owned seven
big farms. After he'd cut the timber he rented these farms to
men who farmed light burley tobacco. And they paid him one-
half the money they got for their tobacco. Soon, Jeff Hargis
was one of the "richest men in Darter County." He had over
fifty thousand in the bank; he owned land, livestock, teams and
wagons.

His neighbors looked upon him as having "a good head for
business." Here was a model man in their midst who didn't
drink, cuss or smoke. He didn't even drink such a strong drink
as coffee for breakfast. He drank milk instead. He couldn't stand
the taste of chewing tobacco nor could he stand the smoke from
this fragrant weed. When a cloud of it came near his nostrils,
he would fan it away with his big hand. There was only one
thing that interested him about tobacco, that was the money he
made from his share-croppers who "raised the stuff" on his
farms. Instead of swearing he would always substitute the word

"sugar." He said that word served just as well as taking the Lord's name in vain. But there was one thing, when he got a taste, he couldn't find any substitute for. . . .

One cold morning when his team drivers were hauling lumber for him, they were passing a jug of pure corn around to "take a few sips to warm 'em up fer the cold weather" and they passed the jug to Jeff. "Just fer the fun of hit, I'll take a sip of the stuff jist to say I've tasted hit," Jeff told them. And from that time on he never stopped tasting "the stuff." Here was this model man without any vices, who had been prolific accumulating wealth and prolific to beget a family of eleven, starting now to "sow his wild oats." His neighbors thought he had waited a long time to sow them and at his age he would sow plenty.

For four years no one saw Jeff sober. And while he was drunk, his farms grew up in brush again; his cattle died; the dogs killed his sheep; his yowes went untended at lambing and the greenbriars on the pasture hill gathered most of his sheep's wool. . . . His mules' manes and tails grew long like horses'. They went unshod and their hoofs grew long and broke off. His barn roofs sagged. His renters didn't bother to give him his share of the tobacco. "What's the use?" they said. "He'll put hit down his long gullet!" His wife couldn't attend to all these duties for she had all she could do trying to keep the family together.

In addition to this, while Jeff was drunk, men would bring him notes to sign and he would endorse them not knowing what he was doing. These men hadn't any thought of paying the money to the bank after they had Jeff "to go thar security"! He had these notes to pay. It didn't take him long to run through all the money he had in Darter County Bank. Then he sold one of his farms and his sawmill. And gradually he sold his livestock, sheep, mules and wagons. "Jeff's a-goin' down the hill of success as fast as he come up," one of his tenants said. "He'll soon be a gone goslin' jist becaze he took a drink of pure corn.

He oughta have more will power." But Jeff didn't have. He drank like he had once worked to make money.

As his children grew up they left home. Not one stayed at home until he was twenty years old. He left home with bitterness toward his father. When one of the older boys drifted away to a "furrin state" and married, he sent for his mother, his two younger brothers and sister and left Jeff alone in the big house. The whole family had moved away and left him. But this didn't bother Jeff. He sold his farms one by one and put them down his "long gullet." He sold them down to the "old home place." And he sold scraps of this four-hundred-acre farm down to four acres around the house. Then he sold all the plows, harrows, corn planters, rakes and garden hoes to buy his high-priced pure corn. But he wouldn't sell the house where he slept. People wondered how he had drunk up so much in less than twenty years. But they knew he was a big man, well over six feet and weighed more than three hundred pounds, and that he had a great capacity. He easily drank a quart of expensive pure corn a day; some days he would drink two quarts. And in the last days when his fortune had dwindled to almost nothing, Jeff started drinking the cheap sugar moonshine which he bought for two dollars a gallon. After he'd traded off his tools, sold all his land, spent all his money, he couldn't buy this. And no one in Darter County would hire him to work. They looked upon Jeff as sort of a superior; they couldn't realize that this model man had been reduced from riches to rags. And, furthermore, they didn't think a man who had been drunk as long as Rip Van Winkle had slept was capable of doing an honest day's work.

Without prestige, honor, money or friends, this big man dressed in overalls so ragged he could hardly hide his nakedness, left Darter County "hoofin' it" one September morning. He knew he could not go to his children. He knew they were all "dry as chips" and they wouldn't take him back after he had deserted them. But he had a sister living in Blake County he hadn't seen for twenty years.

People who saw their once "first citizen" leaving Darter County knew that even wealth was as uncertain as the wind. Here was a man who had once had more of the worldly goods than any man in his county now on the road "a-lookin' worse than any beggar I ever saw." They didn't know where he was going nor did they bother to ask as they watched him shuffle his brogans down the dusty wagon trail, leaving vacant dreams of his home, wife, family, and his life's illusions behind him among the hills that had given him nurture from his birth.

In Blake County, three days later, Roy Gantz came across the mountain and told Sallie Powderjay there was a big man, who said his name was Jeff Hargis and that he was her brother, in their barn. Roy told Sallie that he was down drunk in a stall in their cowshed and they wanted him taken out so they could put the cow back in her stall. Said they didn't like to let the cow stand out at night in the raining weather. Sallie had her sons to harness the mules, hitch them to a sled and go over the mountain to get her brother Jeff from the stall. Finn and Shan Powderjay had a rough journey and a tough time rolling their Uncle Jeff from the stall and getting him upon the sled where they roped him down like they would a sack of feed or any dead weight before they started over the mountain. They had found their uncle with three empty jugs around him and straws where he had siphoned the sugar whiskey when he was too drunk to lift the jug to his lips. But they took him over the mountain though the sled stood on end and almost turned over when the runners hit the big rocks. They had almost sobered their Uncle Jeff by the time they got him home.

Mick Powderjay didn't want his brother-in-law Jeff. He said Jeff was an incurable sot. And furthermore he hadn't forgotten when Jeff had plenty he had never bothered to visit his "poor kinfolks." But Sallie told Mick she wouldn't turn her brother out in the cold, homeless and no place to go, she didn't care what he had done. "But he aint a-drinkin' around here," Mick made it plain.

It wasn't long before Jeff had become a part of the Powderjay family. Mick, who hadn't wanted him at first, was now his closest friend. He said he didn't want Jeff working on his farm for nothing so he started paying him. As soon as Mick paid him, he walked across the ridge to Blakesburg with Mick. That Saturday afternoon when Mick was ready to come home, he couldn't find Jeff. He went home without him. He thought Jeff had gone back to Darter County since he had made a little money. But on Sunday he heard a man singing upon the hill. It was Jeff. He was stretched on the ground singing beside two empty jugs.

But Mick said if Jeff would only do a little drinking on the week ends and if he would work for him during the week, he would be glad to have him stay. And this was a bargain. Mick would pay Jeff on Saturday morning and he would strike out for Blakesburg. If he didn't have a big pay, he would get back Sunday night where he slept in the hayloft. Jeff still didn't smoke and it was all right for him to sleep in Mick's hayloft. This worked well, for Powderjays needed Jeff's help, and Jeff needed the pittance they paid him so he could have his sugar whiskey on the week ends. And this is how Jeff Hargis got to know Blakesburg, a city he adopted and loved.

Before it was known that Jeff would become a steady customer, patronizing one or more of the sixty-eight sugar-whiskey bootleggers, since Jeff couldn't afford pure corn on farm wages, he was arrested by the town marshal and locked up in jail. Mick Powderjay had to pay his fine, which he deducted from his future earnings, to get Jeff out of jail to work. But since Mick was a Greenough and his party was in power, he went to the marshal and told him "thar ain't a bit o' harm in old Jeff! He's just a big man and when he gits drunk everybody's afraid of 'im."

Mick's help was all Jeff needed. He'd get drunk and all the children in the town would gather around him to watch his strange actions. Though he weighed over three hundred pounds, was sixty years old and his hair as white as clean sheep's wool, he could down a pint of sugar whiskey at one drink without batting an eye. After he had downed the pint he would jump up into the air and crack his heels together three times before he came down on the street. He would wave his big hands in the air and go, "Woo-woo!"

Jeff Hargis knew each Blakesburg street and tree and he loved the city. He loved the people and he immediately claimed the city for his own whether the people wanted to accept him or not. When he got himself a jug of sugar whiskey, he would walk from one street to another, often talking to himself, waving his arms and going "Woo-woo." Then he would walk the streets with Liam Winston or follow Tid Fortner until Tid started for his harem, and there he told "Big Man" to turn back. Jeff Hargis wondered why he had lived forty miles away from Blakesburg all his younger life and had never discovered a city so kind, with so many forms of recreation and enjoyment, and as he often said "so many fine people."

Thursday, September 18, 1941, Jeff hadn't eaten his dinner with Powderjays. He only drank some buttermilk. He wanted the sugar whiskey to have a real effect on him. He had missed three Saturdays in a row due to the hay harvest when they had to work while the sun shone. Now with his pocket full of money, with the hay in the stack, he was off to Blakesburg for a celebration. Jeff had worked many long days just to get on a big drunk, walk over the Blakesburg streets again, and see his old friends.

While many of the people were at work in Blakesburg on this Thursday, Jeff walked the streets. He was in one of his happiest moods. The city looked better to him than it ever had. He not only jumped up and cracked his heels together three times for the children but he danced for them and they put a ribbon on his white hair. The town marshal saw him but he let "Big Man" have his fun. He'd never harmed anyone in the town. He was just on one of his sprees spending his money in the town and that was all right. It was a beautiful sunshiny day; people were having fun everywhere. There wasn't a sign anywhere in the sky that pointed to rain, storm or anything that would stop his pleasure as he hopped gleefully along the Blakesburg streets.

Where Jeff was when the lights came no one knows. Liam Winston said he saw him look at the sky from the courthouse square and take off hard as he could go through the crowd. And that was the last that had been seen of him for he had taken out a back alley toward the Produce House. But on that night something happened at Spittie Holcum's shack, which was on the outskirts of Blakesburg beside the path Jeff traveled on his way to Mick Powderjay's.

"Aint there somebody in this room?" Nerva asked Spittie as they lay in bed for they had pulled their shades and gone to bed early.

"Ah, what makes ye so skeery?" Spittie asked Nerva. "Ye know they aint nothing in this room but us!"

"Seems like I hear a 'woo-woo' or something like that," Nerva said faintly as she lay back down in bed beside her husband.

"Woo-woo," Spittie repeated. "Ye hear the wind, Nerva."

Then Spittie laughed and laughed as he pulled the thin cover back up over himself and his wife which she had jerked off them when she arose in her fright.

"Maybe I didn't hear anything," Nerva said. "Maybe it wuz the wind. Maybe, I's jist a-dreaming."

"Woo-woo! Woo-woo! Woo-woo!"

"Hush," Spittie said, raising up in bed. "That wuzn't the wind!"

"I told ye I heard somethin'," Nerva said.

"If thar's anybody in this room, I'll shoot ye!" Spittie screamed. "Just make that sound again!"

"Woo-woo!"

"Light the lamp, honey," Nerva said.

Spittie was one of the men in Blakesburg who didn't believe in electric lights and indoor plumbing. He got his pistol from under his pillow first. Then he reached for the match box on the chair beside his bed, got a match and struck it and lit the lamp.

"Oh, my Lord," Nerva screamed as she saw Jeff standing near the head of their bed. He had his big arms up toward the ceiling and he had a wild scared look on his face. His big black hat looked as big as an umbrella to her. She didn't know him; Spittie was scared too badly to recognize him.

"What are you a-doin' in my house?" Spittie asked Jeff. "Who are you anyway?"

"Woo-woo," Jeff said.

Spittie's hand shook so badly he could hardly hold his pistol.

"I'll shoot ye," Spittie said, getting out of bed.

"Woo-woo," Jeff said.

"Is he crazy?" Nerva asked Spittie. "Can't he talk?"

"He might be drunk," Spittie said, looking the big man over. "He aint a-tryin' to fight us. He acts like he's skeered too! Somethin's wrong with 'im!"

"Woo-woo," Jeff said, jumping up and cracking his heels together three times.

Then Jeff pointed to the window.

"Wonder what he means?" Spittie asked Nerva.

"I don't know," she said.

Spittie kept Jeff covered with the pistol while he backed to the window and with his free hand raised the shade to let in a flood of light that made the yellow glow of lamplight look dim.

"My Lord, Spittie," Nerva screamed. "What is it?"

"Blakesburg must be on fire," Spittie said, running to the door.

"Woo-woo!" Jeff screamed.

"Come, Nerva," Spittie said as she jumped from the bed in her nightgown and ran to the door.

"What is it, Spittie?"

"Thar's fire in the clouds," he screamed. "Heaven is a-blazin'!"

"Woo-woo," Jeff said.

"Reckon he is a stranger sent to us as a warning?" she said.

"Must be," Spittie said. "Let's go!"

They didn't take time to get their clothes. They ran out in their night clothes with Jeff behind them. They ran down the road screaming and Jeff waddled behind them like an awkward goose waving his big hands above his head shouting, "Woo-woo."

29

TEMPERANCE AND Ollie Spradling were one of the best known couples in Blakesburg. Temp and Oll, the people called them, were often seen on Main Street. They could tell if Temp and Oll were drunk or sober by the way they walked. If they were sober, Oll always walked five or six steps in front; if they were drunk Temp walked in front. Never were they seen holding hands like many of the couples walking along the street. And one had his first time to see Oll have Temp by the arm walking beside her. When sober, Oll walked a few steps ahead like the men in Blake County did with their wives. Only there was this difference, Oll didn't have to walk ahead of his wife like a man did in Blake County along a path with a club in his hand to watch for snakes. There weren't any snakes on the streets of Blakesburg. This was an old practice Oll had acquired before he moved from Dogwood Ridge to Blakesburg. Just when Oll was drunk would he walk behind his wife. When Temp was drunk the world belonged to her. She wasn't afraid of anything or anybody. She wouldn't let Oll walk in front of her like the Blake County Red Neck men did their wives.

This couple had moved to Blakesburg when they were very young. Oll had brought his fiddle with him as well as his habits. Though he wasn't as good a fiddler as Uncle Sweeter Dabney, he knew many more of the old dance tunes than Uncle Sweeter. He fiddled for drunk horse traders when they wanted to dance. He fiddled on the courthouse square for anyone who wanted to dance. And he fiddled for the Red Necks on the big celebration days. He would go anywhere to play his fiddle where the people danced but he didn't like to have people who sat around him to listen, people whose feet couldn't tap the tunes his fiddle was playing on the ground or the street or the platform planks. Never did he take money for his fiddling. All he asked was pure corn to drink. And he wouldn't take a promise for pure corn. He had to have it before he played his fiddle. But he knew his weakness and he wouldn't touch the corn until the dance was nearly over and then he would go to his jug, what was left. Temp, who didn't draw a fiddle bow over the strings, didn't have to keep sober. And she couldn't "leave a jug be unstopped at Oll's feet." She would sit and sip from the jug and enjoy the cracking of brogan shoes and slipper heels on the dance floors as the couples circled and promenaded to her husband's fast dance tunes. This was the greatest enjoyment Oll and Temp could have. And they were not only a familiar couple on the Blakesburg streets but they were well known throughout Blake County.

In Blakesburg this childless couple had a reputation no other couple had. People knew they were devoted to each other. They had heard Temp say many times they had only one son and his name was Pure Corn. They would get a jug of pure corn from Tid Fortner, take it to their little cottage and between them they would drink the contents. Then they would go down the street, Temp in front and Oll behind her. They'd make for the spot where the greatest number of people were congregated. Then Temp would demonstrate the power of her fist. She would be walking in front of Oll and she would stop in front of the group and wait for him. When he approached her she would knock him down.

"I love ye, honey," Oll would say as he was getting up.

"Whow," Temp would knock him down again.

And Oll would start up again. Temp would knock him down. She would knock him down until she had him knocked out. She would do it without a reason. This was good entertainment for

the people who wouldn't have this couple in their homes. They
would always gather on the street to watch a Temp-and-Oll
fight. It was something to see a man trying to rise from the
street telling his wife he loved her and to watch her floor him
with her powerful fist. They never fought anybody else. Oll had
never had a fight with any man and Temp had only had one and
she struck only one lick. She had hit Mary Blanton once when
Mary, so she thought, was getting a little too affectionate with
her Oll. She caught Mary square on the chin and brought this
big two-hundred-pound woman whose affections were bestowed
upon many men, married and single, to her knees. Mary Blanton never again spoke to Oll. That one lick shattered her affections for Temp's husband.

On Thursday, September 18th, Oll had finished filling Attorney Joe Oliver's bin with dry seasoned willow kindling he
had split from the dead willows down under the river bank. He
had worked all week splitting kindling for this important
Blakesburg attorney and now he went down to Joe's office and
got his pay. This meant a little celebration. After he'd finished
a job for one of the town's people and got his pay, this always
meant a celebration. As soon as he got his money from Joe,
he went down Main Street where he found Tid Fortner and got
himself a quart of pure corn. Then he hurried home to Temp.

Inside the cottage Temp and Oll sat with the horsequart between them. After Temp had had a shot from the bottle, she
would pass it over to Oll. He'd take a drink and pass it back to
Temp. And while Temp drank Oll would sit and lick his tongue
over his lips to get any precious drop of this magic moonshine
that might otherwise be wasted. Temp's lips were so tight
around the horsequart-bottle neck when she drank it was impossible for a drop to escape. And sitting close to each other, passing
the quart between them, each took a drink as the urge came,
which was often, until they had "kilt the horsequart."

After they had emptied the horsequart, Temp got restless and wanted to go down the street to find a group of people. She got up, staggered a little, but walked well enough to the door. Oll got up from his chair and followed her outside the cottage. And down the street he followed her, walking as straight as any sober man. When the crowd gathered at the Drug Store saw them, they knew Temp and Oll were drunk. And here enough spectators were gathered to interest Temp. She stopped, about-faced and waited for her Oll. And without saying a word to him, she swung an uppercut with so much power she lifted her body from the street. She caught Oll on the chin and down he went.

"I love you, honey," Oll said, as he scrambled on the street with his feet and hands, getting up.

"Whow," she hit Oll again just as he had gotten to his feet and down he went again.

Everybody gathered in front of the Drug Store clapped his hands and laughed at this real funny entertainment.

"If Temp'd been born a manchild instead of a gal youngin," beardy-faced Sam Porter said, "she'd a been another Jack Dempsey. She wouldn't 've been as disappointin' as Bill Simpson!"

"I love you, honey," Oll said as he arose from the street the third time.

"Whow."

Oll sank back to the street.

When he told Temp he loved her again and was trying to rise, Temp took him by the hand and helped him up. But just as soon as she got him up, she socked him on the right jaw with her fist. Down he went like a fattening hog shot between the eyes with a rifle.

"What a wallop," Findley Higgins said.

"Woo-woo," Jeff Hargis said as he walked up to the scene, jumped up and cracked his heels together three times and then went on down the street.

This time Oll was slower about getting up.

"Come on, honey," Temp spoke kindly as she helped the weakening man to his feet.

"Whow," she struck him on the left jaw, with such a lick she lifted herself into the air and spun half way around.

"That got old Oll," Findley Higgins said. "He's down for the count."

But no one counted ten for him to rise. Oll lay on the street while everybody laughed. Temp turned to the spectators, looked at them with her eyes that looked like big pale green apples stuck out on tiny stems. Her face was sliced-beet red and her hair had come down across her face. Her clothes were twisted on her short stout body. She stood there with her fist still ready for action, looking at her cheering spectators. She was the winner; Oll was down on the street and in his dreams he was probably wandering somewhere among the scented flowers. Temp had the look of victory and confidence in her face.

"Look," Sam Porter said, pointing toward the sky. "Aint that somethin' peculiar?"

"Hit's a-lookin' strange to me," Findley said, as long bright rays shot across the sky.

Not anyone now paid any attention to the victor standing before them, nor to the defeated lying relaxed on his back on the street. They stood observing the strange display of brilliant lights that had suddenly come into the sky while they were watching the fight. They watched these lights grow brighter minute by minute. The like they had never seen before. Many got so nervous their teeth knocked together when they tried to talk.

"Lord Jesus, what is it?" Flossie Herald, one of the women spectators, asked.

"I don't know," Findley said. "But hit's somethin',"

"Might be a token," Sam Porter said, running his hand over his beardy face.

By this time people had started running up and down the street shouting and screaming.

Temp turned from facing her spectators. She took one look at the burning sky.

"Oh, God," she screamed, pitching headlong on the street, completely passed out.

"Is she dead?" Sam Porter asked. "Did Temp jist keel over like a beef?"

"I don't know," Findley said. "She hit the street tolerably hard."

"We'd better see," Sam said as he got down beside Temp and held her pulse.

A few people were watching Sam but the majority of them had their eyes turned toward the sky.

"She ain't gone, yet," Sam said. "But her pulse's a-beatin' softer than a grub-worm. We'd better take her to the doctor."

Sam waited for someone to volunteer to help him carry her but no one came.

"Who's a-goin' to hep me?" Sam asked, looking at Flossie.

"I wouldn't touch that sinful woman," Flossie Herald said.

"Ain't ye a Christian?" Sam asked. "I've seen ye a-goin' to one of the best churches in this town."

"I'm a Christian but I won't have nothin' to do with 'er," Flossie said. "Get some of the men!"

"I'll hep ye, Sam," Findley said. "I've danced too much to old Oll's magic fiddle not to hep take his wife to the doctor!"

By this time Oll was coming to his senses and was struggling to get upon his feet.

"But we need two more," Sam said. "We need somebody on each arm and leg and hit wouldn't hurt to have somebody at 'er head!"

"What's the matter with Temp?" Oll asked as he got to his feet. "Did I git her this time?"

"No, that sky got 'er," Sam said, pointing to the sky.

Not another one of the spectators would volunteer to help carry her to a doctor. They had enjoyed her fighting but they wouldn't lay a hand on this sinful woman in a time like this. After they observed the sky for a minute, they took off in all directions like scared rabbits.

"Lord God," Oll said, after he'd observed the lights.

"That sinful old trollop," Bertie Caldwell said as she ran past Temp lying in the street.

Bertie Caldwell was a worker in one of the best churches in Blakesburg.

"Leave 'er be," Roy Oliver said to Damon Thombs, both deacons in a church, as they hurried by.

"But we got to get 'er to a doctor," Sam pleaded. "If she's a child of the devil she's still one of our people!"

"One of our people," Clara Henson repeated. "She's a fightin' old . . . I won't call 'er what she is . . ."

And she hurried on fleeing for her own safety.

"Thar's Boliver Tussie," Findley said. "Come over here, Boliver, and hep us carry Temp to the doctor. Her pulse is low and a-gettin' lower! Fetch somebody! Oll aint in no shape to hep us!"

When Boliver came he brought Tid Fortner. Boliver and Tid got an arm each, Sam and Findley each carried a leg and they rushed to the doctor's office with this sinful woman while her relaxed neck let her head sag. Her mouth was open and her disheveled hair almost dragged on the street as they sped with her down Main Street while Oll followed the best he could behind the procession.

30

WHEN BOLIVER TUSSIE had helped carry Temperance Spradling to Doc Hinton's office, he stayed only a few minutes, where a dozen or more people were lying senseless on the floor, waiting to be revived by the shots from Doc's magic needle. Boliver watched Doc shoot Temp twice in the leg. And while Doc went on shooting others in the leg, Boliver watched over Temp for a sign of reviving life as eagerly as Oll watched from his swollen eyes. When Temp's eyelids started coming open and her lips started twitching, the men were pleased.

"Oh, God, what has happened to me?" were Temp's first words. "Where am I a-wakin' up?"

"In Doc Hinton's office, honey," Oll said.

"She's a-comin' to all right," Boliver said to Oll. "I'll be a-runnin' along!"

Boliver with a cud of light burley leaf under his red-beardy jaw, stepped carefully across the sprawled bodies on the office floor, pushed between the crowd of hysterical bystanders weeping for their people, touching them softly as he made himself a path to the door. He opened the door quietly where he met four people carrying another woman into the office. But he got out into the open air just before they started in at the door. He was glad he got to the fresh air before they got into the doorway and blocked it. For the smell of medicines in Doc Hinton's office was poison to his nostrils as the stagnant air had been in the jailhouse where Boliver had served many sentences when the jail had been overcrowded with sweaty men.

But now he walked calmly down the street chewing his light burley tobacco, spitting onto the street, and rubbing his big hand over his beardy face while people ran past him screaming. Many people were running at such speed they couldn't stop, didn't try to stop, but ran smack into him. But this didn't bother Boliver. It didn't interfere with his philosophy of life. His philosophy, though he had never bothered to tell anybody about it, was to "let come what may and every day provide fer itself." This was the way Boliver had lived. And he had enjoyed his life as much as any man. His philosophy of life had worked for him, whether it had always worked for his family or not. As long as he was out of jail, had enough to eat, tobacco to chew, something to drink, life was good to him.

Boliver had received his Relief as long as his Pappie Press Tussie had wielded influence enough to see that he got it. And that was a long time. During these years Boliver claimed he was down with his back. Said he had hurt his back jumping over a rail fence when he was a young man. But as soon as the Relief was taken away from him, he went to work building roads for the WPA. And anyone who worked with Boliver could tell you there was not another man in Blakesburg or Blake County who was as neat with a shovel cutting a ditch or as neat with an ax cutting down a tree. He could chisel a stone almost as smooth as a concrete block. There was hardly anything he couldn't do with dirt, wood and stone. He was the most skilled worker the WPA had in Blake County when he would work. And he was one of their best road builders. On the country roads where they split saplings and built little bridges across the creeks, people would go to look at a bridge Boliver had built.

But Boliver would not always work. And it wasn't because of his back either. When he was on Relief he got along better. But when he was put to work on WPA, something he didn't want but had to accept, he made money which he didn't always spend for food. Nor did he spend it with Tid Fortner. He spent it with the "sixty-eight" for sugar whiskey. When he got his check, he got himself a two-gallon jug of sugar whiskey and got on a "daisy." He would get drunk, go home and fight with Crissie, who, since she had heard Brother Hank Redfern preach the gospel one time, had become a "saved woman," and would no longer use her fist on Boliver when he came home drunk. Before she became a saved woman she would knock Boliver down with her fist faster than he could get up.

The first thing Boliver would do when he came home fightin' mad and didn't find his big boys home, was to bite a hole through a galvanized washpan or bite a hole through one of Crissie's brand-new galvanized water buckets. And when he started this, Crissie knew it was time for her to "grab the young-ins and start." She would take off to the nearest place where she could find safety. And that was one reason why she was so "agin WPA." Boliver could make money and get paid and buy sugar herbs and come home and beat her up. And that was another reason why she hated to move from Blakesburg two miles into the country. When Boliver had beaten her up while they lived in Blakesburg, if he "bit a piece outten 'er" or "blacked her eyes" in a fight, she went after the Law and had him arrested. But if she knocked him out for the count, there was never a word said about it. But if Boliver won the fight, he was arrested, and fined.

When he was brought into the Blakesburg City Court he would say "I'm guilty" just as he entered the door. They would raise his fine and jail sentence a little each time he was before them until the fine had jumped from ten to a hundred dollars, the jail sentence from one to ninety days. He would have the money to pay the fine but he could work his time by cleaning streets, digging sewer lines, trimming trees for two dollars a day. He had done more free work for the city than any other man who had ever lived within its limits.

As Boliver walked down the street he had so often swept, he had the feeling that it belonged to him. He would occasionally look up to see if the rolling flames of light were getting nearer to his beloved city of which he was so much a part. He felt no malice about the many times he had been fined and jailed and about all the free work he had done. This gave him a greater love for Blakesburg. For every way he looked through the bright light, he could see a tree he had trimmed, a fence he had repaired, a rock he had chiseled into shape and put into one of the buildings to replace a crumbling one. His blood was in the stone, the concrete, the trees and actually the dust on the streets of this city. And now he knew something was going to happen to it but his philosophy of life, "let come what may and every day provide fer itself," kept him from getting excited. Although he had several drinks of sugar herbs under his belt, he didn't feel mad at anyone, not even at Crissie.

When Boliver left the street he made for the courthouse square where many groups had gathered. Here was the center of confusion in the town. Many of the old men, whom he had sat and whittled with, were gathered here watching the strange omen of the northern sky. On this spot Boliver had whiled many happy hours away with his pocket knife whittling for the biggest shaving, which he usually could get. He walked past Charlie Allbright who at that time had his eyes focused on the heavens. And Bass Keaton, who was sitting on one of the political seats, said to Boliver as he passed by, "Boliver, our town's a goner!"

"Hit does look like it," Boliver said, pushing through the crowd until he reached an open space beneath an elm shade tree. Here Boliver stopped and looked at the jailhouse, a second home to him, now lighted as he had never seen it before. He saw the prisoners' faces at all the windows. And he listened to them yelling while others paid no attention to their cries.

"Looks like we oughta git outten this goddamn'd hole now," he heard a husky voice scream above the noises of the town.

"I hope to hell this damned dump's destroyed!"

"Let the damned town sink!"

"Let the world end!"

"Glory to God, this old dump's a goner!"

And he heard the men laugh, shout and scream only for a few minutes. Then the light went out inside the jail. The prisoners' faces could no longer be seen at the windows. Then Boliver saw the beardy-faced prisoners running out and mixing with the shouting people of the town. They had been freed! Jailer Ottis had opened the doors in a time like this!

"Hit's a hell of a poor time to free us now," he heard one prisoner say to another as they ran under the tree where he was standing.

But there was another sound Boliver heard that quickly drew his attention. He heard the rattle of a jolt wagon and the click of mules' steel shoes against the concrete and he turned to see a scared mule team with their mouths wide open and foam-spittle dropping in big flecks from the corners of the bits as the tall driver leaned back against the leather checklines to hold the charging mules.

"Have ye seen Pap?" he heard the driver ask Bass Keaton as he brought the charging mules to a stop and the three standing up riding in the wagonbed almost toppled over on their faces.

"Whose boy are ye?" Bass asked, looking at the six-foot-eight driver.

"Boliver Tussie's boys we air," the driver said.

"He's a-standin' right thar under that tree," Bass said, pointing with his cane.

"Is that ye, Pap?" the driver asked.

"Yep, hit's me," Boliver said. "What are ye a-doin' in here, Snail, with Powderjay's mule team?"

"Ma sent me here to get ye."

"She wants ye at home, Pap," the second boy said, who was standing behind the tall driver with his hands on his shoulders.

"What does she want with me, Erf?" Boliver asked.

"She wants ye to be at home when she goes to Glory," the third boy said, who was standing behind the second one with his hands on his shoulders.

"But I ain't a-goin', Houndshell," Boliver said.

"Oh, yes ye're a-goin', too," Snail said. "Why do ye think we brought this team and wagon fer?"

"We aim to haul ye home, Pap," Erf said.

"Come on, Pap," Houndshell said. "Ma wants ye!"

"But I aint a-goin' to Glory," Boliver said.

"But ye can be thar when Ma goes," Houndshell said.

"And ye will be thar," Snail said. "Ma said fer us to fetch ye!"

When Boliver knew his tall sons meant business, he ran across the street toward a wire fence that surrounds the jail. When Snail saw him break into a run, he gave the checklines to Erf to hold the mules and he leaped over the wagonbed onto the street. Then Erf gave the checklines to Houndshell to hold the mules and he leaped over the wagonbed onto the street and took after Snail.

"Ye'll never make hit to that jailhouse, Pap," Snail said as he stretched his long legs out after his father.

But Boliver had another idea. He knew the power there was in his set of teeth that were as sound as a silver dollar and even and sharp enough to cut a silk thread. He ran up to the fence and grabbed a barbed wire in his mouth and held to it with his teeth and his hands.

"I aint a-goin' a step," he mumbled since the wire was in his mouth and he had clamped down on it with his teeth.

"But ye are a-goin', Pap," Snail said, putting his hand on his shoulder to pull him from the wire.

"Be keerful, Snail," Erf warned, "Ye mought hurt Pap's mouth. Ye might jerk his teeth out."

"Come on, Pap," Snail said, pulling at Boliver.

But Boliver held on. Snail couldn't shake him loose.

"Ye'll pull Pap's head loose from his body," Erf warned, "and he'll never loose that hold. I've got the idear!"

Erf pulled his pocket knife from his pocket and opened the big blade.

"But ye'll ruin that good knife," Snail warned Erf. "Ye'll break the blade before ye'll be able to pry his mouth open. Ye couldn't any more open his mouth with that knife blade than ye could pry a snappin' turtle's jaws apart!"

Erf closed the blade and put his knife back into his pocket. He was standing behind Snail and happened to see the file with a corncob handle sticking up from Snail's hip overall pocket where he had carried the file to sharpen their scythes while they mowed sowbeans that afternoon.

"I've got the idear, Snail," Erf said, taking the file from Snail's pocket and pulling the cob handle from the sharp strong end. "Here, put this sharp end betwixt his teeth. Hit's stout enough to pry his jaws open!"

Erf gave Snail the file and Snail pushed Boliver's lips apart and shoved the small end between his teeth. Boliver fought against Snail's getting the file into his mouth by kicking and butting his rear backwards while he held onto the wire with his teeth and his hands for life. But after Snail worked the file handle into Boliver's mouth where he could get good leverage, he started prying and he loosed his mouth from the wire. But when he got his mouth loose, he started to pull his hands loose and Boliver nailed onto the wire again with his teeth. Snail put the file in his mouth again and Erf stepped up closer so when they got him loose from the wire, Erf doubled a finger back on each hand until Boliver had to let go. Erf and Snail carried their father toward the wagon while he kicked, squirmed, and tried to bite their hands. They threw him over the rim of the wagonbed like they would a two-hundred-pound weight. Then they jumped up into the wagonbed and held him while he fought back. But Houndshell gave the impatient mules the rein and they charged around the courthouse square, snorting, charging, foaming at the mouth, while the people cleared the streets to make way.

31

"**H**ELP! HELP!"

When Joe Dingus heard these words he was running down the road with his hat in his hand. He had seen the lights in the northern skies and he knew something was wrong. He didn't know exactly what was the matter with the world. Some inner voice had told him to take off and he'd obeyed. But he stopped when he heard the cry for help. While he listened for it again, all he could hear was his own breath coming and going like that of a horse with the thumps and his own heart beating like a triphammer.

"Help! Help! Can't somebody hear me!"

Somebody a-needin' hep all righty, Joe thought as he got the direction of the sound.

The sound came from a wooded section near the river where the Oldline Special Railway once had a turning table and big storage depot. But that was long ago when the boats came up and down the river, stopping here to haul commerce the Oldline Special had picked up along its thirty-six miles of railway. Now, the Oldline Special was no more; its tracks had been torn up and its T-rails used for scrap iron. Its big storage depot was gone and there was only a deep hole where the turning table used to be. The place had grown up with saplings and this was a spot near Blakesburg where bootleggers and gamblers hid from the law. And it was a place where much illicit loving was carried on.

"Help! Help! In the name of God, won't somebody come?"

Joe heard the cry again while he stood debating whether to go into a spot like this on such a night.

"I'm a-comin'," Joe shouted before he had made up his mind. "Stay until I git thar!"

"I'll be here when you come all right," the voice answered.

Joe ran out a little road just wide enough for an automobile. This road would have been dark on any normal night. But on this night the light seemed to penetrate the leaves on the tree tops above Joe and flood the road until it was brighter than day. When Joe neared the place where he thought the voice came from, he slowed to a walk and looked behind every tree thinking it might be a trick somebody was playing to call him into this forlorn spot, waylay him, and rob him.

"Where air ye?" Joe asked, stopping dead-still in his tracks.

"Right over here," a pleased voice answered.

Then Joe walked around a thick clump of trees to where the old turning table once was. And before him, he saw something like a house with all the chinking and daubing knocked out and the bright light filtering the cracks.

Something new, he thought.

"Where'd ye say ye wuz?" Joe asked, his voice trembling.

"Right in here," the voice came from inside the funny-looking house. "I'm fastened up in this contraption!"

Joe Dingus, a little suspicious, stood two steps away and looked through the crack. He saw a man and an automobile inside.

"Who air ye?" he asked as he walked up closer.

"I'm Alex Scroggins," the man said.

"Which one of the Alex Scroggins?" Joe asked. "Farmer Alex 'r County Attorney Alex?"

"County Attorney Alex," the man said.

"Then we've met before," Joe said. "And I'm a-goin' to leave ye where ye air!"

"Who are you?" Alex asked.

"I'm Joe Dingus! Don't ye remember me?"

"Yes, I do, Joe," Alex spoke softly.

"Yer words drip like honey now," Joe said. "But ye remember the time ye prosecuted me and stuck me fer sixty-two bucks and costs when I oughta come clean! Now, as fur as I'm concerned ye can stay in thar and sweat!"

Alex Scroggins! Memories flashed through Joe's mind. It took him back to World War I. He remembered when the war was on "across the pond" and many of the Blakesburgians were fighting on "fureign soil," there was also a war being fought in Blakesburg. And Alex Scroggins like himself was a boy wearing short pants at that time. Only, Alex was "a big general" in the opposing army, who led the West End boys against the East End in Blakesburg. At first they had dug trenches in Hezzy Blair's cow pasture. Each had dug a communication trench up to the frontline trench where a supply of rocks could be carried to the front. And when a man raised up from one of the trenches a shower of missiles was thrown at him.

When Hezzy learned what had happened to his cow pasture, he made the boys fill up the trenches. But the next day, they came back for open field fighting. Several brought their air rifles and plenty of BB's with them. Those who didn't have their rifles went back after them. Before their armies clashed, they made an agreement not to shoot anyone about the face and head. They agreed to stand behind where their old trenches used to be and shoot it out, after the signal for the shooting had been given. When the East End boys opened up on the West End boys, General Alex Scroggins got a good sprinkling up and down the body and legs. The East End boys tried to knock out General Scroggins the first one. He threw his air rifle down and took off across the pasture screaming and cursing. This was considered a cowardly act by his own men for he deserted them in time of battle. But a little later General Alex Scroggins was back on the scene, just in time to save his troops from being thrown into a

rout by the East Enders. He brought with him a piece of ar-
tillery, a double-barrel shotgun.

When he pointed the double-barrel shotgun and cocked both
hammers, his enemies learned quickly he meant business. They
started to take off in a body toward the other end of the cow
pasture but General Alex didn't let them get very far until he
opened up with both barrels, sprinkling and routing their entire
army. When they took off toward Blakesburg screaming, Alex
Scroggins smiled.

Joe remembered two shots had hit him and that he carried
them under his hide behind at this minute. And he remembered
when he played shinny at the Blakesburg Graded School, Alex
wouldn't play the game fair. He wouldn't play it any fairer than
he had played the game of war. He would come to school wearing boots to protect his legs. When the two teams lined up with
clubs in their hands and the tin can between them, Alex would
never strike at the can with his club. He would hit the closest
opponent across the shins with his stick pretending he had missed
the can. He would send his opponents one by one screaming as
he cracked their unprotected shins. Joe remembered how he had
sent him from many a game of shinny with blue spots up and
down his aching shins.

Another night Joe remembered was when he and Alex went
up on the high hill slope south of Blakesburg to steal Nellie
Blake's peaches. They had discovered them ripe and ready to
be picked that day.

When they walked silently into the orchard after darkness
had covered the earth like a blanket, they met a woman dressed
in white except she didn't have a woman's head. She had the
head of a rooster on her shoulders and when they met her face
to face, she quacked, cackled excitedly and crowed once to them
like a rooster speaking to his flocks of hens. And she kept coming
straight at them. Joe remembered that when he about-faced in
a hurry and took off toward Blakesburg, Alex was twenty feet

or more ahead of him, screaming, and running wildly down between the rows of peach trees. He took out after Alex, who had been his leader in suggesting they steal the peaches. He ran as he had never run before until he was on Alex's heels. He didn't notice which way Alex was going until he was in the hallway of Nellie Blake's big ancestral home. But Alex didn't stop running and Joe was beside him now. They ran through the hall, jumped off the high front porch, still on their feet running like tomcats until they reached the electric lights of the city. They later learned the woman was Nellie Blake. She was dressed in white and she was carrying a white rooster, from where he had been roosting in a peach tree, to the henhouse.

Many years later after Alex had been elected County Attorney, he had unmercifully prosecuted Joe, who was charged with stealing a keg of locust-blossom wine from Liam Winston. Alex said in his prosecution that one reason he had amounted to so much in life was, he had lived a clean and wholesome life, that he had not only refrained from such indecencies as petty larceny, but due to his early character training at home and in the schools of Blakesburg, he had become immune to such character degradations. When Joe jumped from his chair to remind Alex of the night they went to steal Miss Nellie's peaches, Sheriff George Nance pounded his gavel and called for order in the courtroom.

I've got old Alex where th' hair's short now, Joe Dingus thought. Once I wuz at his mercy; now he's at my mercy.

"You mean you can't help me out of here?" Alex said. "I gotta git back to my work!"

"What time do you think hit is?" Joe asked.

"Must be three in the afternoon," Alex said. "Looks like from that sky we're going to get a storm!"

"Hit's nighttime," Joe said. "And from the looks of that sky we're a-going to git more than a storm!"

"Am I dreamin' 'r am I awake?" Alex asked Joe. "It's still daylight to me."

"If ye ast me I think ye must be crazy," Joe said. "Don't ye know the world's a-comin' to an end?"

"Now I know I'm dreaming," Alex said.

"Then dream on, Alex Scroggins," Joe Dingus said. "Ye'll wake up in hell in the mornin'!"

Alex, like a caged animal, ran around the wall of old crossties that were stacked upon each other, making a pen around his car. The pen was covered with long switch ties. He ran around until he found a convenient place for toe and hand holds between the ties and then he climbed up where he could put his face to a broad crack that faced the north. For a minute he watched the great lights flash across the northern skies. And while he watched the skies, Joe watched Alex through a broad crack. Then he watched Alex scale down the wall like a cat and run back over to a crack where he could look out at him to talk.

"Lord, somethin' is happening, Joe," Alex said excitedly. "Can't you get me out of here?"

"I don't know," Joe said hesitatingly. "You prosecuted me because I didn't belong to yer Party!"

"No, that wasn't the reason, Joe," Alex pleaded. "I was elected by the people and I had to do my duty for the county. I took an oath that I would do my duty when I entered office. I prosecuted the Dinwiddies same as I did the Greenoughs!"

"But ye never did tell me how ye got in that pen," Joe said.

"I don't know how I got here," Alex said. "I usually go down and get me a few beers, drive out here in the afternoon, park my car and drink them. I did that this afternoon and when I woke up, I was fenced in!"

"Somebody played a mean trick on ye," Joe said.

"Well, I don't mean to say anything against your party, Joe," Alex said. "But I believe men in your party knew I came out here and they caught me asleep and built this fence around me to hurt me politically!"

"They could've done hit," Joe said. "But ye must've been mighty sound asleep! Ye must've been more than asleep!"

"Well, I expect I was," Alex said. "May've had one too many beers!"

"I spect that wuz hit," Joe said, laughing a little. "Ye ought to remember yer home trainin'."

"Now, how am I goin' to get out 'n here?" Alex said. "I'll be ruined politically if the people find this out!"

"Yer a-bein' ruint politically won't make no difference now," Joe said. "If I thought ye'd be back a-runnin' agin fer office, I wouldn't hep ye nary bit! But ye won't be a-runnin' any more! I'm shore of that!"

Joe took a couple of steps forward and then he started up the wall. He climbed to the top and looked the crosstie pen over.

"Well, the Greenoughs done a good job," Joe said. "Alex, ye'll haf to stick a five dollar bill up through the crack before I'll begin to tear down what men o' my party has built."

Joe waited until he saw Alex's hand come through the crack between the switch ties with a five dollar bill. Then Joe rolled the big tie, after much struggling, from the roof and let it roll over the side.

"Five dollars for the next one now," Joe said.

Alex gave him another five.

Joe rolled another big tie from the top.

"Ye'll have to shell out again, Alex," Joe said. "If ye don't ye'll stay in thar!"

"I don't have any more fives," Alex said. "Looks like ten dollars is enough?"

"Not fer me," Joe said. "Don't ye have some tens, twenties 'r a fifty?"

"Well I have a little more money," he grunted.

"Then let's have it," Joe said.

"But you said the world's ending," Alex said, as he handed Joe a twenty. "What will you need with money now?"

"But I'd as well have back whut rightly belongs to me even if the world does end," Joe said. "I'll take off four ties fer this twenty!"

When Joe had removed the twelve big switch ties from the top, it had cost Alex sixty dollars.

"Now I'll hep ye git the crossties down from the wall fer a dollar a-piece, Alex," Joe bargained. "Ye'll haf to git yer car out!"

"But this will cost me a hundred dollars before I'm through," Alex said.

"But don't ye think hit's worth it?" Joe said. "Ye'll be lucky if it don't cost ye more 'n that!"

"I think I can finish this myself now," Alex said, after he was able to climb out the top of the pen.

"All right," Joe said, standing watching Alex.

Alex Scroggins took hold of the end of one of the water-soaked heavy crossties. He struggled and grunted painfully but he couldn't begin to budge it from the wall.

"You win," Alex said, giving up his task. "You finish the job!"

"These little ties aint nothin' to whut them switch ties wuz," Joe said as he began to roll the little ties from the wall. "Ye've been in that office too long, Alex. Ye ain't in no shape to lift. I've been a-loadin' green oak crossties on railroad cars."

Joe had to move sixty-one more ties before Alex could move his car.

"Lucky for me that I got paid today," Alex said as he grudgingly shelled off three more twenties from his roll and scraped up enough pocket change for the extra dollar.

"Hit shore wuz," Joe said as he counted his money, fondling each greenback tenderly. "If ye hadn't a-had eny money ye'd a-still been in that pen!"

"My heavens, I've got to get back to my office," Alex said, making a wild dash for his car. "I've got to beat this storm! It's a-goin' to rain to beat hell in a few minutes!"

"Hit's a-goin' to do more than that," Joe said but his words were drowned by the roar of the motor when Alex gunned his car and took off toward Blakesburg through the bright midnight.

32

WHEN HORACE BLEVINS' graduating class in Blakesburg High School voted the graduate "most likely to succeed in life," Horace didn't get a vote. He'd never been a popular member of his class. He was just an average student and he'd never made an athletic team. He had only one or two friendly associates. No one ever suspected this youth's having enough initiative to create a business for himself. The girls in his class at that time didn't realize some day each one would be trying to court his favor to buy his irresistible products. If they had realized back in these early days what his business was to be in the future, they would have been kinder to him.

Horace was a Blue Blood. But unlike Willie Deavers he didn't go around bragging about it. He was probably thinking about how Willie Deavers would make a living someday. He knew he didn't have the chances of many of the young men in Blakesburg whose parents had money and a thriving business. Tim Blevins, Horace's father, had never been a prosperous man. He had worked by the day wherever and whenever he could find something to do until Bass Keaton, his old boyhood friend, got him interested in trading. He wanted to see Tim do well and he took him on trading excursions through Blake County. Then Tim Blevins became a cattle buyer. He would buy lean cattle in the spring, rent a pasture and "grass" his cattle all summer, then put them on the market in the fall. He often made a good turnover.

Young Horace probably thought of following in his father's

footsteps after he had finished Blakesburg High School. For like most of the other boys of his generation and the succeeding generations, he didn't want to leave the town of his birth, the town he had become a part of, nor did he even care to visit beyond the borders of Blake County to buy cattle, since Blake County cattle were always better. But while Horace was on one of these trips with his father learning how to buy and sell, a thought came to him. As he said years later he "just put two and two together and they made four."

Since he had visited in many of the old homes in Blakesburg, especially in Willie Deavers' big home with all of its antique furnishings, he knew the value the Blakesburg women put on old furniture. And while he rode over Blake County with his father and spent nights at the old Blake County homes, furnished with old furnishings, he learned the Red Necks didn't put any value on this old furniture. In fact he learned by talking to the Blake County women they'd be willing to sell their old furniture for very little, almost nothing, and refurnish their homes with more modern furniture. They said they were tired of the old spinning wheels, their Jenny Lind beds, their grandfather clocks, dropleaf walnut tables, wild cherry three-cornered cupboards, and other "sicha worthless plunder." At one home he visited, they had carried out a Jenny Lind and had split it up for kindling. And when Horace saw this, he knew his cattle-buying days were over.

He rented himself an empty dwelling house in an obscure part of Blakesburg and put up his shingle, ANTIQUES FOR SALE HERE. He bought old beds and ladder-back chairs, for a few dollars. He expected to advertise his antiques among the Blakesburg Red Necks since he figured they would want to have old furniture in their frame houses, such as the Blue Bloods had in their stone-crumbling ones. He had expected his own people, the women with blue blood in their veins, to laugh at his idea. He never dreamed one would as much as step inside his store.

He thought they had enough antique furniture to do them the rest of their lives. But here is where he made a mistake. He made a great business miscalculation. When they heard he had these ladder-back chairs, for gossip spread quickly in Blakesburg, women from the old families raced to his store in big automobiles, ran inside and started bidding for the ladder-backs. He sold them to the highest bidder for twenty times as much as he'd given. Horace was surprised at his first success. He knew he had a future if he didn't have competition.

At first he took a spring wagon with a team of mules to Blake County and bought these antique furnishings that the Blake County Red Necks were getting rid of in a hurry. And Horace hurried from shack to shack to get them. As soon as he drove back to Blakesburg a long line of big automobiles would follow his wagon to store. Women had their spies out to know when he left after a load and when he would get back. And many of them drove their automobiles out over the rough roads to meet him and bargain with him. They would drive as far as it was safe out the country road and often beyond where it was safe. But Horace would shoo them off until he got back to Blakesburg. But he would always have trouble when he unloaded. Women would lay their hands on this piece of furniture and that piece and as many as five or six would claim one piece. The only way he could settle the disputes was to sell to the highest bidder.

Horace made money "like dirt" with his new business. He scoured Blake County and got the antiques before the people in Blake County had time to learn their value. His business grew by leaps and bounds. He sold his mule team and his express wagon and bought himself a truck so he could buy the antiques in a hurry. For he had the turnover. Often he got fifty times as much as he gave for one of these old pieces. The Red Necks could find rich pine stumps to get their kindling and let Horace have a three-cornered cupboard made of wild cherry or black walnut for a couple of dollars. And finally they learned his secret and raised the price. But Horace could give them the price they asked and still sell for big profits. He learned that any old dish, even stoves, candle holders, apple butter kettles, apple butter stirrers—just about anything—would sell. And he bought everything that was loose. Horace didn't know their makes and values but the women did. They carried books and magazines with them and checked the value of these antiques.

Just one thing made Horace a little sad despite his making money like dirt. Women who had been friends since they were children fell out and pulled hair over his antiques. Not all of them did such unwomanly things as pull hair—not until the Blakesburg Red Neck women started buying. But they had trouble and it got the men into trouble over their wives. Mrs. Marvin Clayton and Mrs. Franklin Foster had words over a grandfather clock. Each put the price sky-high trying to outbid the other. Mrs. Marvin Clayton got the clock at $1000. No one knew what Horace had paid for it but someone in Blake County said he paid $10.

Though Horace had often said he didn't care to go beyond the borders of his home Blake County for anything, he changed his mind. After he had ferreted out the antiques "as clean as a hound dog's tooth" he took his truck beyond the borders of Blake County where there was greener picking. His customers demanded more and more; he couldn't supply their wants. He was able to hire help now, a man to go with him and his truck to help load and unload and someone to stay in his store which he had renovated, and he had a sign painter imported to paint his windows. "Horace" was a household word in Blakesburg. He was the most popular merchant in the town and was sought after at parties. Each woman interested in antiques tried to be nicest to him. "Horace Blevins has done more to beautify the Blakesburg homes than any one person," Bruce Livingstone wrote in the *Greenough Gazette.*

Men in the town scratched their heads at their wives, fussing over this "worthless house plunder, and paying big prices for it" when the chairs were dangerous for them to sit on. The old dishes were chipped and cracked and the clocks wouldn't run. But they had to buy them for their wives. Many of them said they felt like choking Horace for starting this business when the craze was still unknown to their wives. One of the antique base rockers had fallen with one of the prominent merchants of the town and hurt his hip, one of the beds had fallen when a prominent couple was sleeping on it and had hurt the woman . . . but such minor things didn't hurt the business. Horace ransacked four adjoining counties and then he went into a "furrin" state in quest of more antiques.

Though the people of Blakesburg knew the natives in the state where Horace went after his antiques were "furriners" to them, they gladly accepted their discarded furniture as antiques. Antiques from this "furrin state" were in great demand. Horace would take his truck to the auctions and return with it loaded as long "as he could tie a cheer on." And when the truck arrived in Blakesburg there would be a crowd of women waiting. Just as soon as he would drive to his store and stop, these restless antique-hungry women would swarm around it like hungry chickens after cracked corn. Each would lay her hand on a chair, bed, dresser, and claim it. And as usual, many hands would hold to the same piece. But there was never a man in sight except Horace and his helpers. And these three men would try to keep peace among their customers.

Late Thursday afternoon, September 18th, Horace arrived with one of his biggest hauls. His truck was surrounded by half the women in Blakesburg. Each had gotten a tip Horace was to bring "a grand load this time." There were Greenough and Dinwiddie Blue Bloods among them; Dinwiddie and Greenough Red Necks were there too. Blood lines were forgotten when the truck arrived and each woman fought for herself. She had the beauty of her own home to look after.

In this particular load, Horace had bought barrels of dishes. The furniture on top the truck was unloaded first. The women didn't make a mad rush for these pieces as they formerly had. They had their houses and attics well supplied. But what they wanted most were the barrels of Haviland, cranberry glass, cobalt blue lamps, milk-glass vases, mixed with restaurant dishes, cheap dishes, old milk-glass mustard dishes and a hundred other assortments. There was some sort of an antique to suit every woman in the crowd. And all these women wanted to do was each to get herself a barrel and start digging into it. But there were more women than barrels and this was where the trouble first started.

"Please, ladies," Horace begged, "let me put the barrels in the store this evening and you can come back in the morning at seven!"

But they wouldn't listen to his plea. Women held to their barrels just as soon as one was lifted from the truck into the street. Six or seven women would pounce on each barrel and start digging. They pretended they hadn't heard Horace's plea. It was tonight or never with them. Many of the women had their cars parked near to haul their "catch" home. Many had walked to the store from different parts of the town. They were here to get their antiques from the North, and they wouldn't go home disappointed.

Before Horace and Andy rolled the last barrel down the truckbed and lifted it carefully onto the street, from six to ten women who didn't have their hands on a barrel rushed madly in and took the barrel over. A few sharp words were spoken among them. One woman slapped another who was on the other side of the barrel. Several women were "shocked" at the language these women used while they went digging down into the barrel claiming this dish and that one. Then they started jerking dishes from the others' hands saying they had the first claim on them. Two women pulled on a cranberry lamp until

Horace and Andy had to separate them. They were afraid a fight was going to break out among them over this precious load.

While they fussed, slapped at each other and used "shocking" language to one another over the dishes, one of the more reticent women who had been pushed back from her barrel had time to observe the nature of the strange flood of light from the burning skies. The electric lights above the truck looked dim in comparison. Maybe the screams let out by people over the town turned everybody's attention to the skies above them. Women slowly looked up from the barrels from which they were pulling varied assortments of dishes and what-nots until they observed something was wrong.

Those who had quarreled and fussed looked at each other with a strange light in their eyes. Their faces grew pale; their lips started trembling. Suddenly one woman dropped the precious antique she was holding onto the street, let out a shrill cry and took off. And then another and another while still a few gripped dishes so tight in their hands they couldn't put them in the barrels or drop them on the street. They started off with them in their hands as fast as they could run. Now they were hearing shouts from everywhere that the end of time had come.

When Mrs. Franklin Foster left, as ambitious as she had been over antiques, every woman knew something was going to happen. Each relinquished her right to the barrel to anyone who wanted it. They took off like wild birds before a storm, screaming as they went with their hands above their heads.

33

TIDDIS FORTNER wasn't old enough to fight in World War I. But when the boys came back and found a "dry county," he was one of the first to think of the great enterprise to "wet thar gullets." The way he got into the business was by riding a mule from Cave Branch to Blakesburg, taking a day to make the trip and a day to return, carrying four gallons of pure corn in his saddlebags. He soon had competition by moonshiners who made sugar whiskey and sold it for twenty bucks a gallon. But this didn't bother him. He raised his price above forty dollars a gallon and people clamored for his pure corn product.

"That showed me somethin' right thar," Tid later told Jeff Hargis. "People will pay if they know the product is good."

Then he went on to tell Jeff no one ever went blind from drinking his moonshine. He said a man could drink a quart and be so drunk he didn't know which end was up, yet he could go to bed and sleep and the next morning he would wake up without a hangover or a headache.

Tiddis Fortner found himself so popular in Blakesburg he decided to stay in the town and have his shiners make moonshine and bring it to him. He had only two shiners and one mule at first. But as his business increased by leaps and bounds, he hired more shiners and more mule toters until nearly everybody on Cave Branch was working for him.

In these trying days when the Law was going out after the men engaged in this profitable industry, Tid Fortner didn't have anything to fear but the "Revenooers." He didn't have them to fear as much as the men living on Hog Branch and Buck Run who made the sugar whiskey. The County Sheriff and his deputies were after these men. But they didn't bother Tid or report him to the "Revenooers." Tid had the business of all the Blake County officials. When his caravan of mules started toward Blakesburg with saddlebags across their backs, no one dared to bother this important load on its way to wet the dry gullets of important Blake County officials and Blakesburg business men.

This caravan always reached its destination which was a little house on the outskirts of Blakesburg. When "Revenooers" were coming to Blake County to raid the Red Necks' stills, which was very often, mule caravans never left Cave Branch. Tid knew when for them to come and when they should stay at home.

Tid lived in his cottage alone at first and conducted his business. To show himself as a model citizen, he stopped taking a drink before and after each meal. He never touched it. This might have been because his pure corn was as precious among drinks as diamonds were among stones. He got sixty dollars a gallon for the average run. For some of his expert runs, he got as much as a hundred dollars from people in the big money in the roaring Twenties.

When Tid met women from the old Dinwiddie and Greenough families on the street, he learned to tip his hat and smile cordially. He spoke friendly to the men, shook hands with them and patted them on the back. It was said of Tid that he was a gentleman with the ladies and a good mixer among the men. He didn't claim any political faith after he got in business for he had to be good to everybody. He went first to one church and then the other to show them he wasn't a partial man. He helped support the churches. He was as loyal and faithful to his newly adopted city as he had been and still was to his native Cave Branch whose soil had nurtured him from birth until he went to Blakesburg.

Tid became one of the best dressed men in Blakesburg. He

wore a different suit of clothes every day and each suit was the newest in fashion and design. He wore silk shirts of various loud colors and flashy neckties and fashionable expensive shoes of all colors and combination of colors and designs. He had to go well-dressed because he kept company with all classes of people from railroad section men to lawyers, preachers, teachers and especially men in public offices of both county and city. In the winter he wore overcoats to match his hats; even in summer he wore light topcoats to match his hats.

He was never without an overcoat winter or summer and everybody thought, though no one questioned "Old Reliable Tid," that he had large built-in pockets. For when he passed men on the streets they often said they heard the half-pint bottles rattling. He not only sold to the top-notchers in Blakesburg Society, to the business men and the town and county officials, but he sold to "the little fellar on the street" if he had the money to pay the price. The majority of these men drank sugar moonshine instead of the pure corn. But when one of the little men had the dough, which was plentiful in the Twenties, and desired some "better stuff that won't blind a body" he'd approach Reliable Tid and they'd walk away together.

Tid wouldn't sell a man another half-pint after he got to the place he had to hold to a tree or lamppost. He had his code of honor and ethics. He was known to be the most ethical of anybody in his profession around Blakesburg in the twenties. His customers knew he was the most ethical man in his profession. Only his competitors complained by saying that they could be ethical too if they could sell to the rich and if they had the Law on their side. They were envious of the class of customers Tid had and of the money they thought he was making. Everybody thought he was making as much money as anybody in Blakesburg during the prohibition.

But despite Tid's good clothes, his prestige, money and power, it would have been as hard for him to have married one of the

local girls from one of the old families as it was for Poodi Troxler. Besides, the Blakesburg girls had heard the rumors about
the women who came to Tid's bachelor home which wasn't as
fine a home as Poodi Troxler had before he took unto himself a
bride.

What the Blakesburg women had heard were not merely
rumors. He not only had one woman but he had several women
in his cottage. And they were not all young single women. Many
of them were older than Tid. Several of them were younger.
A few were his age. Many of them had children born in wedlock
and out of wedlock. They had deserted their husbands or their
husbands had deserted them. When they heard of "Reliable"
Tid, they left their disgrace behind them and brought their
babies and came. At Tid's cottage they found food, shelter,
clothes and the solace of friendliness, happiness and comfort.

People in Blakesburg knew that his cottage, which he had to
rebuild many times to house all the unfortunates, had become
the mecca for women and their children who were left to the
mercies of an inhospitable world. They didn't criticize Tid for
his generosity but not any girl would have wanted to marry him
and go into his home which was running over with women and
children. Many of his competitors said he was running a harem;
but his friends stuck by him and he had many friends. They just
let Tid run his own affairs. Not anyone bothered to investigate
as long as the situation didn't concern him.

People knew Tid dressed the women well. They could see
them go over town together, go to the stores and buy groceries
for their home. People knew Tid sent their children to school,
grade school and high school and never was one of them reduced
to charity. They wore good clothes he bought for them. He
bought their books and hot lunch at noon and this was more
than many parents could do for their children born in wedlock
within the confines of the laws of God and man. These children
would approach Tid as if he were their own father on the street

and ask him for spending money. He never would refuse one. He would pull his purse from a secret built-in overcoat pocket and sometimes would hand "his children" folding money to spend. If anyone ever insulted one of "his children" by calling him a bad name, he went to the root of the situation and made it right or else. . . .

Often there would be talk of a new woman who had come to Tid's or a woman who was reconciled to her husband and had departed with her flock. Of course everybody wondered if Tid lived with only one woman, two or all of them or none. This was a question that was always in the minds of the Blakesburg women. Tid to them was a polite gentleman on the street but his domestic life was something of a mystery. Men would get a few drinks and argue over Tid's domestic life. Many of them wanted to date his women but they were afraid of Tid, his prestige, money, and his power with the Law. They knew he had everything on his side. But many of them admitted he was doing a wonderful work. They agreed his place was better than the poorhouse where there had been much gossip about the women and men all thrown together, their morals, their clothes and their keeps. The people did some mild gossiping about Tid's place for they were curious about what went on inside.

When the Depression came, it looked as if Tid would be run out of business. They knew he had overrun his competitors but everybody thought he had done this by getting the breaks. They knew he had the Law on his side. Now Tid would have to come down on his price. This would mean that his business would be reduced to a mere pittance of subsistence for himself and his big family. Already, there were sixty-eight moonshiners peddling sugar whiskey for two dollars a gallon.

But Tid had better business ability than many people thought. He reduced his pure corn to eight dollars a gallon and came through the Depression better than any business in Blakesburg except the undertakers. He could buy more with his money now.

People struggled to buy their pure corn the same as they did their bread. Tid kept his ever increasing family with ease.

In 1932 when Prohibition was repealed, after Tid had weathered the Depression with his competitors trying to undersell him to run him out of business, he found himself facing Government competition. Everybody thought Tid would be "ruint." People just knew everybody would lay off the moonshine whiskey in Blakesburg. They knew the little men would no longer drink sugar whiskey which was still selling for two dollars a gallon. They knew Blakesburg Society, business men, the county and city officials would no longer pay eight dollars a gallon for Tid's pure corn. The sugar whiskey bootleggers were reduced from sixty-eight to five or six; but Tid held on with his pure corn. He sold in competition with the owners of three legal whiskey stores who fought bravely to survive.

Since Old Reliable Tid more than held his own in Government competition, he kept his children in school, his women well dressed and his big family with plenty to eat. He wore a new suit and silk shirt every day. He walked the streets with his hands in his pockets. He survived the Thirties still protected by the Law and was one of the most important citizens in Blakesburg when the Forties began.

On the evening of September 18, 1941, Tid was walking over familiar Blakesburg streets with his hands in his topcoat pockets when he saw the lights. He stood watching them a few minutes while the people about him started running and screaming for their lives. But Tid was not moved. Many of the people who thought he lived in sin in his harem, who knew his business as everyone did, thought he would be one of the first to take off screaming, praying and shouting. Instead of running himself, Tid would grab a man by the arm and try to hold him while he spoke words of comfort.

"Take hit ezy, Windie," Tid said, catching Windie Griffee

by the arm when he tried to run past. "Take hit ezy, man! This iz only a token!"

"Take hit ezy hell," Windie shouted, jerking loose and running down the street.

Then he tried to catch Muff Henderson but he two-stepped into the crowd and disappeared.

"Why are ye a-runnin', Bertie?" Tid asked Bertie Scroggins.

"I'm a-huntin' for Alex," she said. "Have you seen 'im?"

"Naw, I aint," Tid said.

"He's been gone all afternoon," Bertie wailed, then ran hysterically down the street.

"Don't try to stop me," Mart Lambert said when Tid reached out with his long arm to catch him. "I don't want none o' yer pure corn. Not in a time like this nohow!"

He ran past Tid down the street like a stiff-legged rabbit.

"Take hit ezy, people," Tid cried out. "The world aint a-goin' to end!"

"That's what you think," Bruce Livingstone said, as he ran shouting to the people to gather on the courthouse square.

"Don't try to sell me none of that hooch now, Tid," Eif Garthee said, when Tid tried to lay his hand on Eif's shoulder to stop him. "This aint no time fer hooch!"

Tid watched his old customer take out a back street toward Lonesome Hill, his hatless bald head shining like a mirror in the bright moonless night.

"Where ye a-goin', Breezy?" Tid asked trying to stop a young man who was running down the street.

"To hell, I think," Breezy Baylor said. "Stay outten my way!"

"Take hit ezy, people," Tid shouted to the people who were now stirred up like a swarm of bees.

"Take it ezy nothin'," Viddie Pratt said. "Ye've fed our men yer rotten corn licker fer twenty-five years! Ye've got enough to do to look out fer yer own salvation!"

"I say ye have," Sibbie Lavendar said. "What about yer harem! Ye'd have enough to do if ye attend to the lost souls o' yer own darned strumpets!"

Sibbie followed Viddie down the street, like two hens running from a rainstorm.

"I've jist seen yer wimmen and yer youngins a-leavin' the house, Tid," Cackleberry Spriggs said.

"What 've ye been a-doin' out around my house?" Tid asked, since he knew Cackleberry, who was one of his best customers, had often wanted to go home with him and stay all night.

"I's jist out thar, Tid," Cackleberry said. "I wanted to see what'd come outten the house in a time like this!"

Tid faced Cackleberry and looked at him with mean eyes.

"I hope you found out, Cackleberry," Tiddis said, gritting his teeth like a snapping hound.

"I did find out," Cackleberry stammered as he watched Tiddis Fortner putting his hands into his side overcoat pockets feeling for something. "I saw eleven wimmen a-n-d f-o-u-r-t-e-e-n y-o-u-n-g-i-n-s. . . ."

Before Cackleberry could finish his sentence, he knew that Tiddis Fortner's actions were very unfriendly.

He's a-reachin' fer a gun to shoot me with 'r a bottle to hit me over the head, Cackleberry thought as he about-faced and took off as fast as his long stave-bowed legs would carry him. He ran until he was ready for his second wind before he stopped to look back. When he looked back through the flood of bright light over Main Street, he saw Tiddis in his bright-colored topcoat running from the excited crowd toward a side-street which was in the direction of his harem.

34

"I'M NOT SURE about what's a-goin' to happen, Bass," Charlie Allbright said as he leaned forward on his crutches, observing the flaming sky with big blue prophetic eyes. "I don't know whether it's the real McCoy or not! But I do know," he went on, "sich signs 've never appeared in our skies before."

"Yer right, Charlie," Bass said. "It aint nothin' like Halley's Comet!"

When Charlie first observed something was happening in the sky to the north, he was sitting beside his old friends and fellow philosophers on one of the seats donated by Alex Scroggins— County Attorney Alex Scroggins, who had before his election donated a dozen or more of these seats to be placed over town to advertise himself. His name was on the back of each seat in big capital letters. Though Charlie wasn't a Dinwiddie in political faith, he and other Greenoughs and Dinwiddie philosophers made good use of them in their philosophic discussions of the town, county, state and Republic. They had agreed the world was in such a mess, it could no longer go backwards or forwards or even stand still. Their conclusion to this doleful situation was, the end of time was drawing near.

While Charlie quietly leaned on his crutches, observing the sky, people ran around the courthouse square, screaming, shouting and praying. They screamed out the names of their loved ones who were lost in the mad shuffle. If Charlie for one minute could have taken his eyes from the picture of doom that was gradually focusing in the sky, he would have seen many of his fellow citizens sprawled on the ground kicking and moaning unintelligible words. But his ears were deaf to all the sounds about him and his eyes were blind to the contortions of his people. His eyes were glued to the signs in the fiery heavens.

"Why is everybody runnin'?" Boliver Tussie asked. "They'll haf to answer fer thar deeds nohow!"

But Charlie didn't hear Boliver. His prophetic eyes were pinned to the sky. He wanted to be sure this time, for no doubt he remembered back in 1916 when he heard something clattering in the sky like a mowing machine. He ran to the door and saw something he never dreamed he would see in his lifetime. In the meadows of the sky, he saw his first "man-made bird." He called Roxie, his wife, to the door and pointing to the man piloting it, he said: "Roxie, when man can defy the Laws of God Almighty and ride through the air on wings, the end of time is nigh."

This gave Charlie something to talk about to his friends on the courthouse square. He was going there in those days but he was not expounding much philosophy. But after he saw his first airplane, he did prophesy the world would come to an end in 1930. Day after day, year after year, he made his trips from his old home on the outskirts of Blakesburg to the courthouse square where he sat and whittled with Blakesburg's many gray-bearded philosophers until 1930 brought the depression and not the end of the world.

1930 brought more than a depression to Charlie. It brought the death of his wife. Charlie was left alone in the big decaying brick house that was handed down through his family from generation to generation. He was the only male heir left of his family to inherit it. When the bank crashed it wiped out the little nest egg Charlie had inherited from his father. People wondered how he would live since he didn't know how to work. They knew Charlie had never done a day's work in his life.

Suddenly Charlie was taken ill. For three months he lay in bed until Doc Hinton "pulled 'im through."

"Just somethin' got the matter with my legs," Charlie told Liam Winston. "If it hadn't a-been fer old Doc I'd a-kicked the bucket!"

Charlie's sick spell changed him. Though he was still in his forties, he grew a long goatee, let his mustache grow into long handlebars and let his hair grow down nearly to his shoulders. He became a venerable old sage, something he had always wanted to be, overnight. Just as soon as he was able he hobbled on crutches back to his favorite spot of earth in his favorite city and among his favorite crowd of people.

"It's like what I think a-goin' to Heaven would be to git back here," Charlie told Old Glory Gardner on his first trip back to the square.

Then Charlie spoke on the value of young men taking out insurance.

"I would be up against it in my old age if hit wuzn't fer insurance," he warned them. "If it hadn't a-been fer my sick spell I don't know what I'd a-done. I happened to have an insurance policy with a disability clause in it. Now I can go on living the rest of my days without a worry! And I'll have enough left to bury me in the end! Insurance is wonderful. Just be dad-durned shore if ye take some, ye have a disability clause in it!"

When Effie Dood, who had been married three times and had outlived all three husbands, heard of Widower Charlie Allbright's plight with his stiff legs she went to his house with her home-made liniment that she said was good "fer stiffness in the jints." She bathed Charlie from the waist down three times a day for three weeks. When it was rumored that Charlie had thrown his crutches away, two well-dressed men came suddenly to Blakesburg and inquired for Charlie's house. Booten Winston heard their inquiries at the Drug Store and he ran to Charlie's house to warn him. When these insurance men found Charlie he was on his crutches.

"He'd a lost his insurance in spite o' hell if it hadn't a been fer me," Booten Winston later told Tid Fortner. "I jist saved old Charlie!"

But Charlie wasn't thinking now about the insurance check sent him each month as he watched the sign God had put in the northern sky. He didn't see Bass when he jumped up from the comfortable Alex Scroggins political seat and took off. He didn't hear Old Glory who was giving his last patriotic oration on the American flag standing in the seat near him. Charlie was too busy looking for Christ in the clouds. He was looking for more than that. He was sure now, as he watched the lightning darts of brilliant multi-colored lights intermingling in the heavens, that "the time had come."

Charlie didn't pay any attention when the jailbirds had been freed and had passed him yelling and cussing because the jailor had waited until it was too late before he turned them out. Even when Boliver Tussie, who had gotten under one of the elm shade trees with a big bushy top to protect himself from the bright splinters of light, had from time to time asked Charlie what he thought the verdict was, another comet or the ending of the world, Charlie hadn't heard him. If he had, he'd never answered Boliver.

Liam Winston was at this time running around the courthouse square. Boliver Tussie's three tall sons were driving a mule team, charging and foaming at the mouth, hitched to a joltwagon to take Boliver home. Bass had gone; Old Glory was at the apex of his oration. Tid Fortner was trying to calm the people on the streets and Sister Spence was preaching the time had come to repent on the courthouse square. And the brilliant lights seemed now to be swooping down to engulf the city in flame.

"I know it's here this time," Charlie let out a wild scream. "The end of the world is here!"

Charlie threw his crutches away and ran like a gray fox across the courthouse square.

"If the world don't end, Charlie's shore as God lost his insurance this time," Booten Winston said to Boliver Tussie as Charlie passed by them like a shot out of a gun.

"How can Charlie Allbright run like that?" Cackleberry Spriggs asked Denver Callihan. "I heerd his legs wuz stiff at the jints!"

Before Denver could answer Cackleberry, Charlie was out of sight.

"Why does Charlie run like that?" Steve Powderjay asked Nando Wampler as he fondled his long white beard with his wrinkled skinny fingers. "Atter a-hearin' 'im talk fer so many years, I'd a-thought he'd a stood by and faced eternity like the rest of us!"

"But where can he go?" Nando asked Steve. "Thar's no place he can git that the light won't fall upon 'im. He caint git outten the focus of the eyes of God Almighty!"

"Aint nobody a-goin' to git noplace by a-runnin' now," Spruce Winters chimed in to Nando and Steve but they didn't pay him any attention as they hobbled away on their canes.

But Charlie didn't hear any of their conversation. He didn't care what they said about him now that he had crossed Main Street and was heading out the alley toward the Produce House, where Didson Caudill was opening the doors, turning out the geese, turkeys, chickens, guineas and ducks. There was no need to keep them in captivity now. The end of time had come and the people in Blakesburg would not be phoning for a dressed Thanksgiving turkey, guinea chicken or duck, or a Christmas goose. A flock of old hens, long in captivity because the people preferred eating younger chickens, regained their freedom and flew over Charlie's head through the bright light with cackling sounds.

When Didson Caudill saw crippled Charlie Allbright running on two good legs with his hat in his hand, his long locks of gray hair floating in the wind, and really making time out the dirt turnpike with a cloud of dust rising every time his foot hit the ground, he yelled: "Is that you, Charlie?"

"Hit shore is," Charlie grunted without looking back.

35

"LISTEN, FOLKS," Jad Hix shouted to the hysterical people gathered in front of the Winston Boarding House, "this ain't the end of time."

"Then what is it?" a woman screamed hysterically.

"Stand by fer a few minutes," Jad told her. "Ye'll see letters come into the sky. This is a token of something big!"

"How do you know so much?" a man asked Jad, walking over close to him, looking up into his face. "Do ye think ye're greater than God Almighty?"

"Naw, I don't think that," Jad said, looking down at the little man. "But I've done a lot of travelin'. I was in Michigan in 1916 a-cuttin' cordwood and I saw the lights come into the sky. Jist like tonight. Only they weren't as bright!"

"Did the lights ye saw thar bear a token?" the weeping woman asked Jad as other frightened people gathered closer to listen.

"They shore did, lady," he said. "We saw red, white and blue colors in the sky!"

"But what did that mean?" the woman asked.

"Hit meant war," Jad said. "Ye remember 1917, don't ye?"

"I shore do," the woman said. "Brother Jack went away and he didn't get back."

"Now just stand by," Jad told the little crowd gathered around him, "and watch fer some sort of signs. They'll be here shore as the world. That's the way a country gits a token!"

Now Jad Hix and his followers stood watching the sky, looking "fer some sort of a token." They stood silently watching the great flashes of light crisscross each other on the heavens that seemed to be rolling mountains of flames. There were various colors of clouds, light yellow, geranium red, and wildrose-petal pink. Various shades and colors intermingled before their straining eyes across the heavens. But the people stood beside Jad because his words were of solace in this trying hour. They were impressed by his size for Jad Hix was a mountain of a man. This big wood chopper was almost too broad to go through a door without turning sidewise and tall enough to have to stoop under the average door.

"Thar's a burnin' mountain in the sky," the woman said. "Hit looks like a hillside on fire when ye burn a clearin' in the spring."

. "Hit's more than that, lady," Jad said.

"And thar's a river a-runnin' acrost hit," she said. "The water is on fire!"

"Hit's more than that, lady," Jad said. "I go by signs. I live by them."

"I do too," the man said, more contented now as he rubbed his long white beard with his hand. "I plant my corn in the dark of the moon so hit won't grow tall and will have big ears. And I plant my 'taters in the light of the moon so they'll grow nigh the top of the ground and will be easy to dig! And I kiver my buildin's with clapboards in the dark of the moon so they won't curl up at the ends. . . ."

"Watch fer the signs in the sky, Mister," Jad warned. "What ye do aint got nothin' to do with this!"

"But the light's so bright hit hurts me eyes," the old man said

"But keep watchin'," Jad said. "Don't miss the sign. Look! I see hit a-takin' place!"

And Jad pointed at the sky with his big index finger.

"Yes, I see somethin'," the old man said.

"Shore ye see somethin'," Jad said. "Keep watchin' and ye'll see more."

"What do ye see?" the woman asked.

" 'W,' " Jad said. "The letter 'W.' "

Then the woman looked out Jad's long arm and pointing index finger as if she were sighting over a gun barrel at an object.

"I see hit," she said. "I see the 'W.' See, hit's made of flames as red as blood. See hit against that gray cloud! Hit's a 'W' if I ever saw one!"

"Do ye see hit?" Jad asked the old man.

"Yep," he said. "I see hit!"

"Everybody can see that, Mister," said one of the men in the crowd of listeners.

"Now watch fer a letter on the right of the 'W,' " Jad warned.

"Thar," the woman said.

"Right," Jad said to the old man. "God is a-writin' hit thar. Hit's a white letter writ on a dark cloud. Do ye see what hit is?"

Now the old man sighted out Jad's arm like he was sighting over a double-barrel to shoot a rabbit.

"Yep, I see hit," he said. "Hit's an 'A' all right!"

"Now watch fer the next letter," Jad said.

While they watched the sky and Jad kept pointing at the letters, more people began to gather around them for their calmness was sort of a haven for the hysterical people. And when they gathered they asked Jad, the woman and the old man what they were looking at. And they pointed out the letters 'WA' to them in the sky.

"Keep on a-watchin', all of ye," Jad warned. "Watch fer the next letter!"

"Thar's somethin'," the old man shouted. "Dog-my-cats if hit ain't."

"What is hit?" the woman asked.

" 'R,' " the old man said. "Hit's a blue letter writ on a red-lookin' cloud!"

"Red, white and blue," the woman said. "Th' colors of our flag!"

"Hit shore 's 'n 'R' all right," Jad said. "What does that spell?"

"*War!*" the woman shouted hysterically. "And I've got five boys!"

"*War!*" the old man shouted. "Hit means *war*."

"That's what hit means," Jad said. "Hit's a token fer our people!"

"*War!*" everybody screamed and then they scattered in all directions, leaving Jad standing there looking at the sky.

36

W HEN REVEREND JOHN WHETSTONE heard the loud commotion outside his window, he was sitting in the study of
his dilapidated parsonage reading his Bible. At first he thought
it was a group that had gathered to watch a Temp and Oll
Spradling fight. But as he listened to the singing of hymns and
the many prayers coming from strange voices he had never
heard pray before, he closed his Bible.

Wonder what is wrong? he thought as he picked up his cane
and walked out.

As soon as this retired minister from one of Blakesburg's
churches of an old and well-known established religious denomination stepped onto his porch, he saw the highly inflamed
sky. Then he looked down Main Street through the bright flood
of light and he saw something he had never seen in his lifetime
before. He saw people running, bumping into one another on
the street. He heard their weird lamenting cries; he heard them
singing and he heard their prayers. And along the street he saw
people bending over to pick up a comrade overcome with excitement. He saw a steady stream of people carrying the fallen to
Doc Hinton's office. He knew this commotion wasn't caused by
Temp and Oll now for he saw five men carrying Temp toward
Doc Hinton's office.

I must do something to stop this, he thought as he limped
across his porch and walked slowly down the steps. As soon as
he was out on the street, he was almost knocked down by a
panicky group of people.

"Take it easy, people," he said, waving his free hand. "This isn't anything! It's only an aurora borealis!"

No one paid any attention to this old white-haired minister, who had been allowed since his retirement from the ministry to live on in his parsonage. Since the Northern and Southern branches of his church, split since the Civil War, had been reunited after a century had passed, it left his parsonage and the church where he had preached to be sold at auction now that everybody of his faith would be going to one church. His empty church house was the one where DeWit Addington was now on his knees pounding at the locked doors entreating God for entrance. DeWit didn't know enough about the churches to know which had closed and which were still open.

Nearly everybody in Blakesburg knew Preacher John for he had preached twelve years at his church, and for three years after his retirement they had seen him doing little odd jobs about the town to supplement his small retirement pay which was not enough to keep body and soul together. During the summers they had seen him with his goose-neck hoe across his shoulder going to hoe his potatoes in the big garden he raised to give nutriment to his and his wife's aging bodies. Many times they had seen him walk down the street with Rufus Litteral, each with his long-handle hoe across his shoulder, going to hoe potatoes. And now this old minister tried to raise his declining voice above the roar and confusion of the people so he would be heard and at the same time clear the street when panicky people came toward him.

"This is not the end of time," Reverend Whetstone shouted. "This is only the northern lights!"

Not one would stop to listen to him as he walked down the street tapping his cane every alternate step, waving his hand, trying to calm the people by telling them what was happening.

"Won't you listen to the truth?" he shouted as he came near the Winston Boarding House. "This is only an aurora borealis!"

"Roary Boryaliss, hell, Parson," Liam Winston grunted as he ran into the boarding house with his tongue out, panting like a tired foxhound. "Hit's the end of the world!"

Aunt Viney Porter came running down the street getting her breath hard. When he tried to stop her she looked at him with wild staring eyes.

"Viney," he said, reaching out his hand.

"Don't you try to stop me," she warned him.

"But don't you know me?" he said. "I was your minister for twelve years!"

She didn't answer but waddled her heavy body up the street as fast as her rheumatic legs and her gasping breath would allow her.

"It's only an aurora borealis," Reverend Whetstone shouted again.

"First time I ever heerd th' end of time called that big word, Parson," some man shouted, who was running so fast Reverend Whetstone failed to recognize him.

"Glory be to God, Reverend," Bert Edgewater said as he ran up dressed in his best clothes and pulled Reverend Whetstone's hand down from the air and pumped it half a dozen times fast as an automatic could shoot. "We're a-goin' home to Glory tonight, Brother John!"

Bert Edgewater, a short duck-legged man with a heavy body, apple-red cheeks and a shock of ripe wheat-colored curly hair, had been a member of nearly every church in town. He had once been a member of Reverend Whetstone's church until the Reverend had stopped Bert, who had his license to exhort, from shouting in the middle of his sermon until he couldn't go on preaching. Then Bert left his church saying that it was cold as a cucumber and a man couldn't get happy and shout. He had gone to other churches and jumped over seats and had climbed the walls and the stovepipes when he "burned from the fire within."

"Don't get excited, Bert," Reverend Whetstone said calmly. "This is only an aurora borealis! You're not goin' anyplace to-night!"

"You're as cold-blooded as a snake in the wintertime, Parson John," Bert said, drawing away and quickly letting loose of the minister's wrinkled hand. "May God have mercy on your soul! You, a professed minister of the gospel of Jesus Christ, out a-trying to misinform the people on this night when the world ends!"

"You'll see when morning comes, Bert," Reverend Whetstone said. "All your exhortin' will 've been in vain!"

"Save a soul, Brother," Bert said, which had always been his way of greeting the saved or the sinner on the Blakesburg streets instead of the usual "good morning." "Thank God fer old-time salvation," Bert went on as he departed running toward the courthouse square, "and for the good old Greenough Party!"

Reverend Whetstone walked up the street, the way Bert had run, and when he reached the corner by the Blakesburg Bank, where he could see over onto the courthouse square, he saw Bert running circles and shouting as the sinners fell at Sister Spence's feet.

"Why not tonight?" Sister Spence, a buxom, attractive woman, shouted above the wailing guitars, singing of hymns and the wild moans and prayers of the repenting sinners writhing on the ground at her feet. "This will be your last time to repent! Oh, why not be saved before it is too late! A home in Glory and the promise of everlasting life is better than a-goin' to a Devil's hell to spend your eternity in fire and brimstone! Would you rather live forever," she went on, "or burn forever? It is up to you! Why not now? Make up your minds! You won't have long to decide! Where will you spend your vacation? In the joys of Heaven or the discomforts of Hell?"

Reverend Whetstone watched for a minute. He saw many surge forward and fall to earth, confessing sins, praying, wailing to God to save them. Strong men who stood in the background shook as if they were having chills.

"Strong men will quiver before the wrath of God," Reverendess Spence said, looking back at these trembling men.

"God is not wrathful," Reverend Whetstone shouted. "God is not a God of wrath but he is a God of love!"

"How do you know so much?" some beardy faced man asked Reverend Whetstone. "Ye'd better fall to yer knees, ye weaked old sinner, and be saved."

"I've preached the Gospel for fifty-nine years, my friend," he said. "I'm not talking through my hat!"

"Ye don't act like a child of the Lord to me," the man snapped back.

"Repent before it is too late," Reverendess Spence shouted, pleading with her hands and opening her mouth in a pleasant smile wide enough to show two rows of white teeth. "Yes, I say strong men will tremble before the wrath of God as the end draws nigh."

"It's only an aurora borealis, people," Reverend Whetstone shouted, trying to make himself heard above the din of confusion. "It's only the northern lights!"

"It's the end of time," Bert Edgewater shouted, as he jumped up and down and joyfully clapped his hands. "Glory to God, the time has come. This weaked earth shall be no more!"

"God is not a God of wrath, I tell you," Reverend Whetstone shouted again, waving his hand. "God is a God of mercy and of love!"

But Sister Spence and her followers would have none of the old preacher's words. They looked upon him with unkind expressions. Beardy-faced men looked at him with sharp mean eyes. One ordered him to leave the ground.

"We don't want no hypocrites around here in a time like this," he told Reverend Whetstone. "Be gone and pray fer yer own salvation if ye don't believe as we believe!"

"I tell you that this night will pass and these lights will die as quickly as they have come," Reverend Whetstone said. "You'll see that what I'm tellin' you is true. You'll know by morning."

Reverend Whetstone turned and walked down the street.

"It's strange but when you tell people the truth they won't believe you," he said as he slowly tapped his cane along the street.

He walked toward the parsonage, side-stepping for frantic people to pass.

They'll know by morning, he said underbreath as he reached his home so tired he could hardly get up the steps.

THE NEXT MORNING

O N THE MORNING of September 19, 1941, the sun arose, reflecting its bright morning rays on the deserted Blakesburg
streets. But the birds were wide awake as usual. They flew down
from their nests under the eaves of the weather-beaten houses
and the new courthouse to find their breakfast on the streets.
And a lazy morning wind rustled the autumn-tinted leaves on
the elm shade trees in the courthouse yard. Bass Keaton, who
had spent the late morning hours in his favorite bed, was awakened by the chirruping of these hungry birds around him and
the lazy rustle of the leaves above him. He raised up on the
Alex Scroggins political bench, rubbing the sleep from his darkly
circled eyes. Then he looked over the empty streets of Blakesburg, filled with an aftermath of debris, which reminded him of
an Independence Day or a Labor Day celebration in Blakesburg.

But Bass had seen people on the streets after one of these
"Big Days" in Blakesburg. Now he saw only one man, Muff
Henderson. He watched Muff two-step slowly across Main
Street toward the Drug Store. Muff tried to get in but the Drug
Store was still locked. He watched Muff turn away, two-stepping
up a deserted alley. Then Bass yawned, showing a few discol-
ored front teeth in his mouth that was a dark cavern for the
morning wind. He lay back on his bench for more sleep.

Shortly, Bass was reawakened, not by the birds and the wind
but by Uncle Sweeter Dabney. He had come to the courthouse
square to find Charlie Allbright's crutches. While Bass rubbed
his eyes, yawned and talked to Uncle Sweeter, Mrs. Joe Oliver

passed on her way to Attorney Jason Broughton's Law Office. Attorney Broughton, who was a "coming young lawyer" in Blakesburg, had the reputation of a successful divorce lawyer. Uncle Sweeter and Bass watched Mrs. Joe, who seemed too tired to move, take little short steps until she reached Attorney Broughton's office.

When the sun was higher in the sky, people began to appear on the Blakesburg streets. Shopkeepers began to open their shops for a new day in business. When DeWit Addington got his first customer, Bass and Uncle Sweeter, who had begun their new day by whittling for the longest shavings, heard DeWit say, "Praise the Lord," every time he described a product to his customer. Just as soon as Bill Haddington unlocked his Beer Parlor, they watched Liam Winston who was shaky as a leaf in the winter wind, shoot ahead of Bill through the door like a bullet.

Not long after the Blakesburg business men had opened their shops, which was shortly before noon, the political officeholders began to arrive at their offices for a day of duty. Among these servants of the Republic, state, county and city was Judge Allie Anderson, who walked very slowly, looking thoughtfully at his feet as he ambled along. At the same time Judge Allie was walking down one street, Rufus Litteral, with a hoe across his shoulder, was walking up the other. Rufus quickly turned his head so the Judge wouldn't notice him as he went to dig his potatoes.

The sounding of the fire alarm for twelve noon was a good sign that life was astir, that the city was gradually becoming alive and breathing again.

While the indifferent wind of September slowly rustled the elm leaves above their heads, Uncle Sweeter and Bass sat whittling. With easy strokes they sank the bright blades of their long knives into the soft elm wood. They didn't look up when Tid Fortner strolled past them with his hands in the pockets of a new bright-colored topcoat. Nor did they see Malinda Sprouse walk into the Citizen's Bank, carrying a fat but dilapidated old purse.

Nor did they pay any attention to Liam Winston when he came from the Beer Parlor without "the shakes." Liam had a gleam in his eye as he walked steadily up the street past the Citizen's Bank toward the Winston Boarding House. But why should Bass and Uncle Sweeter watch Liam when life was so good to them? They were sitting on their favorite spot of earth while Old Glory rippled above their beloved Blakesburg and life went on for them and their city like the slow turning of a paddle wheel pushing a steamboat up the broad river.